SADIE'S SIN

The Zwi Migdal's Reign of Terror

NEIL PERRY GORDON

Dedication: To Annie—my editor, mentor, and guiding light.

Contents

CHAPTER ONE—SADIE WOLLMAN

Professor Alexander Kaminsky's eyes caught hers again. He tried not to linger, but the pause was more than enough for a few students to take notice of his distraction. Mercifully, the young lady offered a twitch of a smile which did the trick, snapping the professor out of his stupor and back to his lecture.

Alex gathered his wits and continued. "Tomorrow we'll begin our studies on what our history books have called the *Miracle on the Vistula*," he said, tapping his hand upon the textbook and placing it in his leather satchel. "Our country's glorious victory over the Bolsheviks four years ago this past August 1920."

His students seemed to know instinctively, once the professor began to put his things away, that class was dismissed. With his back turned, he heard them shuffling their way out of the classroom.

"Excuse me, Professor Kaminsky," came a sweet voice from behind him.

Alex quickly turned and was face to face with that same young female student, sporting luxurious red hair and sparkling green eyes. "Yes, miss?" he said, trying to sound professorial.

"My name is Sadie Wollman," she said, offering an outstretched hand.

Alex, unsure how to respond, looked around, realized that they were alone, and reluctantly accepted her handshake. She gripped tightly, surprising him.

"It's good to meet you, Miss Wollman," he said, swallowing hard at the young woman's boldness.

"I just want to tell you, I'm looking forward to your class," she said, with an engaging smile that featured full lips, interposed by an adorable pair of dimpled cheeks.

"Thank you, Miss Wollman," Alex said, trying not to smile back.

She leaned in a bit and whispered, "If you like, you may call me Sadie."

"Sadie?" he repeated. Then he shook his head and added, "Oh no, that wouldn't be appropriate."

She tilted her head, hitched her book-bag over her shoulder, and said, "You're right. I'll see you tomorrow, Professor."

Alex watched Sadie turn and walk toward the classroom door. Just as she grabbed the doorknob, she turned and looked back at him and smiled.

He flushed and offered a brief flip of his hand as a wave. Once she was gone, he leaned against his desk and sighed. Whoever Sadie Wollman was, he was looking forward to seeing her again.

*

A hero's welcome surprised Alex when he entered the lecture hall for the first faculty meeting of the semester. It had been years since the war ended, and while people occasionally recognized him at cafés, or when strolling along the promenade, most passed him by, not realizing who he was. But here, at the university, everyone knew Professor Alexander Kaminsky—Hero of Poland.

"It's an honor having you on our staff," Professor Baros, the dean of the Mathematics Department, said on the first day Alex arrived on campus. "Poland owes a great deal to you, sir."

Comments like that were typical, and he was flattered by the attention he received from his colleagues, but he hoped it would soon settle down, allowing him to carry on teaching a subject he was passionate about.

Alex had spent the previous summer months preparing for his upcoming classes. The university provided him with an office where he locked himself inside with his many books and research papers, venturing outdoors only to walk home or have a quick meal at a café. He became a happy recluse, ready to devote himself to becoming a university professor.

CHAPTER TWO—KOTIK'S CAFÉ

Sadie made a promise to her father that she would help him out in his wool business in exchange for allowing her to attend the university and earn a degree. But regardless of her enthusiasm, she couldn't convince him why a young Jewish woman needed to take classes in history, mathematics, and literature.

"What's the point?" he argued. "You'll marry as soon as you're done with this nonsense, and be busy raising a family."

Sadie knew that this was probably true, but she wanted a few years of seeing what the world had to offer, at least from the perspective of exciting instructors like Professor Kaminsky.

She also understood that the opportunity of ever leaving Warsaw and traveling to exciting places was not a likely prospect. All she had to do was look at her girlfriends from the Jewish neighborhood surrounding Nalewki Street; most already married and bogged down raising children.

While feeding carded wool onto the wheel, Sadie thought about the handsome professor. Most likely he was only a few years older than her eighteen years. She imagined him to be in his mid-twenties, and hopefully single.

She was looking forward to going out later that evening when she would tell her best friend Sara how handsome the professor was, with his short-cut blonde hair and neatly cropped beard. She amused herself thinking back to the moment they shook hands and how easy it was to disarm him with nothing more than her charm.

But there was one major problem with Professor Kaminsky. He was a *goy*, a non-Jew, which meant that it would not be permissible to even date such a man, let alone marry him. According to Jewish law, and even more important, according to her father, that was a sin. Inevitably, her father would make a matrimonial agreement on her behalf with a marriage broker. That was another reason she wanted to attend university now. *A girl can have a little fun*, she thought. She wanted memories that she could store away, knowing her life would never again be her own, once she began birthing children.

*

"There's one," Sadie said, pointing to a street-side table at Kotik's café.

Sara squeezed her way through the backs of chairs pressed against each other, and in between an assortment of legs and a hodgepodge of crisscrossed feet, creating obstacles along the pathway toward the lone remaining table for two.

Kotik's on 31 Nalewki Street was always busy at this time of night. Sadie liked it because writers and poets gathered there and would occasionally read their latest stories or poems out loud. It was also popular with politicians and intellectuals who would pontificate their beliefs to the critical gathering, as a way to test the validity of their points of view.

But tonight, Sara had no interest in the world around her. She wanted to talk about Sadie's handsome history professor.

Sadie tried to follow Sara to the table, but was stopped along the way by men she knew who offered to make room for her at their table. When she finally arrived, Sara had already ordered for both of them.

"You can have any man in here," Sara said, observing the dozens of eyes still following Sadie as she sat down.

Sadie glanced behind her and shrugged. "None of these men interest me," she said, waving her hand dismissively, "but I met someone who is very exciting."

Sara's eyes lit up. "Oh, tell me everything, Sadie."

CHAPTER THREE—MIRACLE ON THE VISTULA

The moment Alex stepped into the classroom for the second day of class, he saw Sadie seated in the front row, her eyes bright and clear.

"Good morning, Professor," she said, with an engaging smile.

Trying to temper his enthusiasm, he nodded, placed his satchel down, and pulled out his pocket watch. It was the top of the hour; time to begin.

"This afternoon's lecture will be an overview of the Battle of Warsaw, or as those of us who fought in the war prefer to call it, the *Miracle on the Vistula*," he said, and paused to gauge the students' reaction.

"While it was only four years ago, I'm guessing most of you were too young to fight as soldiers," he said, glancing about at the young male students. "But I'm sure you'll remember the panic that spread among us like a virus, as the Soviet Army threatened our city."

Heads nodded. Unable to resist any longer, Alex turned to Sadie. She sat wide-eyed, riveted by his words. He took a breath to calm himself and moved on with the lecture. "I was one of the many proud soldiers who fought under the command of our great commander—General Józef Pilsudski.

"What you will learn in this course, does not come from hearsay, or from some second-hand journalistic account. Instead, what I am about to share comes from eyewitnesses; the courageous men who fought in this great battle."

There were several whispered conversations ricocheting around the room, forcing Alex to pause. When the students settled, he continued, "We can trace the reasons for the Soviet's aggression to Vladimir Lenin, who, along with his chief advisor Leon Trotsky, conspired to export their communist revolution into Western Europe. Their first target was Germany.

"One can understand after losing the war to the Allies, how the population of Germany was ripe for a similar uprising of what occurred in the Soviet Union. Just imagine how easy it could have been to convince disillusioned ex-soldiers and unemployed civilians that a revolution against their weak and feeble government was possible."

His students leaned forward, eager to hear the engaging professor. Alex smiled, sat on the edge of his desk, lifted a finger into the air, and continued, "But to reach Germany, one nation stood in the way, and that was Poland. Which, by most people's assessment, was more of a joke than a problem. We had just become a nation for the first time in one hundred and twenty-three years, and certainly in no military position to stop the advancement of the powerful Soviet Army.

"Because of this, Lenin thought he could also convince the Polish citizens into becoming Communists without a fight," he said and paused, while a few students snickered. "But one man stood in Lenin's way, and that was General Józef Pilsudski, who spent his adult life fighting for the restoration of Polish sovereignty. The general was a man of extraordinary ambition. It was once said when his army's resources were dwindling, the general himself resorted to robbing banks in order to keep the cause alive."

Alex pushed himself back to standing and took a small step closer to Sadie. As he approached, she tilted her head up to look at him. Her lips were slightly parted, as if she were ready for him to lean down and kiss her. However, he stepped away and swung his arm in a sweeping gesture and said, "But to understand the general, we must look back to 1916 during the Great War, when General Pilsudski led a legion of twenty-thousand Poles into battle against the Soviets.

"It was at a time when Germany was desperate against Russia's seemingly inexhaustible manpower, so they reached out to their ally, the Austrians, and persuaded them to transfer General Pilsudski's Polish legion to fight alongside their German Army. But the general refused to take the oath of allegiance required of every German soldier, and as a result, was arrested and his legion dissolved." Alex took a deep breath before continuing.

"On the day Germany signed an armistice with the Allied powers, ending the war, General Pilsudski was freed from prison and permitted to return to Warsaw. Once he arrived, he wasted no time calling upon his followers to join him. They swiftly disarmed an abandoned German garrison in Warsaw, and took control of the capital city of Poland," Alex explained, holding out a clenched fist.

"Two years later, the reconstituted Polish legion of twenty-thousand men under the General's command were hardly considered a match against the formidable communists with an army ten times that. Lenin recognized the opportunity and declared, '*By destroying the Polish Army we are destroying the Versailles brokered peace, upon which rests the whole present system of international relations,*'" Alex said, reading from the text.

"In the summer of 1920, the Soviet Army attacked our city. Under the leadership of General Pilsudski, they forced our troops to retreat westward in disarray, and were on the verge of defeat. Taking advantage, the Soviets, led by General Mikhail Tukhachevsky, encircled Warsaw and planned to cross the Vistula River. But our army counterattacked from the south, disrupting the enemy's offensive, and this time forced the Soviets into a disorganized retreat. General Pilsudski pressed forward and devastated the enemy. At the conclusion of the fighting, over ten-thousand Russian soldiers were killed, thirty-thousand wounded and sixty-six thousand taken as prisoners," Alex said pursing his lips.

"By October of that year, France and Britain pressured both governments into an armistice, and on March 18, 1921, we signed a peace treaty. Lenin reluctantly abandoned his vision of a communist Europe and instead declared that his government would devote themselves to creating *communism in one country to serve as an example to nations everywhere.*

"This battle for Warsaw became known among our people as the *Miracle on the Vistula*," he said, and paused, allowing his words to linger.

"Now," he continued, picking up a book from his desk, "this summarized our country's historic rise to a sovereign nation. Tomorrow we will go deeper with our studies, beginning with General Pilsudski's release from German prison.

"Please read chapters six through eight for our discussion in class tomorrow," he said, holding up the textbook. "That's all for today."

Alex lingered, taking his time gathering his things, hoping that Sadie would approach. But when he turned around, there were only two male students anxiously waiting to speak with him. Sadie had left without a word, causing him to chuckle at the distraction and knowing that he had more important things to do than become romantically involved with a student.

CHAPTER FOUR—OFFICE HOURS

"Where're you going?" asked Sara.

Sadie picked up her book bag hooked over the back of her chair, and said, "Professor Kaminsky has office hours. I want to be the first one."

"Ah, the handsome professor. I've should have known," Sara said, teasing Sadie.

Sadie leaned in and said with a devilish smile, "Wish me luck."

*

Sadie ran up the flights of stairs to the third floor and stood for a moment to catch her breath; she then marched down the wide corridor to Professor Kaminsky's office. A small brass plaque screwed to a heavy oak door, stained in a deep walnut color, identified that she was at the correct office.

Sadie knocked.

"Come in," a muffled voice said from inside.

Sadie fussed with her hair and flipped her long, red locks over her right shoulder and entered.

The first thing she noticed was the smell. It was an indistinguishable assortment of odors that bit at her nostrils, causing her eyes to tear. She rubbed at the irritation, and noticed the top of someone's head poking above several towers of books, folders, and papers, all of varying heights piled upon a battered wooden desk.

The professor stuck his face into a canyon-like space in between the piles and said, "Oh, Miss Wollman, what a pleasant surprise. Please come in."

He rose from his chair and quickly maneuvered around obstacles to reach the other side of his desk. "Let's sit over here," he said, pointing to a small table off to the side with two chairs, also occupied with books.

He lifted the hefty-looking volumes and piled them upon other stacks which were already creating a growing array of tipsy-towers on the floor. He shrugged, and said, "Sorry for the mess. I must get this place organized."

Sadie rubbed the back of her neck, looking at what she imagined was a glimpse into the mind of the man she was pursuing, and smiled. "Perhaps I can give you a hand with all of this," she said, waving her hands.

He bobbed his head. "That would be wonderful," he replied, and gestured to the empty chairs.

Sadie placed her book bag on the floor and sat down.

The early September weather was warm, and perhaps, Sadie thought, this had something to do with the pervasive, sour odors. *Maybe if he opened the window behind his desk and allowed in some fresh air in, it wouldn't smell so bad.*

"So, Miss Wollman, tell me, how are you managing with the assignments?"

Sadie tried to compose herself. Her intention was to charm the professor, not to contemplate ways of cleaning his office. She nodded vigorously, surprising herself at her sudden loss of words.

"That's great," he said, seeming to force an awkward smile.

Sadie squirmed a bit in her seat, and just looked at him.

The professor broke the uncomfortable silence. "Please, Miss Wollman, how can I be of help?"

Sadie sat up tall in the chair, gathered her composure, and said, "Well, I was wondering if you could share some of your personal stories of what it was like fighting against the Russians?"

He put his hand to his chin, and thought for a moment before he said, "I'm teaching the history of our country to honor those who sacrificed their lives so we may live in peace. It would be shameful to sensationalize the adventures of just one man."

"Oh, I agree, Professor," she said, reaching out and touching his forearm. "Perhaps we can find a place where you feel comfortable talking about it. Preferably not in here," she said with a grimace.

The professor pinched his nose and said, "Yes, it is rather stuffy."

Sadie nodded.

Alex thought for a moment, then smiled and said, "I have an idea. How about we meet in Saxon Gardens tomorrow afternoon, Miss Wollman?"

Sadie felt herself blushing now. "That would be lovely, Professor Kaminsky, but only if you call me Sadie."

Alex stared at her for a moment, took a deep breath and answered, "I'm not so sure that's a good idea."

Sadie shrugged, and with a tilt of her head she said, "It's just my name, what are you afraid of?"

Alex chuckled. "You are charming, Miss Wollman, I must say."

"So you agree then?"

He smiled and nodded. "All right, Sadie, I agree, and you may call me Alex."

CHAPTER FIVE—SAXON GARDENS

Alex suggested that they meet by the fountain in Saxon Gardens. He arrived thirty minutes before their agreed time, and while he waited for Sadie, he walked circles around the popular landmark, designed by the famous architect Henryk Marconi.

With his hands clasped behind his back, he dodged children running and frolicking about, and thought about his imminent date with Sadie. During class earlier that day, he could barely keep his mind focused on his lecture. She sat in her usual spot, right up front, her eyes glued to him. Even when he turned his back to write on the chalkboard, he sensed her.

Alex avoided making too much eye contact with Sadie during class, but was certain a few of the other students noticed their growing mutual fascination, especially the two young men seated in the front row, whispering to each other and glancing over to Sadie. This concerned him since he didn't want to give the impression that Sadie would receive special favor.

It was a perfect day, ideal for a stroll and a chat. Alex wondered what neighborhood this young, beautiful woman was from. Sadie's surname was Wollman, a Jewish name, and from what he knew, it was not uncommon for German Jews to take last names describing their occupation. Perhaps Sadie's family were originally from Germany and in the wool business, he pondered while continuing to make circles around the fountain.

Alex wondered if this rendezvous would lead to a relationship. Not only had he never dated a woman as beautiful as Sadie, but he never dated a Jew either. He held no animosity to the Jews, unlike many of his fellow Poles. Alex believed in himself as a free thinker, not judging a person based on one's religion or race.

Lost in thought, he didn't notice Sadie approaching, until she called out his name.

"Alex," she said, waving with obvious exuberance.

He looked ahead and saw Sadie walking toward him. But unlike the simple, white linen blouse and long brown skirt she wore in class, she had dressed in a fitted top, that was cut almost low enough to expose the top of her breasts, along with a navy blue silk scarf, twisted over her neck. A matching skirt, expertly tailored to her curves, finished at her knees, and sitting on top of her red hair, which was tied up this time, was a silver-colored hat, with similarly colored, tiny silk flowers perched upon its brim.

"Hello, Sadie, you look lovely," he said, trying to avoid the temptation of gawking at every inch of her.

Sadie blushed and smiled. "Thank you, Alex," she said, with a slight tilt of her head and a shrug. "Oh," she blurted out and pointed to his shoulder. "It looks like a pigeon left you a gift."

Alex twisted his neck and saw the glistening, white bird poop on his brown suede jacket. "Oh no," he said, reaching into his pocket for his hanky.

"Allow me," Sadie said, taking it from him and dipping it into the fountain's pool of water.

While Sadie tried her best to remove the stain, Alex asked, "I assume you've been to Saxon Gardens before?"

"I have. When we first moved here from Berlin, my parents liked to bring me and my brother here."

Alex nodded. "I thought with your last name that your family was from Germany, yet you have no accent."

"I was only two years old when we came to Warsaw. But both of my parents still have strong accents, and even my brother does a bit, since he's ten years older than me," she said, finishing her cleaning. "You can hardly notice it."

"Thank you," Alex said and gestured that they walk along the pathway. "Have you ever been inside the Blue Palace?"

"Is that the one with the blue roof?"

Alex nodded.

"I've passed it, but I've never been inside."

"Today you will," Alex said, holding out his elbow, and Sadie accepted by slipping her arm into the crook of his.

"Tell me, Alex," Sadie asked as they walked, "why did you want to become a university professor?"

Alex took a breath and said, "I think it's because of my involvement in the war. As an eyewitness and a patriot, is it not my duty to educate Poland's young people on its recent history?"

"It is indeed."

"May I ask you a question?"

"Of course."

"Why did you enroll at the university? I imagine many girls like you plan to marry and raise a family."

Sadie placed a hand to her cheek and said, "Do you find me out of place, Professor?"

"Of course not, I'm impressed in your interest in improving yourself through an education, that's all," he said, feeling his face flush.

"That's exactly why I enrolled," she said with a broad smile. "I want to have experiences before I devote my life to raising a family."

"That seems reasonable," Alex said, wishing he had the nerve to explore what she meant by *experiences*.

As they strolled along the pathway toward the Blue Palace, heads turned from those sitting along the park benches, taking notice of the attractive, well-dressed couple. Good thing, he thought, he decided to wear his finest suit ensemble, consisting of a tailored jacket, now with a slight blemish, a buttoned-up vest, and pants with a sharp crease, that he bought last year at Jablkowski Brothers. He noticed the suit displayed in the storefront window, and decided to splurge, not knowing if he would ever have the occasion to wear such an expensive outfit. He also bought a crisp white shirt and a silk tie that coordinated with the brown and gold woven suit fabric.

When the impressive, immense structure of the Blue Palace with the blue roof came into view, he turned to Sadie. "This is my favorite building in all of the city. Most people pass it by, without ever going inside."

"What makes it so special?"

"The palace was purchased by King Augustus the second for his daughter Anna as a Christmas present in 1726. But it wasn't until 1748 when it was converted into Europe's first public library."

"I had no idea," Sadie said.

"The palace is a labyrinth of rooms, crammed with a treasure trove of antiques and priceless books. I'll show you once we get inside," he said, taking her by the hand, and slipping in between two large hedges.

They stood before an unmarked steel door. Alex banged hard, and said, "A childhood friend of mine works here."

While they waited, Alex continued to clutch Sadie's hand, relishing her soft palm pressing against his. But quickly released it when the door swung open.

"Alex, come in," said a man with strikingly white hair, pale blue eyes, and skin that seemed as transparent as water.

"Allow me to introduce my good friend Jan," Alex said, as they stepped inside.

"You must be Sadie," Jan said, offering his hand.

Sadie smiled and placed her hand in Jan's, where he brought it to his lips and gently placed a kiss. "You are stunning, my dear."

"Thank you, Jan," she said, and looked over to Alex, her furrowed forehead expressing her concern.

"Jan is albino. It's caused by a lack of pigment in the color of the skin."

"I'm sorry, is it painful?" Sadie asked.

Jan let out an infectious laugh. "No, not all. But I am very sensitive to sunlight. That's why I work here," he said and leaned in. "There're heavy drapes on all the windows blocking the light."

Alex pointed down the corridor. "I'm going to show Sadie the collection of French engravings."

"Enjoy, you two. When you're ready to leave, come find me. I'll be on the third floor. We have a leak and need to remove the Latin collection from the shelves before they get damaged."

Alex turned to Sadie and took her by the hand. "Are you ready?"

She smiled, and her eyes sparkled, even in the dimly lit hallway, and she said, "Let's go."

CHAPTER SIX—SADIE'S CONFESSION

Sadie overexaggerated her hand gestures to describe the Blue Palace to Sara. "The main room was breathtaking. It was tall, with wooden columns supporting a domed ceiling. There were several marble statues of famous Polish men and the books had detailed engravings, with jewels encrusted upon them."

"I'm sure it was very nice, Sadie, but what happened when you were alone with him?" Sara asked, dipping her spoon into the sugar bowl.

Sadie looked around, not wanting people sitting nearby to overhear their conversation. She leaned over the small round top table and whispered, "He kissed me."

Sara's eyes lit up. "On your lips?"

Sadie nodded with a smile. "We were talking about my family's wool business, which he found fascinating, when put his hand on top of mine, leaned in, and kissed me."

Sara put her hand to her cheek. "Oh, my, your first kiss. What was it like?"

"He pressed his lips to mine, and we didn't part for several seconds, and when we did, we looked into each other's eyes and said not a word. He put a hand on my neck and brought me back for another kiss. This time longer than before."

"Did you touch tongues?"

Sadie furrowed her brow and said, "Don't be vulgar, Sara."

"Oh, you should. I did it once, it's wonderful."

Sadie sipped her coffee and looked across the street from the sidewalk café to the pedestrians strolling along Nalewki Street. She took a breath and looked back at Sara and said, "I can't wait to see him again. He's all I think about."

Sara's jaw dropped, and with wide eyes, she said, "You do realize the man's a *goy*?"

"Don't you think I know that," Sadie snapped back.

"What would your father say?"

"The same thing as your father; and you better not breathe a word of this to anyone," she said, wagging a finger.

"I promise," she said, placing her hand on top of Sadie's. "When will you see him again?"

"Tomorrow night after *Shabbat* dinner. We're taking a walk along on the promenade by the Vistula."

Sara sat back in her chair, crossed her legs, and pointed to Sadie. "You remember that story about the girl from the neighborhood who wanted to marry that Russian boy?"

Sadie nodded with a frown.

"That didn't go well. People say her father had the boy murdered to stop the daughter from marrying him. Then through a marriage broker, they arranged a match with a man twice her age. I hear she's got six children and is miserable."

Sadie sighed. "I know all about that."

"You will not like what I have to say," Sara said, shaking her head, "but maybe you should break things off with him before this goes too far?"

Sadie folded her arms across her chest and squinted. "Too far? How dare you?"

"It's just a warning between friends, Sadie. I don't want to see you hurt."

"I think you're jealous of me, because I found someone," Sadie said pointing a finger at Sara.

Sara laughed. "Jealous of falling in love with a *goy*? Don't be ridiculous."

Sadie pushed her chair back and abruptly stood up. She put one hand on her hip and wagged a finger at Sara and said, "Maybe it's best that you mind your own business."

She turned and marched out of the café. As she crossed the street, she stomped her foot on the cobblestones. She shouldn't have snapped at Sara. They had been friends since they were toddlers. Their parents had known each other from synagogue, and Sadie's older brother, Hymie, married Sara's older sister Etta. The two families had socialized countless times.

Sadie couldn't blame Sara for reminding her about the taboos of intermarriage. She remembered her own father pontificating on the subject at the dinner table when her brother casually joked about meeting a *shiksa* who struck his fancy.

Father had slammed his palms onto the dining room table, causing everyone to jump in fright. He glared at Hymie, and with a beating vein protruding down the center of his forehead, he said in a near growl, "Being born a Jew is not an accident of birth, but the sum of over three-thousand years of ancestral self-sacrifice. We have countless heroes who gave their lives to keep our lineage intact, and we still fight to do so, even to this day. But what's even more important, is that a Jewish marriage is a contractual bond, commanded by Hashem." He pointed a finger upwards. "It's a merger between a man and a woman into a single soul. Intermarriage is an unforgivable sin."

Sadie knew the outrage she would unleash from her parents, especially from her father if she dared to broach her affections toward Alex. But she couldn't deny her heart, and what her heart wanted was to see Alexander Kaminsky again.

CHAPTER SEVEN—WALK ALONG THE VISTULA

"You promised to tell me about the war," Sadie said, as they strolled down the busy promenade flanking the Vistula River.

Alex sighed—not sure he was ready to discuss this with Sadie. "It's something I don't enjoy talking about," he said with a shrug and dropped his gaze to kick a small stone off the pathway.

Sadie tugged on his arm, forcing him to stop and look at her. "Why is that, Alex?"

He took a breath and grimaced. "Because many Russian soldiers died."

"Isn't that a good thing?" Sadie asked, holding out her hands.

Alex nodded. "Yes, it's good because we defeated our enemy, but taking a life is nothing to be proud of."

"Tell me what happened."

Alex took a breath. He had never spoken of his exploits to a woman before. "What I didn't tell you about Jan and me, was that we both spied for General Pilsudski during the war."

Sadie jerked her head back and whispered, "Oh my goodness."

Alex looked up and down the promenade then said, "Come, let's stand by the water."

As they crossed, a man who looked as if he had been sleeping in the park approached. "Hey, buddy, could you spare some change?"

Sadie clutched Alex's arm.

"Are you scared of me?" the man asked, sticking his face inches from Sadie's.

Alex put his hand on the man's chest and pushed him back. "Take it easy, friend. Sure, I have some change for you," he said, reaching into his pocket.

Just as Alex was about to hand over a few coins, another man appeared, this one brandishing a hunting knife. "Give me that pocket watch of yours," he said, pointing with the rusty blade.

Alex reacted instinctively, grabbing the man's wrist and twisted it upwards, while with his other hand, he pushed back hard on the accoster's elbow, causing the man to yelp in pain and drop the knife.

The two disheveled men stared wide-eyed at Alex, just as a police officer called out, "Hey, what's going on over there? Are those bums bothering you?"

Alex turned and smiled. "No, officer, all is well."

"I've warned those two to stop harassing people," the policeman said, as he moved on.

"It's fine, I'm just giving them a few zlotys for a meal."

After the men took the money, they graciously thanked Alex for his generosity and the favor of not having them arrested and vanished into the crowd. Alex took Sadie by her hand and walked her over to the iron railing running along the water's edge. The river was full of pleasure boats touring the popular waterway under the early evening sky.

"Why didn't you turn those men over to that policeman? They threatened us with a knife, we could have been stabbed."

"That was nothing. Just two poor souls trying to survive. Maybe they'll remember my kindness and offer the same to someone else."

Sadie shook her head. "I don't know of anyone who would have handled that situation as you just did."

Alex shrugged. "Really? I'm not so sure."

"Well, I'm impressed. Now, tell me your story about the war."

Alex nodded, and looked out onto the river and said, "General Pilsudski was looking for two volunteers who could speak fluent Russian in order to infiltrate General Tukhachevsky's military headquarters in Minsk. Jan and I were the first two to step forward."

"You speak Russian?" Sadie asked.

Alex nodded. "Yes, I also speak German, Spanish, and English."

"What about Yiddish?" Sadie asked, jokingly.

"*Vas makhstu?*"

"*Ikh bin gezunt*," Sadie said with a laugh. "You keep surprising me."

"I guess I have a thing for languages, and so does Jan. That's why he works at the Blue Palace."

"What does he do?"

"He translates sensitive manuscripts for the government."

Sadie nodded slowly. "Tell me, what happened in Minsk?"

Alex exhaled a huge sigh, and began, "It was the dead of winter when Jan and I took off for Minsk. It took us two weeks by horseback over snow-packed roads. Occasionally we found roadside inns where we spent the night. But more often we settled for lodgings in barns, sleeping alongside cows and sheep.

"When we arrived in Minsk, we dressed in the Russian officer's uniforms we packed away in our saddlebags. The plan was to locate General Tukhachevsky's headquarters while posing as officers sent from the front with important tactical locations of the Polish Army.

"It was General Pilsudski's idea to offer intelligence of real value, to gain the Russian's trust, which worked better than we hoped. We were able to learn that General Tukhachevsky had conceded that his Red Army was on the verge of defeat, and planned to issue orders for retreat. He wanted to regroup, improve his logistics, and hopefully regain the initiative, and then try to push the Poles back again.

"Since Jan and I had just come from Warsaw, he gave us the orders to carry back to the front, which of course, we purposely never delivered. This resulted in the Soviet armies at the front lines to fall into chaos. Some divisions continued to fight their way toward Warsaw, while others lost their cohesion, panicked, and did their best to retreat. It wasn't too much longer before all organized resistance ceased to exist and the Soviet Army was routed. Thousands of Russian soldiers were killed or wounded, along with tens of thousands being taken prisoners of war," Alex said, staring out onto the Vistula River.

Sadie reached out, grabbed Alex by his shoulders, and turned him around to face her. "You did the right thing, otherwise Poland would be under Soviet domination now. You and Jan are heroes."

Alex smiled. "Thank you, Sadie. I just don't feel like a hero, and if you ask Jan, neither does he. We just did what any other patriot would do."

Sadie shook her head. "You don't give yourself enough credit. There aren't many who could have earned an audience with a Russian general in his war room and gained his trust. What you and Jan did took immense courage and great skill."

Alex smiled, took Sadie's hand and said, "Come, let's walk awhile."

They walked in silence for a few minutes, then Sadie asked, "Can you tell me about your family?"

Alex took a breath and exhaled. "They're all gone."

"What do you mean?"

"Ten years ago, during the Great War, the German airship *Schutte Lanz* bombed our neighborhood, killing my parents, and my younger brother."

Sadie put her hands to her mouth. "Oh my god, Alex. I can't believe that. Where were you?"

"I was out searching for firewood. On my way home, I saw the airship floating over the river," he said gesturing into the distance. "I dropped the wood and ran home. But by the time I arrived, our apartment building was in flames," he said and frowned.

"I'm so sorry, Alex. What a terrible thing to happen. What did you do? Where did you live?"

"Jan's family took me in. I lived with them until Jan and I went off to war against the Soviets six years later."

"You two are like brothers."

"Yes, we are brothers."

"I'm sorry you're all alone," Sadie said with a lone tear running down her cheek.

Alex stopped walking, put his hand around Sadie's neck and pulled her close. "I'm not alone anymore," he said and kissed her.

This time he did so with his mouth open, and Sadie responded in kind. He felt her tongue meet hers, and they explored each other, darting about, nearly causing Alex's knees to buckle.

When their lips parted, they remained clutched in each other's arms. Sadie's tear-filled, green eyes looked up to Alex, her lips pink and swollen. Then she said the words that would change their lives forever. "I love you, Alex."

Alex took his hand, and gently wiped away a tear from her face, and said, "I love you too, Sadie."

CHAPTER EIGHT—ROWBOAT

Sadie spent hours getting ready for her afternoon rendezvous with Alex. She tried on several outfits and fussed with her hair incessantly. Eventually, she decided upon something casual, but still figure-flattering, and pulled back her hair into a ponytail, tying it off with a navy-blue ribbon.

"Where are you going?" her father's voice bellowed from behind her as she grasped the front door handle.

"I'm meeting friends at the market. I'll be back later, bye," she said and hurried out, while her father's commanding voice was cut off in mid-sentence upon the door slamming shut.

Normally the walk to the market along Nalewki Street took about fifteen minutes. Assuming she didn't stumble upon a friend on the way, that would make her about ten minutes late. Sadie had fought back urges to leave sooner; the last thing she wanted to do was to arrive before Alex and ruin her approach.

While at home she practiced her strut and her *spontaneous* reaction upon seeing Alex, while he waited impatiently for her. She imagined spotting him pacing in front of the entrance to the Old Market where she would call out his name.

Sadie also rehearsed her smile—a grand one, displaying her white teeth, which she brushed several times with baking soda.

When she turned the corner, there, as predicted, was Alex marching back and forth at the entrance to the Old Town Market.

"Alex," she said loud enough for several people to turn their heads, including him.

"Sadie," he replied, with a gorgeous smile that caused her heart to beat faster.

They clasped hands, and Sadie pushed up on her tiptoes to give Alex a kiss on his cheek. He looked at her for a moment, squinting his eyes, as if to say—*On my cheek?* Then proceeded to kiss her lips. She wrapped her arms around his neck and took him in, their tongues swimming in each other's mouth, until she caught herself and pulled away.

"Not here," she said, darting her eyes about. Sadie didn't want to consider the consequences if someone recognized her. No doubt her parents would learn of her encounter—*We saw your daughter with a man that didn't look Jewish.*

"Where can we go?" she asked.

"This way," he said, taking her by the hand.

Like young children, they scampered around the outskirts of the Old Town Market until they got to the promenade alongside the Vistula River.

"Where're you taking me?" Sadie asked, catching her breath.

"It's right down here," Alex said, pointing to a wooden staircase.

As soon as Sadie reached the top step, she saw the rowboats. "Are we going in a boat?"

"Don't worry. If we sink, I'm a very good swimmer," he said, bounding down the steps to the small wooden dock.

"I'm not afraid. I've been in one of these before," she boasted, taking Alex's hand and gingerly climbing aboard.

Moments later, they found themselves out in the middle of the Vistula, among other pleasure vessels, enjoying a pleasant Sunday afternoon.

Sadie tilted her head back, allowing the sunshine to beam upon her face, while Alex pulled hard on the oars.

After ten minutes of rowing, Alex swung the oars into the hull of the boat, allowing it to drift with the current. "Come sit next to me," he said, patting the wooden board strapped to the frame of the rowboat.

Sadie pushed herself close to him and rested her head upon his shoulder. Alex wrapped his strong arm around her and squeezed.

Sadie sighed and said, "I don't ever think I've been so happy."

Alex looked at her and said with a smile, "I was just thinking the same thing."

Several minutes later, Alex said, "Let's dock over here. There's a nice café overlooking the river."

They found a table offering a fabulous view of the Vistula River, choked with couples and families in leisure boats enjoying the afternoon.

"Would you like to order a bottle of wine?" Alex asked.

Sadie nodded. "That would be lovely."

After their first glass, Alex reached over and grasped Sadie's hand. "Can we talk about what we said the other day?" he said, furrowing his brow.

"What do you mean?" she asked, placing her hand on her chest.

"You know," he said, lowering his voice, "when we declared our love for each other."

"Oh, that," Sadie said, trying to smile, while her stomach rumbled.

"Yes, that," he said, taking a sip of his wine before continuing. "We must be careful, Sadie. If your parents learn about us, I'm concerned they would be angry."

Sadie turned her gaze to the boats below and said, "This is my life, and I have a right to be with whom I love, not some strange man. I'm not a pound of wool Father can shop around."

"No, you're not," Alex said.

Sadie squinted and paused for a moment before she said, "I'm willing to take a stand, no matter the consequences."

Alex reached out and took Sadie's hand. "I'm touched that you're willing to give up your family for me."

"What about you?" she said, cocking her head toward him. "Are you willing, if it came to that, to give up your position at the university?"

"That's an easy question to answer," he said with a shrug. "I ready to risk my life for you, Sadie."

She stared at Alex for several seconds, her eyes filling with tears, and as they released and cascaded down her cheeks, she smiled and said, "I would do the same."

CHAPTER NINE—WOLLMAN & SON

Sadie had both hands deep in a metal tub filled with hot water and detergent, submerging the raw wool, then allowing it to dry, before beginning the carding process of pulling the wool into long strands, ready for the loom.

In the next room, her father, and brother Hymie, were negotiating with the city's largest manufacturers of women's sweaters. Sadie knew this was an important deal that her father was eager to make.

"The Dabrowski Knitting Company can double our sales," she had overheard her father boasting to Hymie a few days earlier.

The meeting was taking place behind closed doors, and all Sadie could make out were unintelligible conversations. It wasn't until her father, her brother, and the owner of the Dabrowski Knitting Company, Mr. Michal Dabrowski, entered the workroom that she understood the meeting to be a success.

"Mr. Dabrowski, allow me to introduce my daughter Sadie," her father said.

Sadie quickly pulled her bright red hands out from the tub of soapy hot water, clutching two clumps of wool, and said, "It's nice to meet you, sir."

Mr. Dabrowski's eyes lit up upon seeing Sadie. "You have an exquisite daughter, Mr. Wollman."

"Thank you, Mr. Dabrowski," Father said. "Sadie helps with the business. It looks like she will need to work full time, now that we need to increase our production."

"Such a beautiful young woman should get married and start a family, not toil away in a factory," Mr. Dabrowski said, pointing to the wooden tub.

"Soon enough. Once we get our production up to a point where I can afford a new employee to replace Sadie, a marriage will be arranged for my daughter."

"It will be a lucky man who captures this prize," Mr. Dabrowski said, shifting his bushy eyebrows up and down.

*

At the end of the business day, while her father was filling his worn leather satchel with the day's paperwork to review after dinner, Sadie knocked on his opened office door.

"Do you have a minute to speak with me, Father?"

"Sure, come in, Sadie."

"I want to congratulate you on completing the deal with Mr. Dabrowski. It's very exciting."

"Thank you," her father said, looking up from his desk for a moment.

"Can I ask you what you meant when you said I will need to work full time? You know that I'm busy with classes at the university during the day," she said, reminding him.

He looked up and grimaced. "There will be no more classes until I can find someone to replace you, and when I do, it will be high time we find you a husband."

Sadie sat down on a chair in front of the desk and stared at her father, her jaw hanging open. Just as he rose from his desk and turned to walk away, Sadie called after him. "No, Father, I must finish my classes. I need only one more year to get my degree. You promised," she pleaded.

He stopped and looked at her. "Nonsense. You'll stop at once. Starting tomorrow, I expect you to be working full days, starting at seven in the morning," he said, and walked out, leaving Sadie bewildered about what had just occurred.

She lowered her face into her cupped hands and sighed. Sadie had always known that one day this moment would come, though she had hoped to have it put off for another year by attending college. Now, all she could see were troubled times ahead with her father.

*

After dinner, Sadie told her parents she was meeting Sara and hustled out the door before either of them could object. She needed to find Alex and explain to him what was happening.

Alex had told her he lived in faculty housing at the university. But when she arrived on campus and stood before the stone building, she realized she didn't know which apartment he lived in. Observing the architecture and the number of windows, Sadie figured that there must be a dozen floors, with at least a dozen rooms per floor, and she was worried that she wouldn't be able to find his apartment.

She couldn't make an inquiry regarding his residence, because why would a female student be searching for a male professor with evening approaching. Instead, she entered the building's vestibule, hoping to find a directory of its occupants.

Moments later, Sadie stood before the polished brass plaque, and nervously ran a finger up and down each row until she found it: Alexander Kaminsky—Apartment 6C.

She pushed the heavy interior door open and saw a wide, wooden staircase. Sadie took a brief look up and down the empty corridor and charged up the stairs. By the time she got to the sixth floor, her heart was pounding, not only from the physical exertion, but from heartache as well. How was she going to tell Alex that her father was forcing her to drop her classes at the university, and to make matters worse, she would be forced into an arranged marriage her parents were about to negotiate?

The hallway was empty, except for a black cat tormenting a mouse. Each apartment door was marked with a number. She tiptoed past 6A and 6B, and stopped in front of 6C. Before she knocked, Sadie took a moment to contemplate Alex's reactions to her sudden appearance. He wouldn't be pleased that she'd showed up unannounced, and if anyone caught her, a university-wide scandal would certainly erupt. There was also a good possibility that if discovered, they could fire him for such outrageous and inappropriate behavior.

But this was an emergency, and if Alex truly loved her, he would welcome her in without reservations.

Sadie took a breath and knocked lightly upon the wooden door.

CHAPTER TEN—SADIE'S VISIT

Alex thought he heard a knock at his door while lying in bed reading a book on the history of the Native Americans. He put it down, swung his feet onto the wooden floor, and walked over to the door. Just as he was about to turn the handle, a second soft knock confirmed someone was there.

Alex pushed the door slightly ajar and there, to his shock, stood Sadie. "Sadie, what in the world are you doing here?" he said, taking a quick glance up and down the hallway.

"I need to talk to you," she said, with tears rolling down her cheeks.

"Come in, before someone sees you," he said, stepping back allowing her to enter.

She walked in, put her hand to her mouth and pointed down to his legs. Alex looked and realized that he was in his drawers.

"Oh god, Sadie," he said, and bent down to grab his pants lying on the floor. "Come and sit down and tell me what's wrong," he said, pulling up his pants and cocking his head to the two chairs and a small table situated under the window.

"Can we open it a bit, Alex?" Sadie asked, pointing to the window with a grimace. "It's stuffy in here."

Alex leaned over, unlatched the lock on the window frame, and lifted the double hung a few inches, allowing in a refreshing breeze. "How did you know where to find me?" he said, taking a seat across from her.

"Wasn't too difficult. You told me you lived in the Faculty Residence building. I found your name on the directory, and here I am."

Alex exhaled. "You know if you get caught up here, we're both done for."

"Please don't be angry with me," she said, her tears returning. "I didn't know what to do."

"Calm down," he said, grasping her hand, "and tell me what happened."

Sadie explained about the visit by Mr. Dabrowski and how her father ordered her to drop her classes so she could help in the business.

"That's not the end of the world, Sadie. We can still see each other," Alex said, trying to sound reassuring.

"I know, but Father said that he wants to hire someone to replace me once the business sales increase, which won't be long because of this deal with Mr. Dabrowski. According to what Father said, our production will double within a month, then it would be time for me to marry." She looked at Alex with glassy eyes, and said, "I think he's already discussing arrangements with a marriage broker."

"Have you told your parents about us?"

Sadie put her hand to her cheek. "Oh no, that's a conversation I'm dreading."

Alex cupped his hands behind his head and sighed. "Then we need to make a decision."

"What do you mean?" she said, holding her hands out.

"Should we take action to prevent this from happening?"

Sadie sat silent for a good while, then said, "Are you saying we should marry?"

Alex shrugged. "I would have hoped for a longer courtship, but it appears we have no choice."

Sadie nodded. "There's nothing I would want more than to marry you right now, but how?"

"We elope. We could never remain here in the city. I would lose my position at the university for seducing a student, not to mention your father's presumed vitriolic reaction."

Sadie thought for a moment, then reached for Alex's hand and squeezed. "Let's immigrate to America. I hear many people are doing it."

"Are you serious?"

"I've never been more serious in my life," she said, her eyes wide open.

Alex took a breath and straightened his back and took a deep breath. "I need to give that some thought."

Sadie shook her head and held out her hands. "Either we stay here, and Father marries me to some old disgusting man, or we take control of our lives and go to America."

Alex lowered his eyes for a moment while he thought. "Well, I don't want to lose you to *some old disgusting man*," he said, with a smirk. "It's just hard to imagine giving all this up."

Sadie shrugged. "Well, you're going to need to decide what you want, Alex. All of this," she said, waving a hand about, "or me. Which will it be?"

"You know," Alex said, wagging a finger. "My good friend Peter emigrated last year and got a position as history professor at Columbia University in New York City. He's been writing, saying they're looking to expand the department and I should join him."

Sadie's eyes opened wide and sparkled. "That's wonderful, Alex."

"Let me give this some thought. We'll need to make plans. I'll speak to a few colleagues tomorrow morning who know how immigration is done."

"All right," she said, grasping his hand. "Let's meet at that bench by the river at noon."

*

While Alex waited for Sadie, he mulled over the plan he put into motion. Earlier that day he learned that they would need to travel by train to the Port of Hamburg, where they would board a steamship headed for America.

They would leave tomorrow. Sadie would need to pack a small bag so as not to raise suspicions in case someone saw her leaving. He planned to tell Sadie to meet him at the Warsaw Central Railway Station at noon, having already bought passage on the Hamburg-Amerika line at the ticket office in the station.

Alex stared at the Vistula River, where everything of significance in his life had taken place. Now he was about to leave it all behind for the love of a woman. He sighed, pondering his decision. There was no real debate, he conceded. He loved Sadie and would do anything to be with her. His life as a university professor was wonderful, but it would never provide the joy he was now experiencing. Having the love of a woman like Sadie was indeed worth leaving it all behind.

CHAPTER ELEVEN—THE LETTER

Sadie realized she would need to leave a letter for her parents explaining the reasons for her sudden disappearance. Of course they would be angry for her betrayal and humiliated among the large but close-knit Jewish community, but she felt they left her no choice.

To make sure she wouldn't get caught, Sadie planned to drop the letter in the post the next morning, ensuring that it would be delivered long after they sailed from the Port of Hamburg. Satisfied with her plan, she dipped her pen into the inkwell and wrote.

Dear Father and Mother,

It is with both sadness and joy that I write this letter. Let me begin by saying that I love you both very much, and I have tried all my life to have been an obedient and loving daughter. I would never intentionally do anything to hurt or embarrass you. But something has happened that leaves me no choice but to follow a path I'm sure you will disapprove of.

I have fallen in love with a man. He is intelligent and kind, and we have decided to spend the rest of our lives together. I know, if he was a Jewish man, you would find him a perfect match for me. But alas, he is not, and I know this is a marriage you would never condone.

That is why Alex and I have decided to immigrate to America, where we will marry and raise a family. I know this will cause you great heartache, but please think of my happiness. Tomorrow morning we set

sail from Hamburg aboard the SS Amerika for New York. Once we get
settled, I will write to you, and perhaps one day, after your anger has
gone, you will come and visit.

   All my love, Sadie.

With her letter written and sealed, she laid herself down upon her bed and stared at the ceiling. Sleep would not come that night as she tried to imagine what the next few weeks of her life would be like.

She had packed her valise with the barest of necessities, but there were still several skirts and blouses she could not squeeze in. The only thing she could think of was to wear them under her outer garments. This was not figure-flattering, but she had no other options.

Her father had told her that tomorrow would be her last day at the university. "Make sure you tell the administration that you're dropping out from further studies," he instructed.

"I will, Father," Sadie said, trying to sound deferential.

She planned to leave home at her usual time at eight in the morning and on her way, she would drop the letter in the post. After withdrawing from her classes, she would walk home, grab her valise from under her bed, and meet Alex at the Warsaw Central Railway Station at noon.

Hopefully, Alex would have purchased tickets for both the train and the steamship by the time she got there. She imagined that they would board the train bound for Hamburg and find a place in the glamorous dining car for lunch on their way to their first stop in Berlin.

Once they made it to Hamburg, Alex would hail a taxi to bring them to the port, where they would show their tickets and board the luxury steamship. She decided that tomorrow night, once they were safely out to sea, they would indulge in a romantic dinner in the ship's dining hall, after which, when they were both back in the cabin, she would give herself to him. Then afterwards, they would sit topside, where Alex would hold her in his arms, watching the starlit sky over the vast North Sea, as they sailed for America.

CHAPTER TWELVE—TRAIN TO HAMBURG

Alex had two tickets tucked safely in his jacket pocket. He looked up to the board and saw the 12:25 to Hamburg was leaving from track number sixteen and prayed Sadie wouldn't be late.

According to the train schedule, they were to arrive at six o'clock tomorrow morning in Hamburg, leaving them plenty of time to board the SS *Amerika* for their six o'clock voyage the following evening.

Alex paced the floor of the Warsaw Central Railway Station, and thought about the conversation he had earlier with his superior, and head of the History Department, Dr. Filip Duda.

"Are you telling me, Alex, you're resigning your position, just as the semester begins, to immigrate with a student of yours to America?"

Alex nodded. "Yes, that's exactly what I'm telling you."

"This leaves me in an awfully difficult situation. Where will I find a replacement?"

"I'm sorry to do this to you, Filip, but it seems we have no choice but to go right away. The girl's father is ready to sign an agreement with a marriage broker."

"Are you sure you're not rushing into this?"

Alex sighed. "Haven't you ever been in love?"

Filip stood up, and walked over to his window and looked out onto the university's esplanade. "The ironic thing is, this sounds all too familiar. I once fell for a girl my family didn't approve of. She wasn't a Jew, but she was from a poor family. My father complained that she was uneducated and our children would never amount to much, because of some crap about *breeding among people of our station*. I listened to him, and to this day, I regret it."

*

The bells of the clock tower struck the noon hour, snapping Alex out of his ruminations. He looked over to the multiple sets of doorways, hoping to see Sadie walking through one of them. But there was still no sign of her.

He continued pacing, monitoring the giant clock mounted high above in the voluminous main hall of the railway station. It was now ten minutes past the hour. He worried if something had happened to her. *Maybe she got caught leaving, or her parents discovered her plan. Then what would we do?*

Just as he was imagining the worst, she walked in. "Sadie," he shouted, waving his arms. "Over here!"

She ran over, her valise swinging wildly in her hand. "Sorry, I got held up. There was some wagon filled with apples that turned over and blocked the street."

"We need to run. Let's go," he said, grabbing her hand and racing for the door to track number sixteen.

They ran up the staircase to the platform and saw a few passengers still boarding the train. "We made it," Alex said, as they hopped onboard.

51

Sadie slipped into an empty berth, while Alex lifted their valises up onto the wooden rack before joining her.

"That was close," Sadie said, resting her head on Alex's shoulder.

"Did anyone see you leave?"

Sadie shook her head. "No, the house was empty by the time I went back for my valise, and I saw no one I knew on my way here."

"That's good. When we get to Hamburg, you should write a letter to your parents and let them know what's happened."

"Oh, I already did and dropped it in the post this morning."

"You did it already?" Alex asked, leaning forward.

Sadie nodded.

Alex put his hand to his cheek. "You realize they'll get that tomorrow morning."

"So what, we'll be gone by then. It will be too late," Sadie said with a smile and a shrug.

"No," Alex said, shaking his head, "we don't sail until tomorrow night."

Sadie wrinkled her brow and put her hand to her mouth. "Don't we arrive at six tonight and sail at six in the morning?"

"No, Sadie. This train brings us to Hamburg at six tomorrow morning, and we don't set sail until six tomorrow night."

"Oh, my god. That means Father can send a wire to the Hamburg-Amerika Line and stop us."

"How would he know which ship we're on?"

Sadie dropped her eyes and whispered, "Because I told him in my letter."

"Sadie, what have you done?"

CHAPTER THIRTEEN—PORT OF HAMBURG

By the time they arrived in Hamburg, the sun had not yet risen, and neither could Sadie from her seat. She hadn't slept for over forty-eight hours. The first-half in anticipation of her new and joyous new life with Alex, and the latter-half because of her foolish mistake of mailing her parents a letter, that may have put their grand plan into jeopardy.

"Come, Sadie," Alex said, helping her to her feet. "Let's hail a taxi to take us to the harbor. The ticket agent said we can't board the SS *Amerika* until two o'clock, but suggested a few good places for breakfast, and afterwards there's a large hall where passengers can relax before boarding. Hopefully, your father won't open the letter until he gets home after work, and we'll be safely on our way."

Sadie had never felt so vulnerable, and her lack of sleep only compounded her delicate condition. There were no words from Alex that consoled her, though he tried. Many scenarios played out in her mind. The letter could be delayed and show up a day late, which was plausible, since the mail delivery service in their neighborhood was spotty. Or Father would work late, since he was busy gearing up for the pending large orders from the Dabrowski Knitting Company, and would wait until morning before perusing the mail.

But then there was always the chance her mother would check the mail, and read Sadie's letter, and telephone Father at the office. He would certainly take immediate action, putting a halt to her dream life with Alex.

While they waited for hours in the passenger area of the terminal, Sadie kept her eyes glued on the representatives of the Hamburg-Amerika Line walking by. She imagined being approached by one of these men in an official uniform, asking to see their tickets. *Are you Sadie Wollman?* She would nod. *Please come with me.* Sadie and Alex would be escorted into an office where their tickets would be revoked, and the two of them returned to Warsaw.

"Come, Sadie," Alex said, holding out his hand, "it's time to board."

She looked up and smiled. Perhaps they would be all right.

Sadie's nerves returned when she saw the long line of passengers waiting to board.

"Look at that queue, Alex."

"That's for third class. I bought us first-class accommodations. We board over there," he said, pointing to a fabric-covered gang-plank where people dressed like they were going to the opera, were now boarding.

"First class, that must have cost a fortune."

Alex laughed. "That's for sure. I have some inheritance money from my parents and figured that this would be a perfect time to use it."

"I hope you have some left, we'll need it once we get to America."

Alex stopped walking, took Sadie's hand and said, "You need to stop worrying so much. Everything will be fine."

"I hope you're right, Alex."

*

"What do you think? Isn't it magnificent?" Alex said, spreading his arms wide in their first-class cabin.

Sadie felt the softness of the plush carpeting under her feet and ran her fingertips along the polished wooden tabletop reflecting the lightbulbs from the crystal chandelier above and said, "Am I dreaming?"

Alex smiled. "No, this is all very real," he said, pulling back the luxurious purple velour drapery from the balcony door. "Come, let's take a look at our view."

Sadie and Alex stood on the balcony of their suite, observing the crew performing their last-minute logistics before the SS *Amerika* set sail.

"Looks like we'll be fine," Alex said, putting his arm around Sadie's waist.

Sadie exhaled, realizing that he was right. Within the hour, the crew would roll back the gangplanks, and it would be too late for passengers to disembark. She thought of a stopper being pulled from a bathtub as a way to describe the anxiety draining from her. The tightness in her chest let go. She kissed Alex on his cheek and said, "Would it be okay if I lay down for a while?"

"Let's go inside, I'm sure the bed is very comfortable."

"I'm so tired, I think I could fall asleep on the floor."

CHAPTER FOURTEEN—IN THE NICK OF TIME

It took only seconds for Sadie to fall asleep. Alex sat alongside her for a while before he stepped back out onto the balcony, and watched the passengers shouting their *bon voyages* to friends and family standing on the dock.

There was, of course, no one to see them off, and he thanked god for that. Because if anyone did appear, it wouldn't be to offer their fond farewells, but to take him into custody for absconding with the daughter of a prominent businessman of Warsaw.

He would wait until they were well out to sea before he would wake Sadie up. She needed rest. There would be plenty of time for her to enjoy the special attention of a first-class passenger, especially after the ordeal of the past two days.

Alex leaned back onto the wooden lounge chair, closed his eyes and took in the sun's warmth setting over the western section of the large harbor. Just as he felt himself doze off, he heard shrieks of sirens. He opened his eyes, and quickly sat up, and to his horror, he saw several police cars speeding onto the dock.

Alex got to his feet, grabbed on to the railing, and watched, at the foot of the first-class gangplank, three police officers approaching the ship's first mate, whom he had met earlier when he and Sadie first boarded. From his perch high above, he could make out three police officers showing documents, and then being escorted up the gangplank.

Alex knew immediately who they were coming for. He considered the possibility of shaking Sadie awake and finding a place where they could hide. But that seemed futile, as they would eventually be discovered by the ship's crew, and subsequently held in the brig until their return voyage to Hamburg, when they would have turned them over to the authorities.

By the time he awakened Sadie, and explained what was about to occur, there was a knock on their cabin door.

"Open up," came a stern voice.

"What are we going to do?" cried Sadie.

Alex sighed, and said, "Looks like we're going back to Warsaw."

CHAPTER FIFTEEN—CARDING WOOL

"Father, please tell me what you've done with Alex?" Sadie pleaded.

"That man is no longer a concern of yours," he said, sitting in his high-back, velour upholstered chair.

Sadie looked over to her mother for help, but she refused to say a word, keeping an emotionless gaze upon her daughter.

"Let me tell you what will happen now," began her father. "You'll come to work with me each morning and card the wool until it's time to go home. On *Shabbat*, you'll accompany me to synagogue and sit with the ladies up in the balcony. You'll be under my constant supervision until I find you a suitable husband, which," he paused to sigh, "may take a while."

Sadie shook her head, while her father continued to speak.

"This entire incident has caused our family great humiliation and embarrassment. That's all I have to say." He raised his finger in the air and added, "But I have one important question—are you still a virgin?"

Sadie's jaw fell open. She looked over to her mother again, as if she would come to her rescue, but like before, she sat stone-faced. "Yes, Father, I'm still a virgin. I hope that pleases you."

He shrugged. "It doesn't really matter, because the perception is, you're damaged goods. No one respectable will marry you now. Congratulations on ruining your life, and your family's reputation."

By the time they allowed Sadie to go to her bedroom, there were no more tears left to cry, though sadness still consumed her. She fell onto her bed, and while dozens of troubling thoughts battled for her attention, she eventually fell asleep.

*

The next thing she remembered was being shaken by her mother. "It's time to wake up, Sadie. You have thirty minutes to get ready."

"Ready for what?" Sadie said, through the thick fog that she used to call her mind.

"For work. Now get going, you know how your father dislikes being delayed."

Sadie spent the next four hours carding wool. Thank goodness pulling clumps of wool into long strands was a mindless task. Still exhausted from her ordeal, she nearly dozed off several times.

While she combed through dozens of dense, tangled clumps of freshly sheered and washed wool, Sadie worried what would happen to Alex. During their long journey back to Warsaw, under the watchful eye of a Hamburg Police escort, they discussed the consequences and remedies to their predicament.

"We'll figure this out, Sadie," Alex said, observing the young detective assigned to handing them over to the Warsaw Police, once they arrived at the Warsaw Central Railway Station.

Sadie shrugged her hands in response. "We've had our chance. My stupidity caused this. We could have been out to sea by now, on our way

60

to a new life. Instead, I'm heading back home to a future that frightens me," she said while tears flowed down her face.

Alex put an arm around her and squeezed her in tight. "This is not the end, Sadie. I'll speak to your father. It's not like I'm a vagabond. I'm a well-respected professor at one of Europe's most prestigious universities, or at least I used to be."

Sadie shook her head. "That will make no difference. You're not a Jew, and that's the only thing that matters."

Alex shook his head.

"What do you think will happen to you?" Sadie asked, clutching his forearm.

Alex shrugged. "It's not a crime, what we've done, and you're not underage, and I wasn't forcing you to emigrate to America. So, there's nothing they can do, except release me."

"But why would the police prevent us from leaving, if it's not illegal to do so?"

Alex shrugged. "Apparently your father has important friends in high places in the government."

When they got to the station in Warsaw, Sadie's father was waiting for them, along with two police officers. They took Alex into custody and whisked him away, and Sadie wondered if she would ever see him again.

Her father, even though he called her *damaged goods*, insisted he would find a match for her. She overheard him talking to her brother about the marriage broker stopping by after lunch, and how he was eager to make a deal.

"The sooner we get her married, the better. I have too much to do than worry about her running off again," he said.

Sadie could taste the bitterness rise up from deep within her. *How could Father do this to me? He's ruining my life. I will never marry if I can't marry the man I love.*

CHAPTER SIXTEEN—TWO GOONS

After a day-long interrogation at the Warsaw Police Station, Alex was free to go. Except, as he rose from his chair and headed for the exit, the detective in charge told him to wait.

"We've arranged a ride for you, Professor. If you would please follow me," he said, and led him toward the back of the police station, to a dim alleyway where a motorcar was idling. Standing alongside were two broad-shouldered men. "These gentlemen will make sure you get home."

Alex looked at the detective and shook his head. "You want me to get in the car with them?" he said, jerking his thumb toward the two goon-like figures standing in the shadows.

The detective shrugged and walked through the police station's open back door.

Alex surveyed the dark alleyway, seeking a way to avoid getting into a tussle with these two gangsters. With no apparent escape route, he reluctantly slipped into the back seat.

The car pulled out of the alley and down the street. Eventually, they made their way toward the wide boulevard along the Vistula River, and pulled down an access road that brought them under the Poniatowski Bridge.

Alex knew immediately that unless he reacted fast, he was about to be shot and dumped into the river. As the car slowed, Alex reached over to the man seated in the front passenger seat, and locked his arm around his neck, he then used his full weight, and pushed his legs against the back of the front seat, and yanked the man backwards toward him. The man grabbed Alex's arm, as his body was lifted upwards, and collapsed on top of Alex.

Alex tightened down on his chokehold, causing the man to gasp for air, and in a move he learned as a soldier, he momentarily released his hold, and with one hand holding the back of the man's head, he gripped the man's jaw with his other hand and twisted hard. An audible crack told Alex the deed was done, and he released the dead man.

In the meantime, the driver stopped, exited the car and was waiting alongside it for Alex.

"Get out," the man ordered, pointing a gun.

Alex slowly opened the door, and the moment he got to his feet, he rushed the man. He heard a gunshot, but felt nothing as he rammed himself into the assailant, slamming him into one of the immense stone columns supporting the bridge.

The man groaned, and they both fell hard to the ground. Alex quickly pushed himself off, and saw the gun lying on the brick pavement, only a few feet away. Alex pounced on it, stood up, and pointed it at the man.

"Get in the car," Alex commanded.

The man got to his feet and slipped in behind the wheel, keeping a keen eye on Alex the entire time. "Put the car in drive."

Which the man did.

"Turn the wheel toward the river."

Again, the man complied.

Alex took a step closer, put the gun against the man's temple and pulled the trigger, putting a bullet into his skull, and splattering his brains across the upholstery. The man fell over, and as he did, the car slowly rolled forward and tipped over into the Vistula River.

Alex watched the car glided swiftly downstream, fill up with water, tilt vertically and eventually sink, swallowed by the black river. Alex let out a sigh, leaned over and put his hands on his thighs and noticed blood puddling beneath his feet. He quickly examined himself and realized that he had been shot.

He pulled up his shirt and saw where the bullet entered. It was on the left side of his abdomen. He twisted and saw another wound on his back. This was good news, meaning the bullet had passed through him. But now he was in agonizing pain, feeling like a hot fireplace poker had pierced him and was bleeding profusely. He needed attention quickly or he would bleed out.

Alex tossed the gun into the river and found a stairwell leading to the promenade where he and Sadie had just sauntered a few days earlier. But unlike that day, when dozens of people were out for an early evening stroll, there was not a soul in sight.

He stumbled toward the roadway, which was just as desolate.

"I need to make it to Jan's apartment," he mumbled aloud. But he was growing weaker. *I'll just rest here a minute*, he thought, finding a bench. His vision was becoming blurry as he reached for the arm of the bench and missed it. He tried to pull himself up, but the darkness consumed him, and he passed out.

CHAPTER SEVENTEEN—A SURPRISE VISITOR

Days went by without another word spoken by her parents about finding a match. At home, her mother tried to be attentive, but Sadie's anger kept them distant. During work, her brother Hymie acted as an intermediary, communicating any messages between Sadie and her father.

Sadie secretly wished what her father said about her being a ruined woman, and that no man would want her, to be true. Though she was still a virgin and hardly ruined, there was no man she would ever give herself willingly to, unless it was her true love, Alex.

Sadie dreamt about him often. A recurring one was that they made it out to sea, and they strolled topside onboard the SS *Amerika*, arm in arm, on a moonlit night, talking about their plans upon arriving in America. She dreamed of making love to him for the first time and how they would lie together, intertwined in their luxurious first-class suite. Then, of course, there were the nightmares, where she was awakened from her sleep, and forcibly dragged off the ship.

But tonight, she dreamed of sitting in the classroom, watching the brilliant professor lecture about his extraordinary exploits as a Polish spy, saving the country from the dreadful Soviets. Then she heard her name being called, "*Sadie, it's me,*" and the words came from far away. She looked to where it was coming from, but she could not answer.

"*Sadie, wake up.*" This time voice was closer, forcing her to leave the dreamworld. Sadie opened her eyes and saw Alex looking at her.

"Alex," she stammered, sat up and wrapped her arms around his neck, "how in the world did you get in here?"

He put his finger to his mouth, and said, "*Shhh.* I snuck in through the window."

Sadie looked over to the open window. "You climbed up the wall to get in?"

"I would scale the tallest mountain to see you, what's the big deal about a second story?"

"Oh, Alex," she said and kissed him.

Alex groaned and pulled away. "Not so tight, I'm wounded," he said with a grimace.

Sadie put her hand to her mouth. "What do you mean?"

"I was shot trying to stop two men from killing me and dumping my body in the Vistula. I was able to escape, but not before his gun fired," he said, pulling up his shirt and showing her the bandage wrapped around his abdomen.

Sadie's jaw dropped. "They could have killed you."

"Luckily, those two homeless men who accosted us while we were strolling the promenade appeared. They picked me up and carried me to the hospital. I was just released this morning. They said I almost died."

"How did you know it was them?"

"Oh, they came to visit me in the hospital. And you know what else? We served together under General Pilsudski. They said they realized who I was after we parted that night."

Sadie's eyes widened. "Are you serious?"

Alex nodded and smiled.

She kissed him, and said, "I don't know what I would do if I were to lose you. Thank god you're all right."

"While I was lying in my hospital bed, not knowing if I'd survive, I told myself that the moment I could walk out from there, I would come to see you and tell you that no matter what, I would never give up our quest to be together, as husband and wife."

Tears were now rolling down Sadie's cheeks. She gently pulled Alex down to the bed. "Make love to me, Alex, I cannot wait any longer."

*

While Alex slept soundly, Sadie remained awake. She wanted to make sure she emblazoned the experience of their lovemaking upon her mind, an indelible memory to last until her old age.

She wondered what Alex thought about it. It was obvious this was not his first time. He knew how to maneuver himself both slowly and gently, so as not to hurt her, and when he finished, he seemed pleased, and quickly fell asleep.

"Alex, you must go," Sadie said, shaking him awake.

Alex opened his eyes. "I didn't realize I fell asleep. What time is it?"

"It's almost six in the morning."

Alex swung his feet off the side of the bed and sat up. "Sadie," he whispered, "I need to tell you about a plan Jan and I have devised."

Sadie quickly sat alongside him, and said, "A plan for what?"

"A plan to get you out of here, so we can be together."

Sadie twisted herself to face Alex. "What are talking about?"

Alex smiled and said, "In a few days we're arranging—"

"Sadie, are you awake?" her mother said from the other side of her bedroom door.

"*Um*, yes, Mother. I'm just getting ready for work," she said, putting a finger to her mouth to silence Alex.

"I thought I heard voices coming from your room."

"It's just me, sorry, Mother."

"All right, I'll be downstairs preparing breakfast."

Sadie looked wide-eyed at Alex. He nodded, leaned in and gave Sadie a kiss. He stuck his head out the window and looked around, then turned and gave a thumbs up, and moments later he was gone. Just as he disappeared from her view, Sadie realized she hadn't heard his plan for their great escape.

CHAPTER EIGHTEEN—PLAN B

"Are you sure you want to go through with this, Alex?" Jan said. "You may not be so lucky next time with Mr. Wollman's friends."

Alex grimaced as he reached for his coffee cup. "Yes," he groaned, "I'm one hundred percent sure."

Jan pointed to Alex's abdomen. "Did you reinjure yourself acting like a monkey, scaling that wall to see Sadie?"

"Not exactly, but the cause was worth it," he added, with a gratifying smile.

"I bet it was," said Jan with a smirk.

"Have you confirmed the delivery schedule with the Blue Palace?" Alex asked.

"It's all set. The truck leaves the palace on Thursday and heads straight for Berlin. The exhibition doesn't open until next month, but the engravings must get there on time for the curators to do their preparations. Once we're fully loaded, I'll drive the truck and pick you up at the other end of Saxon Gardens, and we'll head over to Nalewki Street, where you'll rescue your Rapunzel from the tower, and off we'll go to Berlin. Once we get there, I'll drop you and Sadie off at the train station where you'll catch the next train to Hamburg. Then you can buy your tickets for America, once again."

"By hook or by crook, we will get this done," Alex said, toasting Jan with his coffee cup. Alex looked around at some familiar faces seated nearby at the café. "I'll miss this city, but I'll miss you most of all, Jan."

"We've made some good memories. Enough to last us a lifetime."

"Why don't you come to America with us?"

Jan raised his eyebrows and pointed to his chest. "Me, no, I don't think so. I was born here, and this is where I'll die."

Alex shook his head. "Don't be so sure. Sometimes things don't always work out as we intend."

Jan nodded and frowned. "Isn't that the god's honest truth?"

After the debacle of being removed from the SS *Amerika* and forcibly returned to Warsaw, Alex had needed to move in with Jan, since he lost his apartment at the Faculty Residence, along with his office privileges at the university, because of his resignation as professor.

Jan had stored all of Alex's belongings, which were mostly books and papers in a spare room in his apartment, intending to ship them to New York once Alex and Sadie got settled.

In the meantime, while waiting to implement his new escape plan, Alex slept in between towers of his boxes and books, grateful for Jan's ongoing friendship from the time they were young. Their years growing up together and then fighting the Soviets had forged an unbreakable bond between the two men, and a deep love for Poland. After the war, both men pursued interests to further serve the future of their young nation. Jan went to work for the government, translating sensitive documents, and Alex became a university professor of history.

Now that he was leaving Poland, Alex was not so naïve as to think people in America would care about the blood of young Polish men that turned the Vistula River red with Soviet blood. But as long as he could educate students of history, he would continue to honor those who sacrificed their lives for the benefit of future generations.

But above and beyond all of this, he was leaving his beloved homeland for Sadie. He chuckled to himself thinking how, suddenly, the most important part of his life, his legacy as a soldier of Poland, was being pushed into the background for the love of a woman.

Alex had a handful of girlfriends over the past several years, though none lasted longer than a few weeks. Many of his dates with young ladies would often end with not-so-subtle complaints about his unusual devotion to his books, along with his unkempt and stuffy apartment.

Eventually, he stopped bringing women back to his place, and he found himself frequenting the music halls and cafés of Warsaw alone, happy to be free from the burdens of a relationship. He was content to live the life of a confirmed bachelor. That was, until he met Sadie.

CHAPTER NINETEEN—CHANGE OF PLANS

Sadie looked out her window every night for hours, hoping for Alex's return, and more than once, fell asleep curled up on the deep window sill.

It was on the third night since she had seen him last, that Alex returned. He knocked gently on the glass, inches from Sadie's face, and when she opened her eyes, it took her a moment to realize she wasn't dreaming.

She hopped off the sill and lifted the window and said, "Come inside quickly before someone sees you."

Alex climbed in and they embraced for a good minute before they kissed for several more.

"I have news. Tomorrow night at nine, go to the Andersa Square, and look for the truck with the plate number DAHVP3. Jan will be driving, and I'll be in the passenger seat. It's from the Blue Palace and will be transporting a collection of engravings for an exhibition in Berlin. You and I will find a spot in the back with the cargo, and when we arrive, we'll catch a train to Hamburg."

"Oh my, Alex, that's quite a plan."

"All right, I shouldn't linger. Just one last kiss to see me off."

They embraced and kissed with their tongues darting about like two swords in a match. When they finally parted, Alex said, "Write your letter and give it to Jan. He'll post it when he returns in a few days from Berlin. *Long* after we've sailed."

Sadie smiled and watched Alex descend like a cat burglar from her bedroom window and disappear into the street below.

Minutes after Alex vanished from her watchful eyes, and with her valise already popped open on her bed, there was a sharp *knock-knock* on her bedroom door.

"Yes," she answered.

"Open the door," said the unmistakable booming voice of her father.

"One second, Father," Sadie said, quickly shutting and slipping the valise back under her bed.

Sadie took a breath to calm herself and stepped toward the door. She slowly turned the handle and saw her father with his hands on his hips, waiting for his daughter.

"Put your best dress on and come downstairs. We're leaving in ten minutes."

Sadie held out her hands. "But why, where are we going?"

"To synagogue."

Sadie jerked her head back, confused. "Synagogue on a Wednesday night?"

"Just do as I say, and you'll see," he said, turned and headed for the staircase. "There's a wedding to go to."

"A wedding? Who gets married on a Wednesday?"

Nearly at the bottom of the staircase, he shouted back, "You, Sadie, you're getting married."

*

The moment Sadie slipped into the backseat of the car she asked, "Can someone please tell me what's going on?"

"Your father already told you, Sadie," her mother said, turning her head to look at her, "you're getting married."

"What are you saying?" Sadie said, putting her hand to her forehead. "Can we just stop the damn car so we can talk about this?"

"There's nothing more to discuss," her father said, keeping his eyes on the road. "I already told you we were looking. The marriage broker called this morning and said he had an offer, but we need to move quickly, because the man's leaving tonight, and wants to take his bride with him."

"Take his bride where?" Sadie shouted, now feeling sweat run off her forehead.

"To Argentina. He's a wealthy businessman from Buenos Aires. You're leaving with him right after the wedding," her father said. "We've made a deal; he's paying a great sum of money for the honor."

"He's very handsome, Sadie," her mother added. "I met him this morning. You'll have beautiful children."

"I'm going to throw up, can you pull over?"

Her father turned, wagged a finger and growled, "You better not mess this up, Sadie. If this turns out bad, I'll make sure you never get married."

"Just pull over," she screamed, "before I puke in the car."

Her father swerved the car to the side of the road. Sadie opened the door and vomited on the sidewalk near two people who were standing on the curb, smoking and talking.

Her mother handed Sadie a hanky. "Here, wipe your mouth with this."

She snatched the hanky, closed the car door, and dropped her head backwards onto the headrest, closed her eyes, and said, "This can't be happening."

CHAPTER TWENTY—EZRA PORKEVITCH

"Go check the street, Dovid. Maybe they're having trouble finding the place," Ezra Porkevitch said, looking at himself in the mirror, and adjusting his tie.

Unlike the other *stille chuppahs*, this silent wedding would be one he would enjoy. That's because, according to the photographs, Sadie Wollman was a spectacular beauty. Perhaps he would break her in himself by locking her away in his cabin during the voyage, rather than in the steerage hold with the other girls.

Ezra knew to temper his enthusiasm until he saw Sadie in person. He had been misled by photos before. Sometimes the girls had beautiful faces, but their bodies were less attractive. But his speculation was about to end upon hearing voices coming down the corridor.

"Right this way," said Itzhak Baranski, the marriage broker, who made the deal between him and Avraham Wollman, Sadie's father.

The door opened, Ezra pulled back his shoulders, ran a tongue across his teeth so his lips would glide easily into a charming smile. In walked Mr. and Mrs. Wollman, whom he had already met, and following behind, was Sadie. The moment she entered the small office space, with a makeshift *chuppah* propped up at one end, where the rabbi stood poised to perform the mock wedding ceremony, Ezra exhaled, realizing he spent his money wisely.

Though she was distraught, her sadness did little to diminish Sadie Wollman's stunning beauty. Ezra had never seen a redhead with the same rich red and auburn coloring of the red fox, an animal that he used to deal in, back when he was in the furrier business. Her green eyes, though bloodshot from crying, still sparkled like emeralds. But what turned up the heat in Ezra's loins was Sadie's luscious body. *She has more curves than an Argentine wine decanter,* he thought.

"If you would please allow me," began Mr. Baranski, "this is the lovely Sadie Wollman, daughter of Mr. and Mrs. Wollman." He turned to Sadie and added, "Miss Wollman, this is Mr. Ezra Porkevitch, your fiancé."

Sadie looked at Ezra, offering no change in her solemn demeanor. Ezra ignored her insolence and reached for her hand, pulled it toward his lips and gently kissed it. "It's a pleasure to meet you, Sadie. You are what Mr. Baranski had said you would be, *a beauty beyond belief.* I am very pleased."

Sadie said nothing and allowed her gaze to settle back to her hands folded in front of her.

"Say something, Sadie," her father barked.

Sadie lifted her head, looked at her father and said with a snarl, "How can you do this to me?"

"It's all right, Sadie," Ezra said, "we'll take this slow. You need not trouble yourself. From now on, you'll be treated like a princess. Just wait until you see our beautiful Jewish home in Buenos Aires. Each room has a magnificent view of the ocean."

*

The wedding ceremony took only minutes, and when it was over, Ezra handed an envelope to Mr. Baranski, who counted the notes on the same table where Sadie was forced to sign the marriage contract.

The marriage broker took his fee, and handed the rest to Sadie's father, who tucked it into his jacket pocket, and nodded that he was pleased.

"We should get going. Our train leaves in twenty minutes," Ezra said, pulling out his pocket watch. "Sadie, say goodbye to your parents, I'll be waiting for you outside."

Ezra shook hands and exited the room. Once the door closed behind him, he heard Sadie's cries of desperation. While the carrying on was annoying, it was nothing new. He had dealt with many belligerent girls before. In fact, there were eight of them already in the holding house in Warsaw, waiting for the train to Hamburg.

CHAPTER TWENTY-ONE—SOLD

"Mr. Porkevitch is a well-respected businessman, and very, *very* rich, Sadie. He will give you the life of a princess," her father tried to explain.

"What if I don't want to be a princess? I met the man I love and want to marry."

Her mother rehashed all the reasons she must marry a Jewish man. "And he's paid a lot of money for you, Sadie. We cannot give it back."

"How much am I worth to you two?" she said, wagging her finger between her parents.

"Six-hundred-thousand zloty, Sadie. Enough to support your mother and I well into our retirement."

"So that's it then, you sold me, like a piece of property. How could you?"

Her father shook his head. "It's shameful you look at it that way, Sadie. I thought we brought up a young lady who respected her elders. I guess we failed as parents."

Sadie nodded. "That's the first thing you said that I agree with. You not only failed as parents, but you also failed as human beings. You disgust me."

Those three words were the last she spoke to her mother and father, before they were separated.

*

"Please, Sadie," Mr. Porkevitch said, gesturing to the open car door of his luxury black motorcar.

Sadie looked down the street and thought about running, but her shoes were not suitable and probably wouldn't make it far, plus Mr. Porkevitch's assistant, Dovid looked fit.

She glared at the man, who was supposedly now her husband, and slipped into the back seat and closed the door.

"There's something you should know, Sadie," Mr. Porkevitch said, seated alongside her, while Dovid drove the car. "That ceremony back there was bogus. We're not married."

"What do you mean? Wasn't that a rabbi?"

Mr. Porkevitch shook his head. "No, he's just an actor."

"I don't understand. If you don't want me as a wife, what's this about?"

Mr. Porkevitch placed his hand on Sadie's thigh and squeezed. "You're about to find out."

*

About twenty minutes later, the motorcar stopped in front of an apartment building in a part of town that Sadie was unfamiliar with.

"Come on, Sadie, this is where you'll be staying until we're ready to move you."

"I'm staying here?" she said, looking out from the car window.

"For a few days."

"But I have no clothes, or things to wash with."

"Everything you need will be provided. But I should make things clear to you," he said, pushing his face inches away from Sadie's. "If you choose not to listen to the men in there," he said, pointing toward the building, "you'll be beaten. But do as you're told, *no matter what you're asked to do*, and you'll be fine. In fact," he continued, stroking her cheek, "I'm considering having you share my first-class cabin with me when we sail to Argentina. What do you think about that?" he said raising his eyebrows suggestively.

Sadie slapped his hand away and grimaced. "I would rather be dead."

Mr. Porkevitch laughed. "Not after the money I just paid for you. Now get the fuck out of my car."

Dovid escorted Sadie into the entrance of the apartment building, where he inserted a key from the multitude on his keychain into the front door and unlocked it. They entered the lobby and faced a man seated on a chair with a rifle resting on his lap. Dovid and the armed guard exchanged grunts as a form of a greeting.

"Walk up the stairs," Dovid ordered.

"Where are you taking me?" Sadie pleaded, grasping the handrail.

"No talking," he said, giving Sadie a push on the small of her back.

Sadie climbed up three flights of what seemed to be an abandoned apartment building, before Dovid said, "This is it."

Sadie stopped and waited for Dovid to lead her down the darkened hallway, where a single double-hung window looked out onto a dimly lit brick wall of the next-door building. As they stepped further down the hallway, Sadie heard muffled sounds of chatter.

Dovid knocked on the door and the voices ceased, replaced by the screeching sounds of tumblers, and the old door with crackled, faded brown paint swung open.

A man stuck his head out and looked at Sadie and said, "Is this her?"

Dovid ignored the question and gave Sadie another nudge, encouraging her forward. Sadie took a breath, closed her eyes, and thought *oh god, please help me,* before she stepped inside.

CHAPTER TWENTY-TWO—SHE'S GONE

Alex sat on the passenger side of the truck with Jan behind the wheel, trying to capture a glimpse of each person's face entering Andersa Square. But so far, there was no sign of Sadie.

"What's the time?"

"Five minutes past nine," Jan said, glancing at his pocket watch.

Alex rubbed the back of his neck and gritted his teeth. "This could be our last chance," he said, keeping his vision focused on the square.

Twenty minutes later, Jan put his hand on Alex's shoulder and said, "Maybe you should go look for her."

Alex nodded. "Good idea. I'll be back soon," he said.

"I'll be waiting for you."

Alex hurried through the square, looking at each person he passed. He took the most direct route to the Wollman's home and minutes later stood in the darkened shadows on the sidewalk staring at Sadie's window. Her room was unlit, as was most of the house except for a gas lamp burning by the home's entrance door.

From what Alex could make out, the house appeared empty. Just as he was thinking of climbing the ivy to Sadie's second-floor bedroom window, the lights of a motorcar appeared, coming toward the home.

He ducked behind a large oak tree in the front yard, as the car pulled into the drive, and Alex saw it was Mr. and Mrs. Wollman. He strained to see if Sadie was seated in the backseat, but when Mr. Wollman opened the car door and the light from the gas lamp spilled into the interior, Alex saw no sign of a third person.

As they exited the car, Alex could hear their conversation from his hiding spot.

"Do you think she will be all right?" Mrs. Wollman said, walking alongside her husband toward the home's front door.

"Mr. Porkevitch is a gentleman; he'll treat Sadie like a princess. This is the greatest gift we could have given her."

"I hope so; she is such a delicate flower."

Alex couldn't believe his ears. *What have they done with Sadie?*

"How long does it take to sail to Argentina?"

"I imagine two weeks."

"Did you get an address so we can write to her?"

"No, but Mr. Porkevitch promised as soon as they settle at his home in Buenos Aires, Sadie will post a letter with the details."

Alex debated jumping out from behind the tree and confronting the Wollmans. But before he could decide, a voice called out from the sidewalk. "You're finally back, I've stopped by before. Where's Sadie?" asked a young woman joining the Wollmans by the front door.

"Oh, she's gone," Mrs. Wollman said.

"Gone? Gone where?"

"Why don't you come inside, Sara, and we'll explain," Alex heard Mr. Wollman say before they entered the home, shutting the door behind them.

CHAPTER TWENTY-THREE—SADIE MEETS THE GIRLS

Sadie had never seen or smelled such an unkempt and decrepit home before. Remnants of once colorful wallpaper clung in ripped fragments to the plaster. Large cobwebs reached from the crystal-less light fixture to the water-stained ceiling. A mustiness hung in the air that Sadie could taste in the back of her throat.

In the center of the large room, huddled in small groups, were six girls, all about the same age as Sadie, a few even younger. Coarse horsehair cushion-stuffing burst through torn holes in the upholstery of a large sofa where three girls were sitting, while the others sat on small mismatched wooden chairs scattered about.

Sadie took notice of the sad expression of despair in each of the girl's eyes. Suddenly, a door swung open and out stumbled a girl, struggling with a button on her dress. A moment later, a disheveled man followed behind her, tucking his shirttails into his pants.

"This one needs a few lessons in fucking. She just lies there like a dead fish," the man said.

"And I suppose you're gonna teach her, Bernie?" Dovid said with a chuckle.

"Yeah, why the hell not? I know what men like, I'm one of them."

Dovid shook his head. "Sometimes I wonder if that's true."

"Go fuck yourself," Bernie said, and looked over to Sadie. "Well, who do we have here? This is some doll."

"The boss said no one's to touch her. He's saving this one for himself."

"I bet he is. But I don't mind waiting. It's no fun fucking virgins, anyway. I like them broken in," Bernie said, picking off a piece of something clinging to his shirtsleeve, and tossing it aside.

Sadie swallowed hard, wondering if she would be the next victim of rape by these disgusting men, just like the poor girls gawking at her.

"Sit down," Dovid said, pointing.

Sadie walked to a space along the wall, far from the other girls, and slowly lowered herself to the floor. "How long are we here for?" she asked.

"The ship leaves in three days. Tomorrow morning we'll board the train for Hamburg. In the meantime, get some rest."

Sadie leaned her back against the wall, while two of the girls spoke quietly among themselves. The others had dozed off, no longer interested in her. Sadie closed her eyes, wanting to rest. Physically exhausted from the emotional turmoil of the past twenty-four hours, she needed to sleep, but remained wide awake, trying to make sense of how her life had spiraled out of her control so quickly.

About twenty minutes later, Sadie watched a cockroach scamper along the floor and crawl under Bernie, who was seated on the floor, with his back leaning against the apartment's only door, snoring away. He wasn't the only one asleep; Dovid had claimed a spot on a couch, and was lying on his belly, his face buried deep into a cushion.

Sadie saw the girl who Bernie had his way with, curled up on an old, threadbare upholstered chair. Two other girls found a spot on the floor, each with a pillow and a moth-eaten blanket.

Sadie pushed herself up to her feet and walked over to the window. *Maybe with everyone asleep,* she thought, *I could climb out of the window and find my way to the street below.*

She tugged and lifted the hefty frame and stuck her head out the window.

"It's too far to jump; that's why they keep us on the top floor of this shit hole," whispered a woman's voice from behind her.

Sadie backed herself back into the room and was face to face with a woman she hadn't seen before.

"My name's Rebecca."

"I'm Sadie. How do we get out of here?"

Rebecca shrugged and said, "Well, we can't climb down from here or go out the door," and pointed over to Bernie, who was now stretched out on his back, his fat, hairy belly exposed from his pulled-up shirt, blocking the door from swinging open, even an inch.

Sadie shook her head.

"Follow me, I know a place where we can talk," whispered the blue-eyed blonde.

Sadie followed Rebecca into a bedroom and closed the door behind them. They sat down on an unkempt bed, where Sadie assumed Bernie had just raped that poor girl, who was now asleep in the large room they had just came from.

"There's no way I'm getting on that train for Hamburg tomorrow," said Rebecca, folding her arms under her ample bosoms.

"What do you mean?" Sadie said.

Rebecca smiled and said, "I'm going to escape. Do you want to come with me?"

CHAPTER TWENTY-FOUR—CONSIDERING SADIE

Ezra sat in a café that looked out onto the square across from the apartment building where the girls were being held. He was pleased that his boss, Mr. Rivlin—the *Balebos* as was called—had agreed to purchase the building as a holding place for the girls before they were transferred to Buenos Aires.

Ezra explained he needed time to visit the Jewish communities in Warsaw and its surrounding villages and shtetls, to recruit suitable girls, or *Polacas* as they were known in Argentina, to make the voyage back home economically feasible.

Ezra was one of the Zwi Migdal's top agents. Besides his intelligence, he was handsome, charming, cunning, and young. He had just turned thirty years old.

Finding talented men like Ezra was a challenge for the Zwi Migdal. Their job as an agent was not an easy one, because of the seriousness of the deception. Not only did they need to lure young, pretty Jewish girls into their web, they also needed to seek agreement from their parents, who were tricked into thinking they were marrying their daughters off to rich Argentinian men. How they did that the Zwi Migdal didn't care, as long as they had signed documents, otherwise the shipping lines would not permit the girls to board the steamship bound for Buenos Aires.

One of Ezra's most successful recruitment efforts was to post advertisements in synagogues, promoting the opportunity of wealthy Argentinian Jewish men looking for Jewish brides. The ad read:

RICH ARGENTINE JEWISH MEN IN SEARCH FOR JEWISH BRIDES

OPPORTUNITIES TO BREAK THE BONDS OF POVERTY

LIVE A LIFE OF WEALTH IN BEAUTIFUL BUENOS AIRES

A REPRESENTATIVE WILL BE AT THIS SYNAGOGUE ON:

....

PARENTS MUST ACCOMPANY THEIR DAUGHTER FOR THE INTERVIEW

The date was hand-written in at the bottom when Ezra would show up and interview the potential candidates. The real purpose of the encounter was to rate the girls on their looks, sexual appeal, and personality. The Zwi Migdal came up with a simple rating system based on points to decide if they would make an enticing offer to the parents in exchange for their daughters to leave their childhood home, for a *supposed* better life.

Ezra presented random photos and fictitious biographies of these men who had paid a fee to find a suitable bride and return with her back to Buenos Aires.

Another method of recruitment was by a referral through a marriage broker. These girls usually came from wealthy families and because of their upbringing, were more desirable to the better brothels in Buenos Aires, which meant a larger commission for Ezra.

When such an opportunity occurred, Ezra would stage the *stille chuppah* with him acting as the husband, thereby raising his chances of closing the deal.

Over the past few years, he established a reputation for landing the best girls. Representatives from the brothels would pay attention when Ezra Porkevitch's girls were auctioned at the market in the Hotel Palestina in Buenos Aires.

Sadie, though, was unlike any of the previous *Polacas* he had recruited, and he was a man with an impressive resume. He had seen many beautiful girls and women, but none as stunning as Sadie. He figured that he would have no trouble placing her in the most exclusive brothel in all the city, *The Tango*.

Ezra also prided himself on never indulging himself with any of the young ladies, while he allowed Dovid and Bernie to *sample the goods* as they liked to call it. It wasn't a lack of temptation, since many of the girls were lovely, but at this point in their journey, they weren't able to give of themselves willingly, and this was something Ezra considered to be beneath his standards as a gentleman.

As he sipped his coffee, Ezra considered nurturing a relationship with Sadie, perhaps even allowing her to have her own bedroom in his first-class cabin. He could force himself upon her, but it would be exciting having a woman of Sadie's caliber give of herself willingly to him. This would be something Ezra desired most of all, and he had two weeks onboard the MV *Alcantara* to make it happen.

CHAPTER TWENTY-FIVE—ESCAPE

With both Dovid and Bernie asleep, Sadie followed Rebecca through a concealed doorway in the pantry closet, behind the kitchen. Rebecca whispered, "These stairs lead to the ground floor and out into an alleyway. I was waiting for the right moment to make a run for it."

The stairwell was nearly pitch-dark except for the moonlight spilling through small windows at each landing. Sadie kept her hand on the wooden railing, only releasing it briefly as the stairs cut back in the opposite direction.

When they reached the ground floor, Rebecca put her finger to her lips and slowly pushed against an unmarked steel door. The hinges creaked loudly, causing Sadie to cringe in fright.

Rebecca cocked her head for Sadie to follow. Both women stepped outside into an alleyway. Sadie looked to her right and saw wooden crates stacked in front of a brick wall. But to her left was a clear pathway onto the square.

The women stepped gingerly. But before walking out of the shadows of the alleyway, Rebecca stuck her head out and surveyed the square. "It's clear. But we should stay close to the buildings."

Sadie nodded and followed Rebecca as she emerged, keeping under the shadows and away from the bright light of the gas lamps. They made it to the first corner when, out of nowhere, Rebecca screamed, "Rats!"

Sadie looked down to where Rebecca was pointing and saw four or five rats feasting upon the ripped-open belly of a cat. Before Sadie could look up, Rebecca had abandoned her plan and dashed across the square like a spooked horse.

"Wait," Sadie shouted. But it was too late. Sadie shook her head and ran after her.

When Rebecca reached the other opposite side of the square, she slipped into a narrow passageway where shuttered shops lined both sides, and leaned over placing her hands on her knees trying to catch her breath. "We made it," she said, looking up to Sadie.

Sadie shook her head. "Now what?"

"We go to the police and tell them we're being forced to immigrate to Argentina as sex slaves."

Sadie shook her head. "Sex slaves?"

Rebecca held out her hands. "What do you think they will do with us when we get to Buenos Aires?"

"I don't know?" Sadie said.

"They will put us in brothels as prostitutes. I heard Dovid and Bernie talking about it."

"Oh my god," Sadie said, putting her hand to her mouth. "But what will the police do? I signed a marriage contract with my parents as witnesses."

"You mean with your parents as accomplices," Rebecca clarified.

"That's right," Sadie said with a nod. "But I don't think the police will help us. We should find Alex."

"Who's Alex?"

"Yes, Sadie, who is Alex?" came a man's voice from the shadows.

Sadie turned and saw, stepping toward her, Ezra Porkevitch, with a pistol pointing at her.

CHAPTER TWENTY-SIX—SARA'S HELP

Alex waited for Sara to emerge from the Wollman's home and step onto the sidewalk before he approached.

"Hello, Sara. I'm Alex, Sadie's boyfriend," he said, stepping out of the shadows and into the gas-lit street.

Sara jumped backwards, putting her hand over her mouth. "You frightened me. What are you doing here?"

"I'm looking for Sadie. Do you know where she is?"

"I was just with her parents. They've arranged for Sadie to marry some rich Jewish man from Argentina. She's heading toward Hamburg on the train tomorrow and then sailing to Buenos Aires."

"Why would they do that?"

"I warned her about you," she said, pointing a finger. "I said you can't fall in love with a *goy* and now look what happened."

"I can't believe her parents would send her away with a stranger to a foreign country, rather than allowing her to marry the man she loves," he said, shaking his head.

"Obviously you don't know her father."

"Do you know where she is now?" Alex asked, grabbing Sara by both shoulders.

Sara shook her head. "No, not even her parents know. At least that's what they told me. What are you going to do?"

"I need to find her before that ship sails," Alex said, his eyes darting about, trying to think of all the possibilities laid out before him.

"Since we don't know where she's being held overnight, I would wait at the railway station."

Alex nodded and pointed at Sara. "That's a good idea."

"I'm coming with you, Alex," Sara said.

"All right, let me run back and tell Jan what's happening. Can you meet me there?"

"Of course," Sara said.

Alex didn't wait until morning. After he spoke with Jan, filling him in on what he knew about Sadie, he went directly to the railway station. Sara showed up a few hours later, and both of them paced the large main hall of the Warsaw Central Railway Station, waiting for Sadie to arrive with her new Argentinian husband.

"You know, Alex, this is all legal. You can't stop them from leaving."

Alex grimaced and pointed a finger at Sara and said, "I don't know how, but I will prevent Sadie from boarding that train."

*

As the time approached for the departure time for the 12:25 to Hamburg, the same train he and Sadie took, Alex became frantic. "Where are they?" he groaned.

"How am I supposed to know?" Sara shrugged. "This is what I was told."

"The train leaves in two minutes, they'll never make it now," Alex said, and then paused as an explanation occurred to him. "Unless they entered the station another way. Hurry, Sara!"

"Where are you going?" Sara said, chasing behind him.

"To the tracks!"

By the time Alex and Sara reached the platform, the doors had closed, and the train was pulling away. Alex ran alongside, beating his fists upon the large cabin windows as the train slowly rolled by.

"There she is," Sara said, pointing.

Alex followed her hand and saw Sadie seated next to a well-dressed man, looking straight ahead. Alex hit the glass window so hard it rattled in its frame, causing everyone in the car to be startled and turn to look, including Sadie who saw Alex. With wide-open eyes, she placed her opened palm on the glass and mouthed his name—*Alex*.

"Sadie!" Alex shouted. But before he could say another word, the platform ended, while the train continued with Sadie onboard, and gone from Alex's life.

Alex stood there, watching it take the turn in the tracks, and disappear from view. Sara put a hand on his back, and said, "I'm sorry, Alex."

"I need to figure out a way," Alex said with his voice trailing off, still staring down the train tracks.

Sara sighed. "She's gone, Alex, how can you possibly save her?"

"Mark my words, Sara. If it takes the rest of my life, I'll not rest until Sadie is safely back in my arms."

CHAPTER TWENTY-SEVEN—THE 12:25 TO HAMBURG

"Let me guess. That was Alex," Ezra said, as the train pulled away from the station.

Sadie nodded, her tears rolling down her cheeks like the two rails running beneath the train speeding ahead toward Hamburg.

"Good to know," Ezra teased.

"You better not harm him," Sadie warned with a fierce scowl.

Ezra held out his hands. "I would never," he said, sarcasm dripping from his words.

The train rumbled ahead. In the car, along with Sadie and Ezra, were Dovid, Bernie, and the eight girls, including Rebecca. Sadie wondered what would have happened if Rebecca hadn't panicked at the hideous sight of the rats gnawing away at the cat carcass. Apparently, her sudden outburst and mad dash across the square caught Ezra's attention, who happened to be on his way to the building just as they were trying to escape.

Ezra escorted them calmly back to the apartment building and up the stairs. But when he pushed his way past the sleeping Dovid and into the apartment, he went berserk.

"Wake the fuck up," he said, giving Dovid a kick in his ribs.

"What?" Dovid mumbled, stirred, and sat up. "What's going on?"

"You know where I found these two?" he said pointing to Sadie and Rebecca.

"What do you mean? They were right here."

"No, you imbecile, I found them on the other side of the square. Where the hell is Bernie?"

Bernie's head popped up over the couch. "Right here, boss," he said, looking dumbfounded.

"Get the girls ready, you fucking idiots. We're leaving in an hour."

*

Ezra had reserved the entire first cab behind the caboose on the 12:25 to Hamburg. This would prevent passengers from passing through the cab, ensuring total privacy and security. When the train made a stop to drop off or pick up passengers, their cab doors remained shut. It was like a moving jail cell.

Sadie sat still, imaging her life like a train entering a never-ending dark tunnel. She looked around and thought that the other girls had similar feelings of hopelessness.

Along the journey, Ezra told Sadie a bit about each girl. All of them were Jewish and came from a variety of backgrounds. Judith was the youngest, barely fifteen years old. She came from a *shtetl* about two hours south of Warsaw. Ezra said that her parents feared for her safety and wanted her to have a better life without the ominous threat of pogroms. "So they promised her to a wealthy Jewish man," he said with a disturbing sense of pride.

Then there was Aliza, a tall majestic girl, with sculpted cheekbones and long blonde hair, that reminded Sadie of the Norse goddess Freya she once saw in a textbook.

Ezra bamboozled all the girl's parents into believing that a bright future awaited their daughters. Sadie wondered why these mostly educated Jewish parents trusted this man whom they knew nothing about. Did they not think of asking for a reference of someone who had also sent their child, and could confirm that it was not a deception? But sadly, like Sadie's parents, they were blinded by the substantial sums of cash Ezra had paid them, and the promise of a life free from poverty for their daughters.

"Listen up," Ezra said, waking up the girls who had dozed off during the fourteen-hour journey. "We'll arrive in Hamburg within the hour. When we disembark from the train, there will be a truck waiting for us to take us to the Port of Hamburg. You are all to put this around your necks," he said, holding up a tag with a cord attached. "This is your pass that will allow you to board the ship. Once on board, you'll be escorted to your accommodations," he said, handing out the tags.

The girls slipped them over their heads.

When Ezra got to Sadie, he held her tag and looked at it before he handed it to her. He leaned over and whispered, "If you like, Sadie, you can stay with me in my cabin, where you'll have your own private room."

Sadie looked up at him and thought about it for a moment. She then looked at the other girls, with the nametags dangling off their necks, and said, "No, I'd rather stay with them."

"Are you serious? I'm offering you a chance to stay in a first-class cabin, with a promise not to touch you without your permission, and you're turning me down?"

Sadie looked up to Ezra and with words that she would later regret, she said, "I'd rather sleep with pigs than be anywhere near you."

CHAPTER TWENTY-EIGHT—ALEX MAKES A PLAN

"They call themselves the Zwi Migdal," Jan said, "and from what my colleague told me, our government knows all about them."

"So why do they allow this?" Alex asked.

Jan shrugged. "Why do you think? These are very rich men with the ability to pay bribes for the politicians to look the other way. The other reason is, our government does nothing because this is a *Jewish problem*. Jewish men taking advantage of Jewish girls. They couldn't care less about them."

Alex knew anti-Semitism was rampant and despised his fellow countrymen who sought scapegoats to blame for Poland's internal economic problems. "But what will happen to Sadie?"

"Once they get to Buenos Aires, they send the girls to an auction, where they'll be paraded naked across a stage for the owners of the brothels who bid on them, like cattle. Then they're sent off, destined to offer their bodies to men more than willing to pay for . . ." he paused and shrugged, "well, you know."

"This is a nightmare," Alex said, dropping his head into his hands.

"I'm sorry, Alex. If there's anything I can do."

Alex looked up and said with wide eyes, "Come with me to Argentina and help me rescue Sadie."

Jan rubbed the stubble on his chin. "You think just the two of us can go halfway around the world, locate Sadie in a foreign city where we know no one, and return her safely back home?"

Alex smiled. "I think we proved our mettle."

"That we did," Jan agreed.

Alex furrowed his brow, and looked at Jan. "Come with me. We'll be a team again."

Jan snickered. "You make it sound like the good old days."

"Will you come?" Alex said with a furrowed brow.

Jan stood up, walked over to Alex, who also rose from his chair, and embraced him. "Of course I will."

Alex grasped Jan by the shoulders and said, "I'll get us passage on the train to Hamburg, and two tickets for the next voyage to Buenos Aires. But first I need to pay the Wollmans a visit and try to learn more about this shark from the Zwi Migdal."

*

Alex stood by the front door of the Wollman's, took a breath to steady his nerves and lifted the brass door knocker.

The heavy wooden door opened and Mr. Wollman appeared. "What can I do for you, young man?"

"Mr. Wollman, my name is Alexander Kaminsky, I would like—"

"What the hell are you doing here?" Avraham Wollman interrupted, his eyes expressing outrage at seeing Alex posed in his doorway.

"I must speak with you and your wife about Sadie," Alex said, stepping across the threshold.

"Wait a moment," Avraham objected, "you must leave immediately or I'll phone the police."

"Who is this man?" asked Jennie, as she rambled down the staircase.

"I am Alexander Kaminsky."

Jennie put her hand to her cheek and looked over to her husband. "Why is this man in our home?"

"We have nothing to say to you," Avraham insisted.

"Please Mr. and Mrs. Wollman, you've been deceived. You must tell me what you know about your daughter's whereabouts. Her life depends upon it," Alex pleaded.

"What do you mean?" Jennie cried out.

Mr. Wollman stood with his arms folded across his chest. He looked over to his wife, who had tears cascading down her face.

"Tell him, Avraham, for Sadie's sake," she pleaded.

Mr. Wollman jabbed a finger at Alex. "This is your fault. If you didn't seduce my only daughter, none of this would be happening."

"I didn't seduce her, sir. We fell in love."

Mr. Wollman growled back, "There's no such thing as love between a Jewess and a *goy*."

"I'm sorry you feel that way. But please, for Sadie's welfare, let's put our differences aside and explain to me what happened."

"That's enough, Avraham," Jennie shouted and turned to Alex. "We were approached by a marriage broker. He said he heard of our search for a husband for Sadie and had a very impressive gentleman interested."

Alex sighed. "I'm sorry to say that Sadie has been taken by the Zwi Migdal, a criminal organization known for trafficking young Jewish girls into a hideous life as sex slaves. There are hundreds of brothels in Buenos Aires, where these poor girls are being held against their will and forced to perform sexual acts."

"Oh my god, Avraham, what have we done?" Jennie cried.

"I want you to know that I'm going to Argentina to find Sadie and bring her home," Alex said, walking over to the Wollman's front door. "If you think of anything new to tell me, leave a message at the university. Otherwise, wish me luck. I'm leaving with my friend Jan on the train to Hamburg tomorrow morning."

Mr. Wollman walked over to Alex and stood before him and said, "If you succeed and bring back our daughter back, I'll be grateful. But know this—I will never let you marry her, *never*."

CHAPTER TWENTY-NINE—SADIE'S CELL

"You," Bernie said, and crooked a finger at Sadie, "come with me."

Sadie looked at the other girls who were claiming hammocks in a small steel-walled cabin and asked, "Why? Am I not staying here?"

Bernie shrugged. "Don't know, I do as I'm told."

Sadie followed Bernie along a narrow corridor and down a metal staircase that vibrated from the ship's engines. He stopped in front of a doorway, inserted a key, and turned the handle. He held the hatch door open, gesturing for Sadie to enter.

"What's this place?" Sadie said, stepping over the lower lip of the hatch and into a small, square, windowless cell.

"Your accommodations, courtesy of Mr. Porkevitch. He said if you don't find this suitable, there's a comfortable, private room available in his first-class cabin," he said, with a smile that featured an array of hideous tobacco-stained, yellow and brown teeth.

Sadie shook her head, took a breath, and said, "This will do," and stepped inside.

Bernie shrugged. "Suit yourself," he said, and closed the door, locking Sadie inside.

The cell was smaller than her bedroom back home. There was an old, brown-stained, lumpy mattress lying on the floor, and a metal bucket stationed in a corner. A gas lamp flickered a soft light on a wooden table, with a lone chair pushed under it.

Once the door shut, the only sound was an incessant humming of the ship's engine. A sudden loud clang of metal against metal, and a violent shaking of her cell, suggested that the ship was leaving port, and any hope for a last-minute, daring rescue by Alex was dashed. She was alone, and it was up to her to figure out ways to survive the ordeal she was about to endure.

Sadie smacked her palm against the cold cell wall and screamed, "How can you do this to me, Father?"

She dropped her face into her palms and wept; resigned to thinking her life was over. Upon arrival in Buenos Aires, she would be sold to a brothel and become nothing more than a receptacle for hideous men, pushing their way into her, spilling their toxic seed, over and over.

The cell vibrated violently, causing Sadie to spread out her arms against the wall and brace herself. She was no fool; she knew that Mr. Porkevitch had isolated her in this cage to break her will and have her begging to join him in his luxurious suite of rooms.

Sadie lay down on the mattress, looked up at the light flickering haunting images of shadows upon the ceiling, and thought of Alex, wondering if he was aware of what had happened to her. Perhaps her parents had confessed their pitiful deed, and he was now contemplating ways of rescuing her.

She allowed herself a brief smile, thinking Alex would come for her. He was a soldier, a spy, a hero no less, who fought and beat the dreaded Russians. Alex could overcome someone like Mr. Porkevitch. But would it be too late? *Will he want me once I've been turned into a whore?*

Sadie took a breath and thought about Ezra's proposal. She knew his promise not to touch her without her consent would be short-lived. Eventually, before the voyage ended, Ezra would lose his patience and demand she give herself to him.

CHAPTER THIRTY—THE LAST ONE

Ezra sat on a wooden lounge chair on the deck of the MV *Alcantara*, watching it slowly depart from the Port of Hamburg and head north along the Elbe River toward the North Sea.

He always looked forward to the return leg of these trips. It provided him a well-deserved chance to rest. After all, it was challenging work, traveling from village to village, luring poor, young Jewish woman with deceptive matrimonial offers for a better life. Though he did have occasional relief with referrals toward wealthy targets, such as the one on this trip, landing him Sadie Wollman.

He admitted to himself there were brief moments when he experienced remorse for these innocent girls, whose parents sold them unknowingly into life as a sex slave. But this guilty feeling swiftly passed when he reminded himself how this unusual profession made him a wealthy man.

All in all, he was pleased with his catch of nine *Polacas*. These girls would earn him a hefty payday, and hopefully, a few months at home resting before being summoned back to Poland and resuming the recruitment process.

But before all of that, he planned to enjoy the next two weeks cruising across the Atlantic, relaxing in his first-class cabin, consuming gourmet cuisine in the elegant dining hall, drinking fine wine, smoking Cuban cigars, and seducing the lovely Sadie Wollman.

Ezra smiled, thinking of how she was now locked away in that hideous cell. He planned to keep Sadie there overnight and have her brought up to his suite in the morning. By then she should be more than grateful for his generous offer. He would allow her to bathe and dress in one of the elegant outfits he had purchased as gifts for his wife while he was in Warsaw.

*

The entrance to the ship's main dining hall was off a rotunda, featuring a ceiling of triangle-shaped windows that supported at its peak, a large crystal chandelier, with gold link chains that kept it steady as the ship gently rocked, while it sailed across the North Sea.

"Mr. Porkevitch, it's good to see you again, sir," said the maître d' standing behind his podium.

"It's good to see you, Mr. Ruiz," Ezra said, shaking his hand, and leaned in to whisper, "Please let me know when I can send one of my girls up to your cabin."

A bright smile lit up Mr. Ruiz's normally somber face. "I will, sir," he said with enthusiasm. "Now, please follow me; the captain is already seated."

Ezra crossed the large dining hall. Along the way, he stopped to shake the hands of men he knew from Buenos Aires, whose wives were left asking, "Who's that man, darling?" Ezra chuckled to himself, thinking, *If they only knew of their husband's erotic indiscretions.*

"Ah, Ezra, it's wonderful to see you again," said Captain Velazquez, rising from his seat, "please join us."

Ezra greeted the other officers, who all stood to shake his hand, pleased he could offer the services of his *Polacas* in exchange for his fabulous first-class accommodations.

Tomorrow he would arrange the girls' visitation schedule, but first, he would need to meet with them to make sure they knew what was expected. The main obstacle was that these young ladies had limited or no previous sexual experiences at all. Some men, he presumed, found this to be exciting, however that was not the case for most. They wanted a woman who knew how to please them, though the ship's officers understood, from previous voyages, that these girls required patience.

Over the years, Ezra had perfected a method of *breaking-in* the *Polacas*. He even gave his solution a name; he called it *el ultimo uno*, the last one. This referred to the one girl he considered the least obedient of the lot, and upon her inevitable provocation, she would be beaten into a bloody mess in front of the others. Fearful that they could be next, the girls instantly understood the meaning of *obediencia*.

Ezra made it a practice to purposely recruit this defiant Jewess, and she was now in steerage below deck with the others, awaiting her call to action.

CHAPTER THIRTY-ONE—LA SUITE PRESIDENCIAL

Sadie awoke to Bernie's bad breath, and gravel-laden voice, inches from her face. "Wake up, princess."

She had just fallen asleep after a torturous night of trying to ignore the mechanics of the ship's engines humming and vibrating through the cell's metallic walls and floor.

"Leave me be," she mumbled, putting her hand over her face.

"Come now, we can't keep Mr. Porkevitch waiting," he said, slipping his hand under her back, trying to lift her up.

Sadie slapped it away. "Don't touch me," she barked, and stood up on her own.

"Okay, I was just trying to help."

Sadie held up her hands, shook her head. "I don't want your help," she said and followed Bernie out of the cell.

They climbed a dizzying array of crisscrossing stairways, taking her from the hellhole bowels of the ship, upwards to the heavenly decks of first-class. Even the sounds and smells improved as they reached the deluxe amenities. They passed a quartet of strings playing a Beethoven concerto, and the unmistakable, alluring aroma of bread baking in an oven coming from some indeterminable direction that danced about within her nostrils, and caused her stomach to growl.

Bernie led her down a wide, carpeted hallway; its walls heavily paneled in a walnut-stained oak, with elaborate decorative moldings.

"This is it," he said, stopping in front of a wooden set of double doors.

Sadie looked at him, not sure what he wanted her to do.

"Well, go on in, he's waiting for you," Bernie said, trying his best to offer a sincere smile.

Sadie nodded, took a breath, and entered.

The moment she stepped within, Sadie felt as if she walked into the foyer of a grand home. The well-appointed, octagon-shaped room featured three bronze statues of soldiers that she assumed were Argentine, standing guard within wooden niches recessed into the wall panels. A crystal chandelier hung over a table, accented with a gold leaf floret design around its perimeter.

"Is that you, Sadie?" a voice called from a room beyond.

"Yes, it's me," she said, and before she could take a step, Ezra appeared.

"Ah, Sadie, I'm happy to see you, please come this way."

She followed him down a hallway to a salon with a deeply tufted, navy-blue, upholstered sofa wrapping itself around the room. Large, overstuffed, embroidered pillows were tossed about.

"So what do you think of my suite?"

Sadie offered a forced smile and nodded.

Ezra gestured with his hand. "These are the finest accommodations on the ship. They call this *La Suite Presidencial*. Now, Sadie, come this way and I'll show you to your room."

Sadie took a breath. From this point forward, she would need to think carefully before she spoke. Every word and every gesture, were crucial to remaining in control, for this man was formidable with one goal in mind, and it was up to her wits alone to delay that as long as possible.

Standing in the doorway, Ezra said, "After you bathe, select an outfit from the wardrobe. I'll come back for you in a few hours. Then we'll take a stroll on the deck, there're some friends I would like to introduce you to."

Sadie smiled. "All right, Mr. Porkevitch."

"And one more thing," he said holding up a finger, "from now on, you'll call me Ezra."

Sadie walked over to him, placed a hand on his chest ,and with a gentle push she said, "I'll see you soon, Ezra," and closed the door.

CHAPTER THIRTY-TWO—SARA'S CONFESSION

The soonest Alex could purchase two tickets for Buenos Aires was for nearly one month after the MV *Alcantara* had already set sail. That meant by the time he and Jan arrived, Sadie would have already been in Argentina for four weeks. This was an excruciating amount of time under arduous conditions, and Alex feared not only for her wellbeing but also for her life.

In the meantime, Jan had an idea of reaching out to a war buddy who worked for the Polish Prime Minister Grabski. His friend Josef was assigned to a team during the recent establishment of the country's diplomatic relations with Argentina, and was directly involved in the planning and opening of the Polish embassy in Buenos Aires.

"From what Josef told me, the people at the Polish embassy know what's going on over there. They're aware how the Zwi Migdal recruits these Jewish *shtetl* girls under the false pretenses of marriage to wealthy men, and sells them to brothel owners as sex slaves," Jan said.

Alex shook his head and opened his palms. "But why don't they stop it?"

Jan shrugged. "You're aware that prostitution is legal in Argentina?"

"But what about slavery? Owning a sex slave can't be legal," Alex asked, curling his hands into fists.

"I'm sure it's not," Jan said. "But these brothels are often frequented by policemen, judges, attorneys, and politicians, to name a few. Not only are they partaking, but they're also being paid off to look the other way. Corruption in the country is rampant. In Buenos Aires alone, there are hundreds and hundreds of brothels. This is big business, Alex, and no one seems the least bit interested in shutting it down."

"So what does Josef suggest we do?"

Jan sighed. "He says when we arrive, we should go to the embassy and speak to the ambassador. As citizens of Poland, he may be able to assist in getting us out of the country, once we locate Sadie."

"But how will we find her? Can't they help us with that?"

Jan shook his head. "They cannot without causing a diplomatic incident. These are very powerful people at the top levels of government behind these brothels. It's going to be up to us alone to find Sadie and sneak her into the embassy. Only then can we ask our government for help."

*

Alex walked along the pathway through Saxon Gardens, heading toward the fountain. He contemplated the new and useful information he learned from his meeting with Jan at the Blue Palace, but was still deeply troubled. Sadie was well on her way by now, traveling across the vast Atlantic Ocean toward South America. Alex tried to imagine the squalid living conditions on board the MV *Alcantara* that Sadie was being forced

121

to endure, including the likelihood of being violently raped numerous times by loathsome men.

He sat on one of the many benches lining the pathway in the park, leaned back, and shut his eyes. *How could her father have been so ignorant allowing his only daughter to be sent off with that man, just to keep her from marrying me?*

Alex worried that Sadie was not strong enough to handle both the abusive physical and psychological stresses she would be subjected to.

"Alex," said a female voice.

He quickly opened his eyes and saw Sara standing in front of him. "Sara, what are you doing here?"

"I've been looking for you. I've just come from the Blue Palace. Jan told me that you just left, and pointed out the direction you were headed."

"Why are you looking for me?"

Sara sat down beside him, slouched her shoulders, put her head into her hands, and sighed.

"What is it, Sara?"

Sara straightened her spine, turned her head toward Alex, and said, "This was all my fault."

"What do you mean? What's your fault?"

Sara swallowed hard, took a deep breath, and slowly exhaled. "I work for the Zwi Migdal as a scout. I've been doing it for years," she said and paused.

Alex grimaced and shook his head. "You're a scout for those devils?"

Sara puckered her brow. "I'm the one who told Mr. Baranski, the marriage broker, about Sadie."

"But why would you do that? I thought you two were best friends."

Sara nodded quickly. "We were the best of friends. There wasn't a day that went by that we didn't see each other. That was until she met you. After that, she ignored me, dismissed me, and I have to confess, I was jealous of her budding romance with you."

"But why would you destroy her life, Sara?"

Sara shrugged. "One day while I was at synagogue, Mr. Wollman cornered me. He shared his fears that his daughter was going to make a mistake of insurmountable proportions."

"You mean by marrying me?"

Sara nodded. "He was distraught. He begged me to talk sense into her. Hopeful that I would change her mind. But I knew that was impossible. Sadie had already told me she was in love with you. As things sometimes tend to happen, I ran into Mr. Baranski at Café Piwna. He was frustrated with me that I had no prospective recruits to introduce him to. I became flustered and told him about Sadie. I even had a photograph of her. When I showed him, he nearly fell off his chair, and he arranged a meeting with her parents right away."

Alex shook his head. "How could you?"

"I didn't know that Mr. Porkevitch was a fraud until Jan just told me. Mr. Baranski led me to believe that he represented rich Argentinian Jewish men looking for wives. When he said he had someone interested in marrying Sadie and bringing her to his fabulous oceanfront estate in Buenos Aires, I thought I was doing her parents a *mitzvah*. That's a good deed, in Yiddish."

"Yes, Sara, I know what a *mitzvah* is. Do you know what a *shanda* is?

Sara nodded. "Yes, it means a scandal. But it's worse than that. It's more like a *shanda fur die goy*, a fuck-up that shames my people."

"I'm afraid it is."

Sara wiped tears from her eyes. "Jan told me that you and he are leaving on the next ship to Argentina."

Alex nodded.

"I want to come with you. I can help find Sadie."

Alex shook his head. "No, Sara, that's crazy. It's too dangerous."

"I owe it to her to at least try. I was thinking that I can pretend to be a *Polaca*, a Jewish whore. I'll be your source on the inside."

Alex scrunched his forehead and said, "You're willing to do that?"

Sara reached out and took Alex's hand and said, "The way I feel right now, I'd sacrifice my own life to save Sadie's."

CHAPTER THIRTY-THREE—THE STAR OF BUENOS AIRES

There was no doubt that Sadie was causing quite a stir among the first-class passengers. Ezra marveled at the reaction of men and women twisting and turning their heads from their deckchairs, to gawk as they strolled by, arm-in-arm.

The crisp white, tailored outfit Sadie chose fit her perfectly, highlighting her ample breasts, thin waist, and attractive concave curve in her lower back that amplified her firm, round buttocks. Ezra particularly enjoyed how her dress tapered down to finish just below her knees, exposing her long, slender legs, and firm calves. His wife would have required serious alterations to accommodate her less shapely figure.

Ezra was also pleased that Sadie needed only one overnight in that hideous cell to change her attitude towards him. He wondered how many more days it would take before he was able to enjoy her in his bed. But he reminded himself to temper his carnal desires. Sadie was an exquisite woman, worth waiting for; as long as it happened at least a few days before they docked at the Port of Buenos Aires.

"Would you like a coffee?" Ezra asked, gesturing toward a café style restaurant off the first-class deck that offered tapas, drinks, teas and coffees, in between the lunch and dinner service.

Sadie smiled and nodded.

"I was told," Ezra explained, "that they designed this room in what's called Louis XIV style.

"It's quite elegant," Sadie said, admiring the floor to ceiling wood paneling and ornamental moldings.

"Well, look who's here," said a heavyset man puffing on a cigar, who rose to his feet to greet Ezra.

"Ah, Henry, it's good to see you," Ezra said, shaking the large man's hand, and then greeted the woman who remained seated. "Hello, Eleanor, you're looking as elegant as ever."

"Hello, Ezra," Eleanor said, while keeping her gaze upon Sadie, "and who is this beautiful young lady?"

"Allow me to introduce Miss Sadie Wollman. She is immigrating to our country, and I promised her parents to make sure she arrives safely."

"It's a pleasure to meet you, Miss Wollman, please join us," said Henry, sweeping his chunky arm toward the two empty chairs.

"Of course," Ezra said, pulling out the chair for Sadie. "Henry and Eleanor Stillman are the owners of *Stillman's*, a wonderful clothing store that sells the latest men's and women's fashions from Europe. I suppose you and Eleanor were on a buying trip?"

"Yes, we try to get to Paris twice per year. While we were there, we took the opportunity to travel to Berlin to visit Eleanor's family. That's why we departed from Hamburg."

Eleanor leaned over the small table and took Sadie's hand. "My dear, what are your plans when you arrive?"

Sadie looked over to Ezra, not knowing how he would want her to answer, so she just shrugged and said, "That's up to Ezra."

"Well, well, aren't you the obedient one," Eleanor remarked.

"Now don't be rude, darling," Henry said. "I'm sure Sadie will find her way."

"You listen to me," Eleanor said, leaning in and wagging a finger, "*Stillman's* can use a girl like you modeling our clothes around the city. You come and visit with me when you get yourself settled, and the first thing we'll do is set up an appointment with my hairdresser. Have you heard of the *Eton Crop*?"

Sadie shook her head. "No, I haven't."

Eleanor gestured around her head. "It's the latest cut from Europe, and with those gorgeous green eyes and sculpted cheekbones, you would look fabulous. Don't you think, Henry?"

Henry took a puff on his cigar, leaned back in his chair, blew the smoke upwards in a strong stream, and said, "You pay attention to my wife, she'll make you the star of Buenos Aires."

CHAPTER THIRTY-FOUR—TEACHING A LESSON

Ezra and Sadie stood before the podium, waiting for Marcel, the maître d' to return.

"My apologies, Mr. Porkevitch. There's been a change in your seating. If you don't mind, the captain has asked if you and Miss Wollman would join him at his table."

Ezra looked surprised. "Sure, we'd be honored," he said and whispered to Sadie, "I've never been invited to the captain's table two nights in a row."

Sadie smiled and wondered if she was the reason for the invitation. Once they reached the table and were introduced to the officers, her suspicions were confirmed. Throughout dinner, each and every officer, including the captain, kept their wanting eyes glued upon her.

"So, Ezra," the captain said during the meal, "as we discussed last night, we've scheduled our dance social for our officers tomorrow evening. I'm assuming your ladies will be attending?"

Ezra pointed with his fork. "Absolutely, they'll be there. In fact, I was planning on reviewing the details with the girls after dinner."

"Excellent, I'm sure it shall be a most enjoyable evening," the captain said and then looked over to Sadie. "I would be honored, Miss Wollman, if you would accompany me to the dance."

Sadie looked over to Ezra, trying to not appear flustered.

Ezra smiled, looked at the captain, and said, "Sadie would love to, Captain."

*

Once dinner concluded and the officers returned to their duties, Ezra accompanied Sadie back to the Presidential Suite. Once they were inside, and safe from anyone overhearing them, she posed the question she kept to herself throughout dinner. "How come I'm getting the impression that this request from the captain will require more than just dancing?"

Ezra ignored her, removed his dinner jacket, and left Sadie standing in the salon while he disappeared into his bedroom. When he returned, she said, "Aren't you going to answer my question?"

"Come, we need to go see the girls," he said, walking toward the door.

Once he stepped by, Sadie spread out her arms, expressing her frustration. But with no recourse to change anything, she resigned her private protest and followed Ezra out of the suite.

*

"Good evening, ladies," Ezra said, as he and Sadie entered the steerage cabin where the eight girls were being held.

Just like at dinner, every set of eyes was glued upon Sadie, curious to know why she was the pampered one, and not one of them.

"How are things?" Ezra asked Dovid, who along with Bernie, slept in steerage with the girls.

129

"Mostly fine, except for our troublemaker," he said, cocking his head toward one of the girls standing alongside him.

"Oh," Ezra said with a nod, "and who would that be?"

Dovid shrugged. "I'm afraid Rebecca has been causing Bernie and me a good amount of grief."

Ezra squinted his eyes, showing concern and flicked his hand at Rebecca. "Come here."

"What do you want?" Rebecca said, with a palatable dose of disdain.

Ezra stepped toward her, grabbed a handful of her blonde hair, and jerked her forward, causing her to stumble and fall.

"Get up," he demanded, and gave her a swift kick to her stomach.

Rebecca heaved a guttural sound, that Sadie didn't know a human could make.

Ezra kicked her again. "Get up or I'll keep kicking you."

Rebecca struggled to her feet and stood face to face with Ezra, who wasted no time. He reeled his arm back and delivered a punch square upon her face. Rebecca spun around like a top, blood spraying out in an arc, and collapsed into the waiting arms of Bernie.

Bernie propped her back to her feet. She looked at Ezra. Blood was pouring from her nose that appeared broken. What was once a pretty face, now looked deformed. The girls, including Sadie, cowered, afraid one of them would be next.

"Get her cleaned up," he ordered Bernie, and without missing a beat, he shifted into a cheerful mood and said, "Now on a more pleasant note.

Tomorrow night, you ladies have been invited to the Officer's Social. You'll be their dates. You will dance with them, admire them, compliment them and then, you will go to their cabins and fuck them."

The girls instinctively huddled together, while Rebecca grabbed an old rag off the floor and held it to her bloody nose. Sadie knew she would need the attention of the ship's doctor. So with all the courage she could muster, Sadie walked over to Ezra and leaned in to whisper in his ear, "Would it be all right if I took Rebecca to the ship's infirmary? This way, she can be ready for the dance."

Ezra looked at Sadie with a furrowed brow and said, "But what about you, Sadie? Will you also be ready to make the captain happy?"

Sadie sighed, looked over to Rebecca, then back to Ezra, and nodded. "Yes, I'll be ready," she said, reaching to help her.

"Take your hands off me," Rebecca snarled, pulling her arm away.

"I'm just trying to help," Sadie whispered.

"By fucking him? How does that help me?"

"That's enough," interrupted Ezra. "Take her to the infirmary, and for the rest of you—let this be a lesson," he said and took a step closer to the girls. "Tomorrow, after you shower, Dovid will provide you with clean dresses. We also have makeup and hairbrushes. Make yourselves pretty and most importantly, make the officers happy." He pointed to Sadie, helping Rebecca out the door. "It would be a shame to *damage* any more of you."

CHAPTER THIRTY-FIVE—A FAVOR

While Ezra thought it unfortunate to damage a pretty face like Rebecca's, her sacrifice was necessary to motivate his fledglings to behave, and to be fearful of what was yet to come if they didn't.

Ezra was not ignorant of the challenges imposed upon these young women being forced into the world of prostitution. They were virgins and even if they were not, Ezra knew they were petrified by the thoughts of strange men violating them in the most intimate way.

Most young women, Ezra imagined, fantasized about making love for the first time on their wedding night. His abduction shattered their illusions, and because of this, he needed to use the time on the voyage to Argentina to break the girls in, so when they reached the marketplace in Buenos Aires and sold at auction, they were ready to work, and he was able to collect his commissions.

While Sadie was busy taking Rebecca to the infirmary for the ship's doctor to stitch up her wounds and reset her broken nose, Ezra met with Henry Stillman in the men's smoking lounge.

"You've found quite a treasure, Ezra. This one belongs in *The Tango*," Henry said, tapping the ashes off his cigar into a silver ashtray.

"That's what I thought," Ezra said, and exhaled a stream of cigar smoke.

"I'm sure you'll have no problem getting her placed there."

"How about you? How did you make out in Paris?"

Henry smiled, took a puff on his cigar, exhaled, and said, "Terrific. I've recruited four young French ladies from Le Chabanais, the most exclusive brothel in all of Paris. I've put them up in my own suite. I'll take you by later. Maybe give you a taste?"

Ezra held up his hand, with his cigar pinched between two fingers. "Ah *une putain française*, there's none better. But I must regretfully decline, Henry. I'm saving myself for Sadie," he said with a smirk.

Henry let out a belly-shaking laugh. "Saving yourself? That's a good one. Well, you better hurry. From what I hear, the captain may spoil her before you get your chance."

Ezra wiggled a finger. "That's why I wanted to speak with you, Henry. Sadie's going to suffer from an awful bout of seasickness, and won't be able to make the dance social. Perhaps you can arrange one of your experienced *putains* to take her place?"

Henry nodded slowly, took a puff on his cigar, exhaled, and said, "I would be happy to help you out, Ezra, and don't worry, once the captain spends a few minutes with Claire, he will soon forget all about Sadie."

"I would be most grateful," he said, reaching over to shake his hand.

Henry smiled and said, "It is my pleasure to help out."

Ezra nodded, knowing that this favor would require a hefty payback one day.

CHAPTER THIRTY SIX—MADAM ESTHER

Sadie gently stroked Rebecca's back while they shared a look at her battered face in the mirror.

"It will take time, but you'll heal," she said, trying her best to reassure Rebecca.

"Look at me, I'm hideous," she said, wiping streams of tears off purple blotches forming under her eyes.

Sadie took a breath to steady herself. Rebecca didn't look good. The doctor had just left after resetting her nose with an audible crack, followed by Rebecca screeching out a gut-wrenching yelp. Sadie took a cloth, ran it under warm water, and tried to dab away crusts of blood clinging to her nostrils.

"Stop, it hurts," Rebecca insisted, pushing Sadie's hand away.

"I'm sorry."

Rebecca stood up, steadied herself by holding on to the edge of the examining table, and pointed a finger at Sadie. "Why are you helping me?"

Sadie held out her palms. "What do you mean? You're hurt, I just thought . . ."

"Why don't you just go back to that monster and leave me alone?" she said and hobbled across the infirmary toward the doorway.

Sadie put her hands on her hips. "That's not fair, Rebecca. I'm in the same situation as you are."

Rebecca turned and pointed a finger. "You can't be serious; you've fucked your way into his first-class cabin, while I'm stuck in steerage with those two imbeciles. I was raped by both of them last night."

Sadie put her hand to her mouth. "Oh my god, Rebecca, I didn't know."

"You want to help me, Sadie?" Rebecca said, grasping onto the frame of the doorway.

Sadie nodded. "I do, just tell me how."

"Take me topside, and give me a hand getting myself over the railing, so I can jump overboard. I'd rather drown than continue to live like this."

"No, Rebecca, suicide is forbidden. It's a sin."

Rebecca took a few steps toward Sadie, and with a furrowed brow said, "Was it a sin moments before the Romans overtook the fortress of Masada, when the Jews took their own lives, rather than to be enslaved by those barbarians?" Rebecca paused to catch her breath and then continued, "Why should I allow myself to be violated in such an unholy manner? And how dare you try to shame me, after you have given yourself to that wicked, wicked man?"

Sadie spread her arms wide. "I have done so such thing, Rebecca, and will never do so, at least willingly."

"We're all doomed," Rebecca said, and walked out of the infirmary, leaving Sadie behind.

*

Sadie pursed her lips in anger as she marched along the Promenade Deck toward the Presidential Suite. She paid no attention to the dozens of passengers she passed, lounging upon the wooden deck chairs.

"Excuse me, young lady," a voice said in Yiddish, piercing through Sadie's internal fury.

Sadie stopped and looked at an elderly woman seated, smoking a cigarette.

The woman took a puff and blew a stream of smoke past Sadie. "Are you traveling with Mr. Porkevitch?"

Sadie looked down the promenade and saw the double doors to her suite. "Yes I am, but I really can't stop to talk, I must get back."

The woman tilted her head and looked up at Sadie. "Why don't you sit down and talk to me for a few minutes; if Ezra sees us, I'm sure he won't mind."

Sadie waved her hands in protest. "Oh no, I must get back right away."

"What's your name, sweetie?"

"Sadie."

"Sadie, please sit with me, what I need to tell you won't take long, and you may find it enlightening," the old woman said, tapping the ashes off her cigarette into the breeze.

Sadie nodded, sat down, and placed her hands on her knees.

"My name is Esther Gimmel. I'm imagining the reason you are here is that your parents were bamboozled by Ezra."

Sadie nodded again. "How did you know?"

"I'm a retired madam. I know a *Polaca* when I see one."

Sadie puckered her face, unsure what Esther meant.

"I used to manage girls like you. Though I have to say, you're a rare beauty. I would imagine that you'll be sold to one of the high-class brothels, like *The Tango*."

Sadie's eyes opened wide. "Sold? That's what I heard. Is it really true?"

Esther shook her head. "I'm afraid so. When you get to the city, you'll be taken to what they call the meat-market. It's a place where the agents, like Ezra, bring their girls. You'll be marched out onto a stage naked and auctioned off to the highest bidder."

Sadie held her hand to her mouth. "Naked? Oh my god."

Esther nodded and wagged a finger. "You should earn Ezra a healthy payday. That's why he's pampering you, while the other girls are down in steerage."

Sadie nodded and looked up and down the promenade before she said, "Yes, that's right. I just came from there. I watched him beat up one of the girls. He broke her nose."

Esther nodded. "This is nothing new. That's how the Zwi Migdal has worked for years. They terrify the girls into submission." She paused to take a drag on her cigarette, before she continued, "I was a *Polaca* once, a long time ago, and just like you, my parents were looking to provide a better life, so they married me off to a handsome man, just like Ezra. I ended up at a decent brothel, nothing like *The Tango*." She chuckled. "Over the years I was able to work my way out of spreading my legs several times a day, into managing the girls as the madam. I earned a good living and was able to put money away and retire."

"Why are you here on this ship?"

Esther shrugged. "I was visiting family in Lodz."

Sadie nodded and smiled.

"I'm assuming that since you're staying with Ezra, he wants you for himself."

Sadie shrugged. "Oh no, he said he wouldn't touch me, unless I allowed him to, which I would never," she said, shaking her head.

Esther laughed. "That's what he says now. He'll only wait so long, Sadie. Mark my words, before this voyage ends, Ezra will expect you in his bed."

Tears welled up in Sadie's eyes. "The reason my father made the deal with the marriage broker was that I wanted to marry another man. Someone who my father didn't approve of."

Esther held up a hand. "Let me guess, you wanted to marry a *goy*."

Sadie nodded, with tears trailing down her cheeks. "His name is Alex. He's a professor at the university."

"My advice, dear, is to forget about this Alex and make sure you impress the *Rufiano* from *The Tango*. They treat their girls like princesses. No more than one man per day. They want their *Polacas* well rested. As for your friends down in steerage, they'll be lucky if they survive the year. The girls in the street brothels wear out quickly, and some of them end up homeless, begging for food. It's not a pretty thing to see."

"I don't understand, how can Jews let this happen to other Jews?"

Esther laughed. "Being a Jew does not make one immune to the bewitchment of money and power. We all succumb to it, regardless of our traditions or religion, and as a result, we make excuses for our vile and sinful behavior, and I'm certain, so will you, my dear."

"This would never happen where I come from."

Esther grunted, shook her head, and said, "Tell me, Sadie, how much did Ezra Porkevitch pay your father for the privilege of taking ownership of his daughter?"

Sadie stared at Esther for a moment, exhaled, and bowed her head in shame.

CHAPTER THIRTY-SEVEN—LEO'S ADVICE

Ezra walked into Sadie's bedroom suite and remained unnoticed while she gazed upon her reflection in the vanity mirror, and fussed with her long, thick locks of red hair.

"You look beautiful," Ezra said.

Visibly startled, Sadie quickly turned her head. "Ezra, what are you doing here? I'll be ready in a few minutes. Please wait for me in the salon," she said, pointing to the doorway.

There was no doubt Sadie was frightened of him. Ever since he taught Rebecca a lesson, she, along with the other girls, cringed in his presence. But Sadie exhibited no signs of submitting herself to him in the way he craved. Even after he concocted an excuse of sea-sickness that prevented her from sleeping with the captain two nights ago, she didn't relent or even offer her gratitude.

"I have shown inexhaustible levels of patience with you, Sadie," he said, curling his fingers in fists. "Do you think your beauty provides you with some sort of special power that protects you?" he said, shaking his head. "On the contrary, it makes you a target. I think you've seen a glimpse of that on this voyage."

Sadie watched Ezra walk over to a table against the wall, where a bouquet of fresh roses was displayed in a crystal vase. "You're like these flowers, Sadie, beautiful but delicate," he said, gripping the vase and flinging it against the wall, smashing it into shards of glass.

Sadie put her hand to her mouth and stared in horror at the dislodged rose petals and stems, scattered upon a puddle of water soaking into the plush carpeting.

Ezra jabbed a finger at Sadie. "Later tonight, when we return to our suite, you will come to my bed, and reassure me that what I paid your father was a wise investment. Otherwise, you'll end up with that lot in steerage, and trust me, Sadie, your regrets will be many."

Sadie stood up, calmly walked over to Ezra, and looked into his eyes, expressing a longing that Ezra had not seen before. She stood up on her toes, leaned in, and kissed his lips. He felt his face go flush, as she parted her lips, allowing their tongues to meet and explore. When she pulled back, Ezra stared at her, his mouth still hanging open.

"There will be more later," she said, taking Ezra by the hand and leading him toward the doorway.

*

Ezra had never experienced such personal pride as when he and Sadie walked arm-in-arm across the dining hall to their table. Heads turned, and hands reached out to greet the glamorous couple. Ezra imagined that this was how celebrities and politicians were ogled over.

Tonight was his last chance to mingle with several influential passengers he had his eyes upon, before docking at the Port of Buenos Aires.

They stopped at the captain's table and greeted the officers. "I hope your dance social was enjoyable," Ezra asked.

The captain kept his focus upon Sadie while he answered Ezra. "It was fine, but I have to say that I was disappointed to hear that you were not feeling well, Miss Wollman. Though it appears that you have recovered," the captain said, taking Sadie's hand and placing a soft kiss upon it.

"Thank you, Captain, I'm feeling much better."

"I understand my ladies provided suitable companionship for your officers," Ezra said, gesturing to the men seated and conversing among themselves at the table.

"I've heard no complaints," the captain said, with a smirk and a wink.

"Excellent," Ezra said and led Sadie to their table.

"I'll be back shortly. I would like to say hello to some people," Ezra said, holding out Sadie's chair.

Sadie shrugged. "Take your time," she said, flipping her hand dismissively.

Ezra first stopped to offer his thanks to Henry Stillman for offering the elegant Claire, as a stand-in for Sadie. "The captain told me he was pleased," Ezra said.

"I'm happy it went well," Henry said.

After saying goodbye to Henry, Ezra looked over the dining hall. There was someone in particular he wished to meet during the two-week voyage, and he had not yet seen him. His name was Leonard Rubenstein, a powerful *Balebos* for the Ashkenazum, an offshoot of the Zwi Migdal.

What Ezra knew of the man was that he was born in Odessa, and after a few years getting his feet wet with the Zwi Migdal, he branched out, starting his own organization, which had grown to an impressive network of over seven-hundred agents. It was well known that the Ashkenazum had judges, politicians, attorneys, and police captains as clients of his brothels.

To Ezra's delight, he spotted the obese Mr. Rubenstein seated at a table with several young ladies, along with a brawny man, who appeared to be his bodyguard. When Ezra approached, the man stood up, blocking his access to the man.

Ezra poked his heads around the large man and said, "Excuse me, Mr. Rubenstein, if you have a minute."

Mr. Rubenstein flicked his wrist in a shooing motion. "That's all right, Benjamin," he said, dismissing his man, as well as the ladies seated on either side of him.

"Hello, sir," Ezra said, leading with his outstretched hand. "My name is Ezra Porkevitch. I'm an agent with the Zwi."

"Ah, Mr. Porkevitch, it's a pleasure to finally meet you. You have quite the reputation."

Ezra smiled at the enthusiastic greeting. "Thank you, Mr. Rubenstein."

"Let's do away with the formalities. Call me Leo," he said, swallowing a gulp of red wine, and cleaning off the dribble running down his chin with the back of his hand.

"You honor me, sir."

"Tell me, Ezra, how are things with the Zwi?"

Ezra shrugged. "Same as it's always been. I'm working as an agent, although I have to confess, I'm getting exhausted from the constant travel."

Leo wagged a finger. "With your experience, you should be working for me as a trainer, instructing our agents."

Ezra nodded. "That sounds interesting."

Leo cut a piece of meat, stabbed it with his fork, and buried it deep into his puffy mouth. "We should talk. But tell me, Ezra, I couldn't help but notice that magnificent woman of yours," he said, pointing with his fork to the table where Sadie was seated.

"Yes, she's my prize. I found her in Warsaw."

"If her manner compliments her beauty, she could be a top earner."

"The manner part I'm working on," he said with a chuckle, "but I think she's getting closer to understanding her circumstance."

"A word of advice, Ezra," Leo said, pausing to guzzle what was left in his wine goblet, "don't fall in love with her. You'll find yourself in an untenable position. I've seen it too many times."

Ezra nodded and wondered if his lust for the beautiful Sadie would evolve into something more.

"And one more thing," he said, reaching into his pocket and handing Ezra a business card. "Give me a call when you're ready to talk."

Ezra looked at the card, then back to Leo and said, "Thank you, sir, I'll consider it."

CHAPTER THIRTY-EIGHT—THE TANGO

Sadie would do her best to ensure the evening lingered on as long as possible; though she knew avoiding the inevitable was futile. At some point, she would return to the Presidential Suite with Ezra, and be expected to surrender to his unbridled, lustful desires.

But to her delight after dinner, Ezra asked if she would like to go dancing, and, of course, Sadie enthusiastically agreed. Perhaps, she mused, he would exhaust himself and prefer to sleep, rather than to take her to his bed.

As they walked down the corridor from the dining hall to the ballroom, Sadie heard the muffled sounds of an orchestra, and understood that this was going to be different from her prior musical experiences, which were limited to the amateur street musicians of Warsaw.

Once they stepped through the opened doorway into the ballroom, Sadie felt an energy that caused her skin to tingle. The orchestra was playing a song that Sadie recognized, though she had never heard it played with such depth and vibrancy. She marveled at the dozens of dancing couples, swirling to the rousing melody, like they were all in a wonderful dream, trying to squeeze out each moment before they awoke.

Ezra took Sadie by the hand into the middle of the crowded dance floor. Her previous experience with formal dancing was with family, such

146

as attending wedding celebrations at the synagogue. But she managed to move gracefully enough, following Ezra's lead.

After their first dance, the orchestra paused and the conductor asked for the floor to be cleared. Everyone backed away, forming a three-sided human wall, and from behind a curtain off to the side of the orchestra, a couple appeared, taking center-stage. The audience gasped, including Sadie. The tall, slender woman wore a blood-red dress that hugged her body like a glove, with a long slit that opened to her hip, exposing the dancer's slender legs.

But it was her hair that mesmerized Sadie. Could this be the *Eton Crop;* the cut that Eleanor Stillman had told her about? Sadie touched her long, thick wavy hair, and imagined the effect of such a hairstyle.

The man, strikingly handsome, with a face that looked as if it was chiseled from stone, was dressed in all black. Even his greased-back hair was jet-black, though his eyes were a disarming sky-blue.

The tapping of the bandleader's baton silenced the audience, who were buzzing with anticipation. "Ladies and gentlemen," he announced, "the tango."

As the tone of the first note sounded, the man stood tall, shoulders drawn back, his gaze mysteriously dead-panned. His partner now tucked stealthily behind him, with only a flare of her red dress visible.

Then on cue, as the music began, she reached around from behind, placing her hand upon his chest. He held onto it for a brief moment, caressing it, before she withdrew, spinning away, causing her dress to cascade outwards. Just as swiftly she returned, collapsing into his arms, her head tilted, looking up into his eyes, but only for an instant.

Then they moved together across the floor, but not like Sadie's clumsy attempt with Ezra, but in harmony; two lovers becoming one.

They explored each other through their touch and intimacy of the dance.

The vibrancy and youthfulness of the tango stirred an unquenchable thirst in Sadie. It was a raw yearning from a part of her deepest core that had been awakened.

She watched as the woman in the red dress wrapped her naked leg around the man's hip, arched her back, her eyes lost within his for the moment. His hands slid along her bare arms until their fingers interlocked. They came together, facing one another, their lips nearly touching, then they parted, gliding across the large dancefloor, in step to the music.

When the dance ended, and the audience cheered their approval, Sadie wanted more. Nothing, except making love with Alex, had ever touched her at such a deeply sensual and erotic place before. Though now that experience with Alex seemed a distant and quickly fading second.

"Would you like to learn the tango, Sadie?" Ezra asked.

Sadie nodded, her eyes sparkled with desire and she said, "Can you teach me?"

CHAPTER THIRTY-NINE—MR. SORKIN

Alex admired the artwork on the walls of the cigar lounge. "Do you think this is a painting of the harbor at Buenos Aires?" he asked Jan.

"I don't know. I'm trying to figure out what's going on over there," Jan said not paying attention to the painting but instead pointing to a man seated in a burgundy upholstered Queen Anne Chair, speaking in a rousing tone to several passengers, under a cloud of cigar smoke.

Alex shrugged. "Let's go see."

It had been a week since Alex and Jan had set sail aboard the SS *Argentinean* from Hamburg. Up until this point, except for a few rough days of weather, the voyage had proven uneventful. This was their first time in the cigar lounge, since Alex refused to take part in any of the luxuries the ship had to offer. "We can't pamper ourselves while Sadie's life is in danger," he insisted, and Jan agreed.

But tonight, neither man could stand the boredom of being locked away in their cabin any longer, so they decided to check out the late-night activities onboard the ship.

"I've traveled from *shtetl* to *shtetl* across Poland, warning rabbis," the man pontificated, as Alex and Jan approached.

What serendipity! Alex thought. He looked over to Jan and nodded. This was an opportune discussion they needed to hear.

"They call themselves the Zwi Migdal, and have been recruiting young Jewish girls as sex slaves for many years, and there's no sign of it slowing down anytime soon. Though I try to do my best. That's why I travel to Poland, warning my people about them.

"Just this past April, after many months, I was able to convince the rabbis in Buenos Aires to ban the *Rufianos*, the Jewish pimps, from their synagogues. But that's not all. I even had them denied from burying their dead in Jewish cemeteries, which I thought would be the beginning of the end for the Zwi Migdal. But you know what they did?" he said, and paused to look over the faces, before continuing. "They built their own cemetery and opened up a fancy synagogue, right in the heart of the Jewish quarter. When you enter, it looks like a traditional place of Jewish worship, but on the second floor," he paused to pucker his face, "there's a brothel. Can you imagine?"

The men gathered around, all gasped.

"But their next act was more than I could endure," he said and paused to cough into a hanky. "During the synagogue's inauguration, their shameful rabbi held the sacred Torah in his arms and led the congregation of *Rufianos* into the street, and paraded around the new building as a blessing. I watched, with other honorable Jews, at this disgusting demonstration, but sadly, we could do nothing to stop it.

"That's why I decided to go to the birthplace of my ancestors and warn them. But alas, I'm only one man, and the Zwi Migdal employs hundreds and hundreds of agents, nefariously recruiting, young innocent girls into their criminal organization as sex slaves."

Alex and Jan waited for the flood of questions and conversations to conclude before they approached.

"Would you have a minute for me, sir?" Alex asked.

"What is it?"

Alex looked into the man's weary eyes, which seemed to express not only his exhaustion but also the sadness of his journey. "The reason my friend and I," Alex said and gestured to Jan standing alongside him, "are heading to Buenos Aires, is to rescue my fiancé from the grips of this Zwi Migdal."

The man looked at Alex, and then at Jan. Jan's appearance stunned the man for a moment, before he regained his composure. "You're albino?"

Jan nodded and offered his hand. "My name is Jan, and this is Alex."

"It's good to meet you both," he said, shaking hands. "My name is Nachum Sorkin. Come, let's find another place to talk. This smoke is bothering my lungs."

They followed Mr. Sorkin to where the plaque over a doorway read THE READING ROOM, which they soon learned was a small library.

"Let's sit here," Mr. Sorkin said, pointing to a setting of a round table with four chairs, in between two rows of wooden bookshelves, filled with novels by Argentine and Spanish writers.

"I like coming here," he said, taking a seat, "hardly anyone ever comes in. We can speak freely. Please, gentlemen, tell me your story."

Alex shared the details of his romance with Sadie, her father's betrayal, and the ultimate abduction by Mr. Porkevitch, an agent of the Zwi Migdal.

Mr. Sorkin listened and nodded. "What you have told me, Alex, I'm sorry to say, is nothing new. It's the same woeful tale, voiced by many young Jewish girls bound for brothels throughout Buenos Aires."

Alex reached across the table and clasped onto Mr. Sorkin's wrist and squeezed. "Can you help me find Sadie?"

Mr. Sorkin shook his head. "I hope you realize, Alex, that you're not the first forlorn lover searching for a girlfriend, a fiancé, or even a wife. There are hundreds of bodies of men, just like you, at the bottom of the Rio de la Plata who had similar intentions. My advice," he said, patting Alex's hand still gripping his wrist, "is to take the next ship back home. The men of the Zwi Migdal are murderous swine, you cannot defeat them."

Alex looked over to Jan and smiled. "Thank you for your advice, Mr. Sorkin, but I have seen murderous swine before. Jan and I fought in wars and we have, as one may say, particular skills. We will find Sadie, and if that means leaving a trail of blood in the journey's wake, so be it."

Mr. Sorkin nodded. "Excellent, then perhaps I can help. Anything to slow down the Zwi Migdal is a *mitzvah*."

"Indeed it is," Alex agreed.

"You speak Yiddish?"

Alex nodded.

"Marvelous!" he said, clapping his hands together. "You'll be able to move around, mostly unnoticed. But, as for your albino friend here," Mr. Sorkin paused to shake his head, "he'll certainly turn heads."

*

"I still think that it was a bad idea not taking Sara along with us," Jan said, as he and Alex strolled along the port side deck, heading back to their cabin. "She could have been useful."

Alex shook his head. "I thought the same thing, but reconsidered, as I am unsure we could count on Sara as a dependable asset, especially after what she did by exposing Sadie to those men."

"I suppose you're right," Jan said, opening the door to their cabin.

Alex patted Jan on his shoulder and walked in, and waited for the door to shut behind them before he spoke again. "When we arrive in Buenos Aires, I think we should take up Mr. Sorkin's offer and set up our base of operations from his apartment. Then go to the Polish Embassy and see what we can learn about Ezra Porkevitch."

CHAPTER FORTY—REBECCA'S REVENGE

When Ezra opened his eyes, Sadie's arm was limply draped across his chest, her head rested upon a pillow, and she was still asleep. He gently removed her arm and sat up. The morning light was setting off a warm glow around the edges of the heavy velour curtains, though the room remained mostly darkened.

It had taken the entire two weeks of the voyage to get Sadie to make love with him, and he was resigned to admit, he'd had better. Certainly, the *Putain Francaise* at *The Tango* provided more refined and exquisite lovemaking. After all, those girls were professionals, and capable of sending a man into uncontrollable, full-body convulsions, and mind-bending orgasms.

But regardless of her mediocrity, Sadie offered an intimacy that none of these French girls could ever provide. Not even his own wife, after many years of lovemaking, was able to touch a chord the way Sadie had.

While their naked bodies intermingled, all Ezra wanted was to please Sadie, rather than seeking personal pleasure for himself, though he wasn't sure he achieved this, as she offered no verbal response to his affection.

These heartfelt feelings were something he had never experienced and wondered what it meant. But he did know one thing for certain—he would not bring Sadie to the market for auction; even it meant forfeiting a massive commission, along with upsetting those at the top echelon of the Zwi Migdal.

Sadie would become his *amante*, his mistress, regardless of the expected consequences. Ezra kept an apartment by the waterfront that his wife knew nothing about. Sadie would live there—which was also a convenient short walk to the exciting nightlife of the city.

Perhaps in a week's time, after a few tango lessons, a wardrobe of the latest Parisian fashions from *Stillman's*, and a visit to *Santiago's*, the city's most exclusive beauty salon, Ezra would introduce Sadie into the upper echelons of Buenos Aires society.

While Sadie slept, Ezra made his way down to steerage. He needed to make sure Dovid and Bernie got the girls ready for disembarking when the ship docked at the port later that day.

As he descended to the lower levels of the ship, the accumulation of fourteen days at sea, and men being crammed into tight quarters, created a pungent smell nearly causing Ezra to gag. He would need to make this a quick visit.

But when he entered the windowless steerage cabin, where Dovid, Bernie, and the girls were being housed, his eyes bugged out of his head.

"What the fuck is going on?" he said.

With arms, torsos, and legs bound with heavy ropes to their bunks, all Dovid or Bernie could do, with gags in their mouths, was to express with their eyes their relief that Ezra had finally arrived.

"They got what they deserved," said Rebecca, standing alongside them, her arms folded across her chest.

"Who did this?" Ezra said, unsure that these eight women were capable of overpowering two strong men.

"Who do you think?" Rebecca said, bending over and tugging on the ropes, binding Dovid's legs together. "These men are animals and need to be treated as such."

Ezra looked over to the other girls, who were casually seated upon the edges of the bunks, seemingly at ease with the reversal of the master and slave roles.

He turned to Rebecca; the bruises from her beating had mostly subsided, though her nose had a sharp bump along its bridge. *A permanent reminder of her disobedience*, Ezra thought.

"Untie them, Rebecca," Ezra ordered, "and get yourselves ready to disembark. We'll be in Buenos Aires after lunch, or do I have to give a beating to another one of you girls?" Though that was the last thing he wanted to do. Taking one girl off the auction block was a worthy investment, one more would be costly and foolish.

Rebecca remained steadfast in defiance. She pointed to Dovid and Bernie. "These men will stay tied up as my prisoners. They'll not be released until I've been safely returned home."

Ezra exploded in laughter. "Are you serious? I can have the ship's security officer down here within minutes."

Rebecca reached into a pocket of her battered and stained dress and brandished a hunting knife. She took a step over to Dovid and poised the blade against his throat. "I'll kill both of them before that happens," she warned.

Ezra shook his head. "Come now, Rebecca. I couldn't care less about these two idiots. You want to murder them, go ahead. But know this," Ezra said, holding up a finger, "you're disembarking at the Port of Buenos Aires. How it's done, is up to you."

"It's over, Rebecca, hand the knife over to Mr. Porkevitch," pleaded Judith, huddled next to Aliza.

Rebecca looked at the trembling girls, shook her head, adjusted the grip of the knife in her hand, and before another word was spoken, she pulled up Dovid's head by his greasy hair, and skillfully slit his throat.

The girls screamed as Rebecca grinned like a madwoman, before releasing Dovid's head.

Ezra stood there, unable to move.

"Now do as I say, before I do the same thing to Bernie," she said, pointing the bloody blade at Ezra.

CHAPTER FORTY-ONE—ARRIVAL

Ezra left instructions for Sadie to disembark the ship with the Stillmans and wait for him at their home. *I'll come for you later. I have some unfortunate business to attend to*, he explained in a note she found on the nightstand when she awoke.

In a way, Sadie was relieved that she was able to have some private time to reflect on what occurred the evening before. Certainly, the stimulating tango performance, followed by the lighthearted, evening-long tango lesson, were the highlights.

While she could guess at the erotic insinuations of the dance, she didn't fully grasp their intensity until the *Bailarin*, the male dancer, had Sadie squeezed against him, her knee pressed against his hip, when he whispered, "Tango, my love, is a vertical expression of a horizontal desire, legitimized by the music."

These words acted like a key inserted into a hidden chamber, deep within Sadie's mind, where her raw carnal urges were no longer chained like prisoners. The doors had swung open, unleashing her sexual energy. Like a young sunflower absorbing the morning light, Sadie lifted her chin, shifted back her shoulders, smiled, and said, "I'm ready."

With this newfound freedom, the *Bailarin* moved Sadie swiftly across the dance floor, capturing the attention of both the men and women who ceased their own dancing to watch.

Thinking back upon it, Sadie imagined this as a journey beyond the confines of her physical body, and more of a dance within the spiritual realm, deep within her consciousness.

Though her movements were far from flawless, they were honest and authentic. When the dancing concluded for the evening, and the first-class passengers retired back to their cabins, Sadie was ready to allow Ezra to take her to his bed.

*

Once alone in the presidential suite, Sadie had resigned herself to the inevitable. Hopefully, Ezra would be satisfied with her body alone, as her mind could never connect with such a hideous man.

She allowed him to kiss and fondle her, though she found no pleasure, and offered no audible or physical cues to encourage him. When he entered her, she closed her eyes, hoping for a quick finish. He not only obliged, reaching an orgasm within seconds, but to her surprise and great relief, he withdrew before climaxing, draining himself upon her belly.

When finished, he got to his feet and went into the bathroom. A few minutes later, he returned with a hot towel and gently cleaned her. He then laid himself alongside her, closed his eyes, and fell asleep.

Sadie figured from his silent response that Ezra found her lovemaking lacking. After all, her only prior sexual experience was with Alex, and even that was her first time, though she knew even with a longer history, she would have performed in a similar lackluster way.

*

Sadie joined Eleanor Stillman along the promenade, as they watched the dockside crew push the multiple gangplanks into position. But to Sadie's surprise, along with many of the passengers waiting to disembark, several police cars with their sirens blasting, entered the docks from multiple points.

"What's going on?" Sadie asked Eleanor.

"I don't know, but isn't that Ezra?" she said, pointing to the gangplank used for the steerage passengers.

Sadie nodded and focused her vision. It was Ezra, and he was standing on the lower deck where she could see the girls who were quartered in the steerage cell, with Dovid and Bernie. She saw Bernie standing next to Ezra, but didn't see Dovid.

"Oh, there's Rebecca," Sadie said, and then realized that she was being escorted by an officer of the ship, her hands bound behind her back.

The sounds of boots clomping up the gangplank shifted her attention to the police now charging up toward the deck where Ezra was waiting. Sadie could see words being exchanged, fingers pointing, then a stretcher with a body, covered by a sheet, suddenly appearing.

Ezra pulled the sheet back, exposing the person's face, and Sadie recognized it as Dovid. She gasped from the sight of the blood-soaked shirt and open gash at his neck.

An arm wrapped around Sadie, causing her to jump. "It's alright, dear," Eleanor said, trying to comfort her, "this business has its rough moments. But not to worry, Ezra knows how to deal with it.

Sadie said nothing, staring at the scene below.

"Did Ezra tell you that you'll be staying with us for a few days?"

Sadie nodded. "Yes, he told me."

Eleanor grasped Sadie's hand and said, "You realize that he's very fond of you, or you'd be down there with those girls."

"Yes, I'm aware."

"You're going to be his *amante*. Do you know what that means?"

Sadie shook her head.

"His mistress, his lover. He's putting you up in his apartment, where you'll be treated like a princess, assuming you do as you're told," she said with a devilish smile.

"I'll do my best," she said, turning her head and rolling her eyes.

CHAPTER FORTY-TWO—HOTEL PALESTINA

Ezra and Bernie ushered the girls into a side room, not far from the *Hotel Palestina's* main ballroom. Bernie handed each of the seven girls a battered, thread-bare cotton robe.

Ezra stood with his hands on his hips, and said, "You'll be naked under your robe. When it's your turn, your name will be called. Walk out onto the stage, face the audience, remove your robe, and place it on the chair. I suggest you practice posing before you get out there. Show off your best features. That means if you have a nice ass, make sure you turn around and let them see it. If you have great tits, play with them, get them aroused. Remember, the more you work up the bids, the better the brothel, and trust me, it makes a difference."

"Why do we have to parade naked?" Judith called out. "Can't we keep our robe on and just give them a peek?"

"We're not selling robes, Judith," Ezra said, dismissing her question. "Now when the bidding is done, you'll put your robe back on. The *Rufiano* with the winning bid will have a holding room where you'll go and wait until the auction is over. Then you'll be taken to your new home."

"What's going to happen to Rebecca?" asked Aliza.

Ezra wiggled a finger. "Now's not the time to worry about her."

The girls muttered among themselves. Ezra had seen this pitiful spectacle each and every time he brought his *Polacas* to auction. But any sympathy he felt for them was quickly wiped clean by the end of the auction when he received his commissions.

"What about Sadie? Why isn't she here?" asked Aliza.

"You ask too many questions," Ezra said, glaring at the frightened girl. "Rebecca is in the custody of the police, where justice will be served. As for Sadie, she's none of your concern. Now focus on what's at hand. I'll be out in the audience watching you, so if you don't do your best, you'll hear from me. But if all goes well, this will be the last time we'll see each other. Good luck to you all," he said and left the girls in the room with Bernie.

Ezra found a lone seat near the front of the ballroom, closest to the stage, wanting to make sure he was visible to his girls when they were *on-the-block*, as it was called.

While he waited, he thought about last night's fiasco and Judith's heroic moment. After Rebecca had slit Dovid's throat and threatened to do the same to Bernie, Judith, who was standing behind Rebecca, grabbed a wooden chair and smashed it across her head. Rebecca fell hard, her head bouncing on the metal floor, causing the knife to release from her grip. Ezra reacted quickly by pouncing and subduing her.

He told Judith to pick up the knife and cut the ropes.

Later on, after security came and took Rebecca into custody, Ezra asked Bernie, "Can you tell me how she was able to get a hold of a knife?"

"We fell asleep, and that's when she went through our stuff and found the knife in the bottom of Dovid's duffel bag," Bernie said, looking down at his feet in shame.

"Next on the block is the lot from Agent Porkevitch," the auctioneer said, snapping Ezra out of his thoughts. He glanced around the room to see if any of the *big players* were in attendance, and to his delight, he saw several of the brothel's top *Rufianos*. He spotted and offered a wisp of a wave to Michael Lipshitz, the *Rufiano* to the *Condor*, a brothel owned by the Ashkenazum. Michael ran a respectable operation, and treated his girls well, even giving them days off for *Shabbat*.

Sitting one row back was Antonio Catalano, the top *Rufiano* in all of Buenos Aires, who ran *The Tango*. Ezra tried not to show any overt enthusiasm at his presence but nodded when Antonio made eye contact with him.

In a flash, he thought about Sadie and cursed under his breath. Was he foolish in keeping her for himself? *Can I afford the luxury of maintaining an amante?* Not only was he forfeiting a potential huge commission, but he was also adding a substantial weekly expense. Ezra rubbed the back of his neck, having second thoughts upon seeing Antonio Catalano with a bid paddle in his hand.

His attention quickly returned to the stage when his first girl, Aliza, clumsily walked barefoot toward center stage, removed her robe, folded it, and placed it on the chair. She squeezed her knees together, lifted her arms above her head, giving her saggy breasts a lift, causing Ezra to chuckle at her clumsy effort.

A paddle went up from someone Ezra didn't know. Soon several *Rufianos* began to push the bidding up, while the auctioneer tried to offer his encouragement by talking up Aliza's slender body and pretty face.

All in all, after his last *Polaca* was sold, Ezra was relieved. Like all of the previous auctions, this was a pitiful exhibition of young, frightened girls, heading toward a future of sadness and misfortune. But regardless of his moments of compassion, Ezra carried on.

He would earn himself a decent payday, even with losing Rebecca and holding Sadie back from the block. After all, his girls were considered to be above average quality, and as such, would be sold to decent brothels.

He settled up with the auctioneer and Ezra headed for the hotel lobby. He was anxious to get home, see his children, and get some rest. He figured that in a few days he would gather Sadie from the Stillmans and set her up in his city apartment.

Just as he was headed out through the grand set of double-brass doors leading to the taxi stand in front of the *Hotel Palestina*, he heard his name being called. "Ezra, one moment, please."

Ezra turned around and saw Antonio Catalano walking briskly toward him.

"Can we talk," Antonio said, gesturing to a set of upholstered wingback chairs set up in a grouping in the lobby.

Ezra sighed, figuring this conversation would be about Sadie. He wasn't surprised that word had already reached Antonio.

"It's good to see you, Antonio," Ezra said, following him to the chairs.

The men sat down, Antonio leaned forward, rested his elbows on his knees, and stared at Ezra for a moment before he spoke. "Where is she?" he said plainly.

Ezra shook his head. "Where is who?"

Antonio sighed. "You know, Ezra, I don't waste my time with these auctions. I came for your redhead."

Ezra smiled. "Ah Sadie, well I decided not to put her on the block."

Antonio sat back and folded his arms across his chest. His furrowed brow offered a hint of his frustration. "Let me guess, Ezra, you're keeping her as your *amante*?"

Ezra looked at Antonio, knowing he would have paid a fortune for Sadie. Probably more than double he received for the entire block of girls he just auctioned off. But Antonio's frustration gave Ezra a burst of pleasure he didn't expect. He smiled and said, "She's a wonderful young lady, perhaps you'll get a chance to meet her."

Antonio opened his eyes wide and tilted his head. "I'm surprised at you, Ezra. I've always thought of you as a sound businessman. Sounds like you're letting your dick do your thinking."

Ezra stroked the three-day stubble on his chin, thinking Antonio was probably correct. But he would never confess such a flaw. His status as a top agent would be in jeopardy if the *Rufianos* and his *Balebos* with the Zwi Migdal thought his actions were costing them money.

"I appreciate your interest in Sadie, she's certainly spectacular, but I'm afraid she's not going to be a *Polaca*. This is a woman to be cherished, protected, and dare I say, admired like a precious work of art."

Antonio laughed and pushed himself up to his feet. He pointed at Ezra and said, "You're in love with her, aren't you? I've seen this dozens of times before. Be smart, Ezra, before it's too late, bring her to me. I'll pay you a year's worth of commissions for her."

Ezra rose up, stood face-to-face with Antonio, and shook his head. "Thank you for your offer, Antonio, but I must respectfully decline."

Antonio pointed a finger inches from Ezra's face. "I'll give you three days, Ezra. If you don't change your mind by then, the offer is off the table," he said, turned and exited the hotel.

CHAPTER FORTY-THREE—THE MAKEOVER

Santiago Romero, the premier hairdresser in all of Buenos Aires, stood behind Sadie seated in his salon chair. "I've never seen such vibrancy," he said, running his fingers through her thick hair. "The color is so rich, it's a shame to cut it."

"Nonsense," said Eleanor Stillman, standing off to the side, "her color will only be enhanced."

"So be it," said Santiago, with a pair of shears in his right hand, and sliced into Sadie's luxurious locks.

*

Sadie sat in the chair, gazing at her reflection. She touched what was left of her hair; now as short as a man's cut. Lying on the floor beneath her feet were her long locks, ready to be swept away.

"You look stunning," Eleanor said, standing behind Sadie.

"Do you think?" Sadie said, evaluating herself in the mirror. She hesitated a moment before rising from the chair and continued to gaze at herself. She gently touched her fashioned hairdo and smiled. As Eleanor had said, the *Eton Crop* suited her. Two flattened curlicues swirled upon her cheekbones, and her newly sculpted eyebrows allowed her wide-spaced, emerald-green eyes to sparkle.

"Come now, Sadie, let's head over to *Stillman's*, and get you fitted," Eleanor said.

Sadie nodded. If she was forced to play along with Ezra until she was able to figure out how to get back to Alex, then she was going to do it with all the power her beauty and charm could wield.

*

The fancy stores in Warsaw offered little compared to the spectacle of *Stillman's*. Sadie gawked upon stepping through the store's grand entrance. Rows of marble columns soared thirty feet, supporting a ceiling painted with stars, like the evening sky. Its walls featured oversized murals depicting various poses of tango dancers.

Customers greeted Eleanor as she and an entourage of her assistants led Sadie across the store's main floor toward the magnificent staircase. Excited shoppers treated Eleanor like a celebrity, rushing toward her for a glimpse, and perhaps to share a few words. But it was Sadie who caught everyone's attention. She took notice of customers pointing at her, and conversing among themselves, apparently trying to figure out who she was.

Eleanor leaned in and whispered, "Wait until they see you in one of my new Parisian ensembles. Come, Sadie, we're going to the second floor, my tailoring team is waiting for us."

*

Sadie was fitted for three evening dresses. Each one exceptional, but the one she fell in love with was made from a soft, black, silky fabric, featuring silver embroidery across its front, resembling feathers of a peacock.

She stood upon a carpeted platform, and admired herself in the three-sided mirror, while the tailor pinned and marked with chalk, his alterations. She amused herself thinking about the likely reactions of both the men and women when she swaggered into the elegant night clubs of Buenos Aires.

"You look absolutely stunning, my dear," Eleanor said, entering the fitting room.

"I've never seen such a beautiful gown," Sadie said, turning around and twisting her head to see how she looked from behind.

"Sadie, I've just heard from Ezra. He will be sending over a car later today to take you to your apartment. Your gowns will be ready in a few days and I'll have them delivered in time for Friday night. Ezra tells me you'll be going to *El Choclo*, the city's premier tango club," she said, shifting her eyebrows. "He's also arranged private tango lessons during the afternoons, so you'll be ready for your debut on Buenos Aires society."

"Eleanor, I don't know how to thank you for all of this," she said genuinely feeling grateful.

Eleanor laughed. "There's no need to thank me. This," she said, wagging her finger up and down, "is a mutually beneficial arrangement. In a sense, you're working for *Stillman's*, as a walking advertisement. I expect to be paid back handsomely for my investment," she said with a tone that sounded intimidating.

Sadie looked at Eleanor and tried to smile. "I hope I won't disappoint you."

"That would be most unfortunate. But I'm not worried. I'm sure you'll be a smashing success."

CHAPTER FORTY-FOUR—EL CHOCLO

The excitement began the moment Ezra's driver pulled the motorcar up to the front entrance of *El Choclo*.

"Wait for me to open your door," Ezra said.

Sadie nodded.

Ezra rose from the backseat of the black sedan, and slowly walked around its front end, savoring the attention from the people gathered on the sidewalk, anxious for a glimpse of the rich and famous arriving at the city's most popular night club.

A few photographers covering the nightlife for the city's papers noticed the new arrival and pushed their way through the crowd in order to position themselves for a clear shot of the glamorous couple, walking the red carpet.

In a grand gesture of an exaggerated bow, Ezra dipped his torso from the waist, gripped the car door handle, and twisted it. As he pulled it open, out of the darkness of the car's interior, Sadie's long, stockinged leg appeared.

The onlookers audibly hushed as Sadie accepted Ezra's hand and stepped from the car. She wore the black silk, embroidered dress from *Stillman's*, beautifully tailored to the curves of her breasts, waist, and hips.

The maître d' of the club left his post to clear the way for the couple. Sadie, with a gesture that surprised Ezra, took a moment to pose for the photographers, by turning her back toward them, placing her hands on her hips, twisting her head over her shoulder, and offering a bright smile that seemed to cause the flashbulbs to simultaneously explode.

Ezra had been to *El Choclo* before with other beautiful women, and found his way to his table gathering nothing more than subdued attention. But with Sadie on his arm, nearly everyone stopped to shake his hand, and get a better look at his date.

But the biggest fuss was made as Sadie and Ezra followed the maître d' across the dance floor to their table. Before they could make it to their seats, the orchestra, who was playing a popular tune, nearly stopped cold. Ezra looked over and saw nearly every musician of the orchestra was gawking at Sadie. Quickly, the bandleader tapped his baton, refocusing his musicians' attention back on the song.

The small round table with two chairs, white table cloth, and a candle was situated at the edge of the dance floor. Ezra pulled out the chair, allowing Sadie to sit. She folded one leg over the other and smiled at Ezra as he joined her.

"Would you like champagne?"

Sadie put her hand to her mouth and giggled like she was about to do something naughty.

Amused at her response, Ezra asked, "Have you ever had champagne?"

Sadie shook her head and said, "No, never."

*

They had nearly finished the bottle, when the conductor tapped his baton and the namesake of the club, the popular tango tune, *El Choclo* began.

Ezra looked over to Sadie, whose nose was turning red from the champagne, offered his hand and said, "Are you ready?"

Sadie smiled and nodded.

Together they joined the other couples who had hurried onto the dance floor. Ezra hoped the three lessons he arranged for Sadie had transformed her into a respectable tango dancer. But the moment she pressed her body against his, Ezra sensed something in Sadie was ready to explode.

Perhaps it was the champagne that unleashed Sadie's raw, uninhibited energy, as she seemed more connected to music, rather than to Ezra. The tango was a dance meant to express the relationship between the two dancers, but Sadie seemed to forget this.

Rather than moving in sync, Ezra needed to catch up. She appeared in a trance, oblivious to her partner and the other couples now gawking at her unusual physical interpretation of the music; hardly what the tango was meant to be.

She pulled away from Ezra, seeming to float away like a balloon, until she was snapped back from his tug upon her arm, and twirled back into his grasp.

When the song finished, Sadie was lying with her back pressed against Ezra's chest, his arms wrapped around her waist, her head tilted back and her eyes fixed upon his. Her chest was heaving from her exhaustive dance.

Ezra took Sadie by the hand and led her back to their table. It wasn't until they were seated that Sadie noticed that people were staring at her. She looked over to Ezra and asked, "Why is everyone looking at me?"

"Is that what they taught you at that tango dancing school?"

Sadie's eyes opened wide. "What do you mean?" she said breathlessly.

"I don't know what that was, but it certainly wasn't the tango, though you did seem to mesmerize everyone," he said, shifting his eyebrows.

Sadie put her hand to her mouth, "I just lost myself in the music. I hope I didn't embarrass you."

Ezra straightened his back and sat up tall. He took a sip of his champagne and said, "The beauty of the tango is that it's a dance of two lovers, not one."

Sadie's brilliant smile faded to a frown. She reached a hand across the table and squeezed Ezra's. "I'm sorry."

Ezra was about to respond when a hand tapped his shoulder. He turned around and saw a man he didn't know. "Mr. Porkevitch, would you and Miss Wollman please follow me. Mr. Rivlin would like to speak with you."

Ezra jerked his head to get a better look at the man. "Mr. Rivlin wants to see me?" he asked, obviously surprised.

The man nodded and said, "Please, this way."

Sadie looked over to Ezra, her blushed cheeks from dancing had drained to a pasty white. "Who is Mr. Rivlin?" she asked, eyes wide.

Ezra ground his jaw and muttered, "Just stay close and keep your mouth shut."

CHAPTER FORTY-FIVE—MR. RIVLIN

Sadie held on to Ezra's hand tightly as he led her through the club. The fear expressed in Ezra's eyes upon hearing Mr. Rivlin's name, spread to Sadie, causing her heartbeat to accelerate even though she had no idea who this man was.

When they arrived at the upholstered banquette, built into the elaborate woodwork, Sadie saw seated between two beautiful women, one blonde, the other brunette, a well-dressed man, with slicked back, black hair, piercing blue eyes, wearing a black, silk suit-jacket.

"Good evening, Mr. Rivlin," Ezra said. "I understand you asked to see me."

"Yes, Ezra, please join us," he said, gesturing to the empty spaces on either end of the semi-circular banquette, next to the two ladies.

Ezra nodded.

"You must be Sadie," Mr. Rivlin said.

Sadie smiled and wondered how he knew her name.

Mr. Rivlin took a sip of wine and said, "Sadie, I understand that you're from Warsaw?"

She looked over to Ezra before answering, "I am."

"We were enjoying your performance on the dance floor. Quite an artistic interpretation of the tango," he offered with a charming smile.

Sadie shrugged. "Oh, I'm afraid I got carried away by the music and probably too much champagne."

"Nonsense, it was fabulous," he said, turning to Ezra. "You've got yourself a prize here, Ezra, one in a million. It's a shame to keep her all to yourself."

Ezra inhaled and glanced over to Sadie, whose hands were shaking. He did his best to smile and said, "Thank you, sir. She is special."

Mr. Rivlin leaned across the table and reached for Sadie's hand. "Are you nervous, my dear?"

"I'm sorry," she said.

"There's no need. I don't bite," he said with a smile that hinted at the opposite. He released Sadie's hand and turned to Ezra. "I was speaking with Antonio from *The Tango*, who told me he offered you a fortune for this young lady, and you turned him down."

Ezra grimaced, unable to speak.

He took a puff on his cigar, and continued, "Antonio is a very important man within the Zwi—not deserving of your disrespect. Why would you do that, Ezra?"

Sadie realized that Mr. Rivlin must be Ezra's *Balebos*, which she previously learned to mean his boss. With a burst of courage, Sadie said, "Ezra and I are in love, Mr. Rivlin, and I came all this way to be with him."

Mr. Rivlin put down his cigar and smiled. "In love?"

Sadie nodded and reached across the table and took Ezra's hand. "Yes, I'm his *amante*," she said, trying to sound lighthearted.

"Is that so? Well, I'll tell you what, Sadie. I'll give the two of you lovebirds one week for your little romance," he said, holding up a finger. "After that, you'll move into *The Tango*." He then turned to Ezra, pointed inches from his face, and said, "You'll make that deal with Antonio, take your commission, then I want you on next month's ship to Hamburg. It's back to work. You understand me, Ezra?"

Ezra looked over to Sadie, who had tears running down her cheeks. He nodded and said, "Yes, sir."

"Good, now let's have some fun," Mr. Rivlin said, dismissing Ezra and Sadie with a wave of his hand.

Ezra led Sadie straight out of the club and into his waiting motorcar. As they drove away, Ezra stared out his window, ignoring her.

"I'm guessing that Mr. Rivlin is your *Balebos*?" Sadie said, breaking the silence.

Ezra turned to look at Sadie and shook his head. "Mr. Bendik Rivlin is more than that; he's the boss of all the bosses in Buenos Aires. He's the most powerful man in the Zwi Migdal. I'm afraid we have a week before our affair comes to its end. I'm sorry, Sadie," he said and turned back to look out the car window, and they rode the rest of the way in silence.

CHAPTER FORTY-SIX—THE POLISH AMBASSADOR

"The ambassador will see you now," said Zofia, the young Polish assistant holding open the door.

"Thank you," said Alex, as he and Jan walked past her and into Ambassador Stanislaw Duda's office.

"Gentlemen, please come in," said the ambassador.

"Thank you for seeing us," Alex said.

"I always have time for my fellow countrymen. Come, let's sit over here by the window," he said, pointing to a table with four chairs.

"My name is Alexander Kaminsky and this is Jan Mazur, we're from Warsaw."

"When Zofia told me who was asking to see me, I was certainly surprised and pleased. I'm well aware of who both of you are," the ambassador said, shaking Alex's and Jan's hands. "Your reputations, gentlemen, are legendary as heroes of the homeland. Please tell me how I can be of service."

"Thank you, sir," Alex said, took a deep breath, and sighed. "Jan and I are here because we need your help."

The ambassador offered a charming smile, held out his hands, and said, "I am at your service."

"I assume you've heard of the Zwi Migdal."

"I have indeed, and say no more." He paused for effect. "You're here to ask for my help in rescuing a young Jewish woman from their grip."

Alex nodded. "Yes, how did you know?"

The ambassador wagged his finger. "You're not the first countrymen to seek assistance from our embassy, and excuse me for asking such a delicate question, but are either of you two gentlemen Jewish?"

Alex glanced over to Jan and shook his head. "No, we are not, but why is that important?"

The ambassador held up his hand and said, "Which one of you two fell in love with the Jewess?"

Alex held up his hand.

"Tell me if I'm wrong," he began with a smirk. "You and your young lady wanted to marry, but the girl's parents disapproved because you're not a Jew. A timely advertisement in the synagogue caught her father's attention from a wealthy Jewish man from Argentina seeking a Jewish bride. A bargain was made through a marriage broker, a *stille chuppah*, as it's called, was performed by an agent of the Zwi Migdal, and your young lady was shipped off to Buenos Aires, headed for a brothel."

Alex sighed. "I gather you've seen this before."

"There have been at least a dozen or so men, just like you, who have sat in these chairs with the same sorrowful tale."

Jan leaned forward to ask, "Were you able to help them?"

The ambassador chuckled and shook his head. "I know both of you have considerable skills as soldiers and have proved it against a

181

formidable enemy. But unlike the enemies you faced during wartime, the Zwi Migdal are not soldiers; they have no honor. They're ruthless, fearless scum who would do anything to keep their brothel trade functioning, and I mean anything," he said pursing his lips.

"Are there not laws in this country that prevent men from making sex slaves out of innocent women?" Alex asked.

"There are, but they have the police, judges, and politicians paid off to look the other way," the ambassador said and shrugged. "Laws without enforcement are useless."

"On the voyage here from Hamburg we met a Mr. Sorkin—that's who we're staying with—who told us something similar."

"Ah, poor Mr. Sorkin. He visits with me every now and then. I tell him, there's nothing I can do. But he's relentless, waging a one-man crusade for years, trying his best to take the bastards down."

"Let me ask you this," Jan said, leaning back. "If we're able to sneak Alex's fiancée into the embassy can you arrange passage for us to get back home?"

The ambassador snorted. "I can protect you within these walls," he said, holding up his arms, "but as far as smuggling the three of you onto a ship back home, that's impossible. The Zwi would know you're here and would keep an army of men surrounding the building. The moment you stepped away from these walls, you'd be captured, and your girl would be sent back to where you found her. The two of you would end up dead. My suggestion is to find a fisherman willing to take you to Montevideo, Uruguay."

"Where would we find one?" Alex asked.

"Down by the harbor. Many people running from the law or from the Zwi, go to Montevideo, where there's a better chance for escape."

Alex nodded and stood up. "Thank you for your time, sir."

"One second, Alex," he said, holding up a finger. "How are you planning to find your *um* . . . you never told me your fiancée's name?"

"Sadie, her name is Sadie."

"All right, what's your plan for finding Sadie? You can't just go from brothel to brothel asking for her."

Alex looked over to Jan, then back to the ambassador and said, "You have a better idea?"

The ambassador reached for a pen, dipped it into an inkwell, and wrote a name on a piece of paper. He dusted the ink, blew on it, and handed it to Alex. "Go find Madam Esther Gimmel. She's retired but knows the underbelly of the brothels better than anyone."

Alex looked at the paper and said, "Where do we find her?"

Ambassador Stanislaw Duda stood up, put his hand on Alex's shoulder, and said, "You'll find the madam at Café Margot. But be cautious approaching her, she's not always forthcoming with strangers. Like everyone in this city, she's suspicious, the Zwi has eyes everywhere."

CHAPTER FORTY-SEVEN—DAY ONE

One week later, Sadie sat in the back seat of Ezra's motorcar, passing by café tables with patrons having their late afternoon coffees before heading home. She saw men and women engaging in lively conversations, laughing and carousing like she used to do with Sara back home in Warsaw.

Sadness consumed her as she thought about how carefree her life had been, only four weeks earlier. But now she was on her way to an existence she could have never imagined. Of course Sadie had heard of prostitutes, and thought they existed in Warsaw, though she had never knowingly met one.

Ezra sat quietly next to her in the back seat, gazing out the window. Sadie felt no need to engage in conversation with him either. In fact, during the past week, while quarantined in his apartment, they hardly spoke even though Sadie saw him every day when he brought over her meals.

To Sadie's relief, Ezra lost his interest in her both socially and sexually. He didn't offer to take her out on the town, or try to lure her to his bed. Sadie wondered if this sudden shift in his behavior had something to do with her becoming a *Polaca* and remembered her father's words of accusing her of being a ruined woman. *I guess he was right*, she thought.

Earlier that day, when Ezra came to pick her up, he explained that she should be grateful. "*The Tango* is the most exclusive of all the brothels in the city. You'll be treated like a princess."

Sadie snapped at him. "A princess has a prince. Not strange men violating her."

"I'm sorry, Sadie. I've tried my best to keep you from this."

"I think you're forgetting that you were the one who ripped me from my home."

Ezra shrugged. "I guess this was inevitable."

Sadie thought of Alex and wondered if they would ever reunite. She thought of the last time she saw him, banging helplessly against the glass window of the train car, as it pulled out of the Warsaw station.

Sadie touched the glass of the car window and thought, *Has Alex given up on me? Even if he wanted to rescue me, how would he even know where I am?*

Even her parents had no address, though Ezra promised to send it once they arrived. Which, of course, was a lie. She sighed, coming to the realization that Alex was not coming to save her. If she was going to get out of this predicament, she would have to figure it out on her own.

The motorcar turned down Lavalle Street and passed *Stillman's* where Sadie was fitted for three beautiful dresses that Ezra had allowed her to take to the brothel. Moments later, the driver made a left turn onto Junin Street and came to a stop in front of a tall, stone building with black, louvered shutters. Sadie saw a glossy, black door with a polished brass plaque mounted off to one side that simply said: THE TANGO.

"This is it," Ezra said, pointing to the front door.

Sadie sat still, staring at the ominous dark entrance, imagining the salacious things going on beyond it. *Ugly, hideous men, spilling their body fluids into the girls, for their own pleasure and disgusting desires.*

Suddenly the car door opened, snapping her out of her thoughts. "Let's go, Sadie," Ezra said, offering his hand, "I'll introduce you to the madam."

Sadie stepped toward the door, and stood there, while Ezra knocked. Her hands started to shake, and her mouth was as dry as on a midwinter's morning. The door opened, and a well-dressed young man greeted them.

"Mr. Porkevitch, please come inside," he said, sweeping his arm toward the darkened interior. "You must be Sadie. It is such a pleasure to meet you. My name is Frederick. The madam will be joining us soon."

Sadie tried to smile, but her nerves made it feel more like a frown. "Thank you," she muttered.

They entered a round-shaped room, so beautiful that Sadie's mouth fell open and she gawked at the decorations and architectural details. The floor, as well as the columns which soared to the towering ceiling, were made of pink marble. Deeply tufted benches, upholstered in blood, red velvet lived in between the columns.

"Right this way," Frederick said, ushering Ezra and Sadie through an archway and into a larger room.

Sadie gasped, and put her hand to her mouth as she admired the luxurious silk draperies hanging off gold-leaf poles, assorted plush cushions tossed about upon velvet upholstered sofas, and a large mahogany table stationed in the center of the room with fresh-cut, yellow flowers rising from a crystal vase.

"It looks like a palace," she said.

"It is a palace," came a woman's voice approaching from behind.

Sadie turned and saw a tall, thin woman, dressed in a perfectly tailored, cerulean blue jacket that ended just above her knee. Her brown hair was long and straight and fell over her shoulders. "You must be Sadie," she said softly, extending her hand.

Sadie couldn't help staring, as she mindlessly shook the older woman's hand.

"My name is Marguerite Paris," she said with a heavy French accent. "I am the madam of *The Tango*."

"I've never seen anything so beautiful."

"It is elegant," the madam said, and gently placed a hand upon Sadie's cheek. "And I must say, my dear, you are even more lovely than I was told."

Sadie tilted her head and said softly, "Thank you."

"You've done well, Ezra," she said, patting him on his back. "I'm certain our clientele will be most pleased with our new addition."

Ezra offered a smile that Sadie suspected was forced. "Thank you, Madam. It has always been my dream to have one of my girls placed here at *The Tango*."

"You are sweet. Thank you, Ezra. Now if you don't mind, I would like to show Sadie to her room."

Ezra nodded and lifted his hand awkwardly. "All right. I guess that's it. Good luck, Sadie, and goodbye," he said, leaning over to kiss her cheek. He turned around and headed for the front door, with Frederick following closely behind.

Sadie watched him leave. He looked like a defeated man, even though he earned a small fortune for selling Sadie to the city's most exclusive brothel. There was a sadness in his eyes and slight slouch in his shoulders. At first Sadie had pity for him, which surprised her. He certainly didn't deserve her sympathy after the terrible ways he treated her and the other girls on the voyage, especially Rebecca.

"He won't be the last man to fall in love with you, Sadie," the madam said.

Sadie nodded.

"Come now, I'll show you to your room, then I'll introduce you to the girls," she continued, taking Sadie by the hand and leading her up the winding staircase to the second level.

CHAPTER FORTY-EIGHT—CAFÉ MARGOT

Every table at the café was taken, but Jan spotted two empty stools at the far end of the bar. "Come on," he said, squeezing through the patrons standing and chatting, drinks in one hand, cigarettes in the other.

Alex followed through the smoke that hung over the café like a puffy cloud and watched as heads turned to gawk at the strange-looking albino man passing them by. Jan never failed to draw attention to himself, be it in Warsaw, Hamburg, or now in Buenos Aires, and to his credit, he never let it bother him; but this was not always so.

Back when they were teenagers Alex had noticed how Jan was terribly sensitive about his condition, and would go to great lengths to conceal himself. He grew his hair long and combed it down to hang over his eyes. He wore clothing that covered as much of his unusual skin as possible, even in the oppressive heat of summer.

Alex knew that Jan had a phobia about people thinking he was a freak. He had confessed it to Alex more than once, especially when the boys found themselves trying to socialize.

"Look as they laugh at me," he would say, pointing to a gathering of girls, obviously amused by Jan's albinism.

But all that changed one day when his grandfather summoned both boys over at a family gathering. They were fourteen years old, and while

Alex was playing with the cousins in the yard, Jan sat under a tree sulking the afternoon away.

His grandfather said to the boys as they stood before him, "Did you know that my father, your great grandfather, was also albino?"

Alex looked over to Jan, who shrugged and shook his head. Grandfather patted the empty space on the bench next to him to join him. He wrapped his long arm around Jan and said, "My father was also like you, Jan, withdrawn about his *condition*. But all that changed when he was walking one day, with his parents and brother in Saxon Gardens. As they strolled along the pathway toward the great fountain, he noticed, coming in the other direction, a tall man, dressed in a magnificent suit. He walked with his shoulders back, his head held high, and as he got closer, my father saw that this man was albino, just like him. Of course, he couldn't help staring at the man, who was walking with such pride, unashamed of his strange appearance. When he caught the eyes of people gawking at him, he smiled, nodded, and tipped his hat toward them. My father recognized himself in that man. Someone, who instead of being ashamed, embraced what god had given him and used it as a strength, rather than as a weakness. From that day forward, my father changed his life, and became a great man, someone I and my brothers and sisters admired. You too, Jan, can be such a man."

His grandfather's words changed his life. The next day both boys went to the barber and got haircuts. Jan even wore clothes suitable for the weather, and instead of living in shame, Jan became proud of his albinism.

They settled at the bar and Alex asked the man sitting next to him what he was drinking.

"What everyone drinks, Quilmes," he said, holding up his mug. "Where you boys from?" he asked, offering a perplexed look at Jan.

"Poland. We're on a goodwill mission with the embassy."

"Poland, *uh*, is that in Europe?" asked the man wiping the froth from his mouth with the back of his hand.

Alex patted the man on his back. "That's right."

The man frowned. "You speak Spanish in Poland?"

"No," Alex said, shaking his head, "we speak Polish."

The man nodded and muttered an unintelligible grunt.

"What can I get for you boys?" interrupted the barkeep.

Alex held up two fingers and said, "Two Quilmes, please."

When the two mugs were thumped on the worn, wooden bar, Alex held out a hand and said, "Can I ask you a question?"

The barkeep shrugged, and said, "Sure, what is it?"

"Do you know a woman by the name of Esther Gimmel?"

"You mean Madam Esther?"

Alex nodded.

"She comes in nearly every night. I haven't seen her yet, but if you hang out for a while, she'll show up. She has her own table," he said pointing behind them. "Once she comes in, we chase away whoever is sitting there."

Alex and Jan turned around and saw a young couple ogling over each other.

"Thank you," Alex said, tossing the man a peso.

*

About an hour later, the barkeep slid up to Alex and Jan and pointed. "That's her."

They twisted to look behind them and saw an elderly woman, with silver hair, waiting for her table to be cleaned.

"Thank you, Carlos," Madam Esther said, as he held out the chair for her to sit.

Carlos nodded and said, "The usual?"

"That would be nice."

As she took her seat, Alex stood up and approached the table. He figured that with her last name of Gimmel, she must be a Jew from Eastern Europe. He offered his most charming smile and asked in Yiddish, "Good evening, my name is Alex. Would you mind if I and my friend Jan," he said, pointing behind him, "joined you?"

Esther looked at Alex, then at Jan, and nodded. "Bitte meine, Herren," she said and gestured to the empty chairs at her table.

Jan grabbed his and Alex's beer and rose to his feet, and both men sat across from Esther.

"Your Malbec, Madam," Carlos said, placing the red wine on the table.

Esther smiled and thanked him. "So I gather you two *goyishe kops* are from my homeland."

Alex jerked his head back at the insult. "It's true my friend Jan and I are *goys*, but I can assure you our minds are not dull."

Esther nodded. "Your Yiddish is good. Please tell me why you're interested in speaking to an old lady. There are plenty of young ones your age," she said, gesturing to the crowded bar.

"Actually, we are looking for a young lady, and we were told that you may be able to help us locate her."

Esther tilted her head, and said, "Let me guess, you traveled from Poland looking for this young lady whose family was tricked into a marriage with a rich man from Buenos Aires."

Alex sighed. "I know it must be an old tired story by now. But to me this is serious and we are here to find her and bring her home."

Esther took a sip of her wine, put the glass down, and pointed her finger at Alex. "The story is nearly as old as me. Another story that's been told over and over is men like you, trying to be heroic and rescuing them, only to end up dead." She paused to lean in and said, "You're dealing with monsters who've built an empire that has made them rich beyond their imagination. No one has ever taken a girl from their brothels. Once a girl is in their grasp, that's the end of the story."

Alex looked over to Jan and said, "Thank you for the warning, but we must try."

"I can get myself into trouble even speaking about this to you," she said, looking about. "The Zwi Migdal is ruthless, even to an old lady like me."

"I'm in love with her, Madam Esther," Alex said, reaching across the table and touching her hand.

Esther lowered her eyes to look at his hand, then raised them to stare at Alex. She squinted and said, "All right, I'm curious, who are you looking for?"

Alex reached into his pocket and pulled out a photo and handed it to Esther. "Her name is Sadie Wollman."

Esther looked at the photo and her eyes opened wide. "I met this *Polaca* on the ship. She's lovely," she said handing the photo back to Alex.

"You've met Sadie?"

"She was with Ezra Porkevitch, one of the Zwi Migdal's top agents. I doubt if you're ever going to see her again."

Alex held out his palms. "Why, what's happened?"

"From what I've heard, she's been sold to *The Tango*."

Alex shrugged. "What's *The Tango*?"

"It's the city's most exclusive brothel. There's no way the two of you are getting inside."

"Why is that?" Jan asked.

194

"It's an exclusive member's only club. You must first be invited to apply by a current member. They do a background check, making sure you're as wealthy as you say you are. Then there're the annual dues," she said with a snicker.

"How much is that?"

"Three thousand pesos."

"How do you know all of this?"

"A long time ago, I too was a *Polaca* for the Zwi, just like your Sadie is now. Eventually, when I was too old to entice customers, I became a madam of one of their brothels. Through my smarts, I was able to save money and eventually retire. With all my years of experience, I learned the inner workings of how the Zwi run their operations. In a place like *The Tango*, not only do they carefully check the clientele, but also the people who work there, like the cleaning and maintenance staff. Even the nurses and doctors who treat the *Polacas* are scrutinized, as well as the businesses making deliveries."

"There must be a way inside," Alex said.

Esther leaned in and lowered her voice. "Normally I wouldn't share this information with strangers," she said looking at Alex and Jan, "but since I met your girl, I feel compelled to help."

Alex smiled and said, "Thank you."

Esther held up a finger. "There is one way. Applicants are permitted to tour *The Tango*, only with a referral by a member in good standing. They only start the extensive background check afterwards. If you can make friends with a member of the club, and get a referral, that would at least get you into the club for a look around. Perhaps you'll see Sadie."

Alex looked and Jan, then back to Madam Esther and smiled. "You have been very helpful, thank you," he said.

"Good luck to you, and if you need to speak to me again, you can always find me at *Café Margot*," she said, gesturing around her.

CHAPTER FORTY-NINE—ORIENTATION

"This is your room," the madam said. "It's small, but you have a comfortable bed. The bath and toilet are down the hall. If you build a successful clientele, which means men are asking for you specifically, then you'll be moved to a larger, more luxurious room, with your own bath."

Sadie cleared her dry throat and asked, "Do I bring men here?"

"Oh no, you'll never entertain members in your room. Come, I'll show you our theme rooms," she said, leading Sadie down a long hallway.

"This is our *Persian Room*," Marguerite said, holding open one of the two double wooden doors.

Sadie stepped inside. "Oh my," she said, taking in the layers of silk fabrics draped in scoops across the ceiling, giving the impression of being under a tent in Persia. Long fabric panels cascaded down from above, dividing the room into smaller vignettes, and within each space were upholstered lounges with thick cushions and dozens upon dozens of large, soft pillows tossed about. Under her feet was an intricately woven, red and gold rug in a geometric pattern, nearly as large as the room.

"I even have Persian outfits for the girls. Do you know how to belly dance?"

Sadie shrugged. "I don't know what that is."

The madam laughed. "Don't worry, we'll teach you."

Sadie toured the *Japanese Room*, the *Roman Room*, and the *Room of a Thousand Mirrors*. As they walked toward the central balcony, the madam said, "There are also special rooms for members who want something different, like bondage or humiliation. But you won't be ready for those rooms until you've been here for a while. Come now, let's meet my girls. They're anxious to see the stunning Sadie Wollman."

When they reached the grand staircase to the main floor, the madam stopped and put her hands on Sadie's shoulders and said, "Before we go downstairs and start your orientation on how to be a *Lady of The Tango*, I want you to know above all things, Sadie, is that we are not in the business of selling sex. Instead, I like to say, we offer our members an *experience*. A chance to escape from their dreary, boring existence. And that's why every wealthy man in Buenos Aires is banging down our door trying to become a member."

Sadie put her hand over her mouth and said, "I think I'm going to be sick," and ran down the hall toward the bathroom.

*

"Here, drink this," said Frederik, "you'll feel better in no time."

Sadie sipped. "This is good," she said and finished the carbonated ginger soda.

Frederik patted Sadie's forehead with a damp cloth as she lay upon a chaise lounge.

Sadie was in the Grand Social Hall, as the madam called it. Unlike the themed rooms upstairs, the décor here was formal, with richly colored, damask fabrics covering deeply tufted sofas, and a crystal chandelier sparkling over a mahogany table with an elaborately carved wooden base.

"Ladies," the madam began, "this is our new girl Sadie."

There were six of them lounging upon sofas. Sadie took a moment to observe each one. Never before had she seen more beautiful women. She put her hand to her cheek and murmured, "Oh my."

"Let me introduce you to our exquisite ladies, we have three French girls and three Jewish girls; four now, including you."

The madam gestured to a slender woman with the longest hair Sadie had ever seen, reaching down to her lower back. "This is Amelie, and in the past year since she first arrived from Paris, she has become *The Tango's* most requested lady."

Amelie offered a barely perceptible smile, and said with a heavy French accent, "It's a pleasure to meet you, Sadie."

The madam introduced the other two French girls: Dominique and Eloise. "Our French girls come to us already experts in the art of pleasing a man. A skill you will have to learn if you want to succeed here."

Dominique stood up when introduced and approached Sadie, swaying her ample hips to each side. "If you need anything, Sadie, come see me," she said, kissing Sadie on each cheek. Followed by Eloise, a voluptuous, platinum blonde, who offered Sadie the same greeting as

Dominique, but when she kissed the second cheek she whispered, "Beware, Sadie, no one here is your friend."

Sadie felt the same nervousness returning that made her sick and quickly took a large gulp of the ginger soda.

"Our Jewish girls appeal to our large clientele of Jewish men who want a relationship as a way to enhance their sexual pleasure. I find Jewish men," she paused to shrug, then said, "unable to separate sex from love, unlike the French. So Becca, Nava, and Shayna have all become *girlfriends* as well as lovers to our rich, Jewish members."

Sadie was introduced to each of the girls, and, unlike the French, they offered a cold, limp handshake. Each of them was pretty and curiously reminded her of her Jewish girlfriends back home, unlike the French girls whose mannerisms and features were exotic and interesting.

"Okay, ladies, off to your rooms, I would like to speak with Sadie in private," the madam said, dismissing the girls with the flip of her hand.

Once they were alone, the madam said, "Let's begin with the rules of *The Tango*. When you're with a man, ready to make love, there's no kissing. That is a sure way of passing on sickness, and once one girl becomes ill, it spreads quickly and we need to shut our doors until we recover. Also, do not let a man touch or lick your vagina. I've seen it too many times that girls end up with some type of infection." She reached into her pocket and pulled out a small tin, opened it, and pulled out an indistinguishable, crumbled up, yellowed thing. "Have you ever seen a sheath?" she said and pulled at it until it came to a shape of a small, thin bag.

Sadie looked at it with a puckered brow.

"This goes over the penis before he puts it inside you. All members must wear them if they want to fuck you. As for blowjobs, that's up to you. Some girls find the taste of the sheath disgusting. Not that a man's penis is a lollipop, but you can decide. But let me warn you, men don't want to put this on. They complain that it diminishes their enjoyment, which is true, but we don't want you getting pregnant or a transmitted disease."

Sadie rubbed her fingers along her forehead and shook her head. "I've only made love a few times in my entire life. I cannot satisfy men, like your French girls."

The madam leaned in, pointed a finger inches from Sadie's face, and said, "I understand that you met Mr. Rivlin."

Sadie nodded.

"He's a man who doesn't like disappointment. In fact, he doesn't believe in second chances, especially with his *Polacas*. Do you know what that means, Sadie?"

Sadie put her hand upon her chest and shook her head.

"It means we all do what he expects of us, and those who don't," she paused to pucker her lips and tilt her head, "they simply disappear, never to be heard or seen ever again."

Sadie thought about Rebecca on the ship.

"Sadie, with your looks you can become the most popular lady here, and you'll be given special treatment, like the best room in the house."

"Do we ever get to leave here—go places?"

"No, Sadie, you'll stay in the house until your time here is done. You're still young; you should expect to be here at least fifteen years."

"Fifteen years before I'm allowed to leave?" Sadie muttered.

The madam nodded. "Many of the older *Polacas*, once their youthful allure has faded, end up living in the city, though some have gone back to their homeland. But that's a long way off," she said flipping her wrist dismissively. "In the meantime, you'll learn from our French girls the delicate art of sexual stimulation, and from our Jewish girls, the skills of companionship that so many men are seeking in their lives. This is what our ladies of *The Tango* offers to our members. Can you do the same, Sadie?"

Sadie's jaw hung open for a good while, until the madam said, "Sadie, are you all right?"

She nodded, though she did it more as a reflex.

"Can you do what's expected of you?" the madam asked, dipping her head to catch Sadie's downward gaze.

Sadie sighed and said, "I'll try."

CHAPTER FIFTY—MR. SORKIN'S HOSPITALITY

Alex and Jan sat with Nachum Sorkin in his kitchen.

"Thank you, Nachum, for allowing Jan and me to stay with you."

"I hope you boys will be comfortable sleeping on the floor. I've been meaning to buy a sofa, but I'm never home."

"No, we're fine and grateful."

"So tell me, what did you learn at the embassy?"

Alex shook his head and scratched at the stubble on his face and said, "Not much. If we can find Sadie and smuggle her into the embassy she can be protected, but as far as getting us out of the country, the ambassador said that was impossible."

"I'm afraid he's right." Nachum nodded. "If the Zwi know you've taken one of their girls, they would use all their resources to retrieve her, and trust me, they are enormously powerful."

"But," Alex said, raising a finger, "the ambassador did have a suggestion that may bear fruit."

Nachum looked at Jan, then back to Alex and said, "Tell me."

"He suggested we go to Café Margot and find the former madam, by the name of Esther Gimmel."

"Of course," Mr. Sorkin interrupted, "I've known Esther for years."

"The ambassador said she was someone who was knowledgeable about the brothels and not involved with the Zwi. So Jan and I went to

Café Margot and spoke with her. She shared with us what she thought was *The Tango's* weak link in its security. Apparently, they don't screen prospects seeking membership. If I could befriend a member who would sponsor me, then I could get inside and see if Sadie's there, and try to figure out a way of getting her out."

"But why would you think she's there? It's the most exclusive brothel in all of Buenos Aires."

"The madam met Sadie on the ship over here from Hamburg. She said with her looks, that's where she'd expect her to be, and if she's not, we'll continue our search for her," Alex said and wagged a finger. "We're not leaving this country without her, Nachum."

"All right, I understand. But as you can see," he said, sweeping his arms outward, "I'm not a wealthy man. I could ask around, but I do not know any members of *The Tango*. How will you find such a man?"

Alex reached over, placed his hand on Nachum's shoulder, gave it a squeeze, and said, "Jan and I will find him, don't you worry."

CHAPTER FIFTY-ONE—HER FIRST

"My name is Theodore," the skinny man said in Yiddish.

Theodore wore round wire-rimmed glasses and sat upright at the edge of the sofa.

Sadie offered her hand to the man who gently shook it with his soft clammy hand. "It's a pleasure to meet you, Theodore."

He looked around, his eyes darting about. "You're new here," he said, keeping his focus elsewhere as he spoke.

"I am," Sadie said, turning around to see what he was looking at.

"I thought so," he said, sounding disappointed and returning his gaze back to Sadie.

"Why are you looking at Dominique with that man?"

"Because the madam screwed up and forgot to write down my date with her. She said she was sorry," he said with a guffaw, "and the only *Polaca* available was you."

Thank goodness, Sadie thought, *perhaps he only wants Dominique and won't ask me to take him upstairs.*

Theodore shook his head, returned his attention to Sadie, and said, "So, Sadie, I gather from your accent, you're from Warsaw."

"I am," Sadie said with enthusiasm at hearing someone speak of her home. "Have you been there?"

"I was born there."

Just as Sadie was about to probe further into his background, the madam appeared before them. "I see you've had a chance to meet Sadie. Isn't she lovely, Theodore?"

"Indeed, Madam, she is, though I was expecting Dominique."

"Theodore darling," she said, bending over to kiss his cheek, "I am very sorry for the mix-up."

Theodore smiled at the respect he was receiving.

"Now, Sadie, you'll be escorting Theodore to the *Room of a Thousand Mirrors*, it's his favorite. Isn't that right?" she said with a sultry smile.

"Yes, it is," he said with enthusiasm.

"Take good care of Theodore, he's a valued member and we like for him to be happy," the madam said, leaving them.

"Of course," Sadie said, sitting up tall. "Tell me, where in Warsaw did you live?"

"Enough of that," Theodore said, beckoning to Sadie, "let me look at you."

Sadie's eyes opened wide. "Excuse me?"

"Stand up, let me see your ass."

Sadie inhaled. She slowly got to her feet and turned around. The outfit she was wearing was a tight-fitting gold lame, flapper dress that highlighted Sadie's curvaceous figure. Theodore reached out and squeezed Sadie's ass, which caused her to jump.

"Nice and firm, I like that," he said with a mischievous grin.

Sadie was beginning to feel warm. The thought of allowing this hideous man to enter her was making her ill again. She sat down and reached for the glass of water sitting on the nearby table.

"You don't look well. Are you sick?" he said, sounding more disappointed than concerned.

Sadie took a breath. "No, I'm fine, thank you. Whatever it was, has passed."

"Good, because I would like to go upstairs," he said, knocking back the last gulp of Scotch whiskey.

Moments before Sadie had met Theodore, the madam had told her, "Have a conversation, make him feel comfortable, then take him upstairs. You'll have thirty minutes, which gives me time to have the room cleaned for the next member."

Though thirty minutes wasn't a long time, she imagined it lasting a lifetime in a situation with a hideous man like Theodore standing naked before her. But when she recalled what the madam had said, *Once a man climaxes, he's ready to head back home to his wife,* Sadie prayed he would be quick.

One of the benefits of *The Tango*, unlike the other brothels, where the *Polacas* could have two or three men in one night, the ladies of *The Tango* entertained only one member per night, no more. So with seven ladies, only seven members were offered the brothel's exclusive hospitality each evening, adding to its allure. But before Sadie could retire to her room, she had to fulfill her duty.

Theodore stood up, displaying his stature of about three inches shorter and ten pounds lighter than Sadie, along with his noticeable erection pushing on his trousers.

"Come now, Sadie, take me upstairs," he said, sticking his face inches from hers.

His breath smelled like garlic and whiskey, causing Sadie to close her eyes and jerk her head back in disgust. "All right, Theodore," she said, swallowing hard, and taking his hand, "let's go."

CHAPTER FIFTY-TWO—SURVEILLANCE

Alex and Jan spent six nights slipping into the shadows of the nooks, alleyways, and streets surrounding *The Tango*. Their training in espionage taught them how to blend in, and go unnoticed among the pedestrians strolling along Junin Street, or by the police paddy-wagons on patrol, and, of course, from the inconspicuous, ever-watchful eyes of the Zwi Migdal.

Their plan was to observe the gentlemen entering the exclusive club and wait for them to exit. Sometimes this would happen in as little as an hour or last several hours, but eventually, they stepped back out onto the curb. Without any form of transportation, Alex and Jan would follow only those men who left on foot.

This usually amounted to no more than one per night, though on the last evening, two took to walking. Once a *Tango* member left, Alex or Jan would tail them to their next destination. Later at night, back at Nachum's apartment, they compiled their notes about where each man went, and upon the sixth night, they accumulated five potential targets to continue to pursue.

Sitting in the kitchen, they discussed the plan with Nachum.

"We have the addresses of these member's final destinations, but no names," Jan explained. "But over the next four nights, Alex and I will split the list and follow each man again, hopefully to a café or a bar, and do our best to meet them."

Alex said, "There was one man I followed last night who didn't go straight home. He left *The Tango* at ten, walked to the corner and turned down *Avenida Corrientes* and another five blocks to a place called *Café La Paz*."

"*Café La Paz*, yes I know it," said Nachum. "It's popular among intellectuals, writers, and poets."

"What was interesting was when this well-dressed, bearded man approached the café, he was greeted like a celebrity. The patrons rose to shake his hand, and pat him on his back. There was a table where ten men were squeezed in. When he was noticed, they shifted their chairs to add one more."

"Did you hear his name?" Nachum asked.

Alex nodded. "They called him Oliverio."

Nachum clapped his hands together. "Oliverio Girondo the poet. He's from a wealthy family that enabled him to study in Paris. No wonder he likes *The Tango*. I'm sure he's acquired a taste for *putains françaises*."

"Well, perhaps Mr. Girondo is a prospect worth approaching."

"He may well be," Nachum said, lighting a cigarette and exhaling. "You realize that this plan of yours may take time. It could be several weeks before you get your invitation."

Alex nodded. "We must be cautious. It will do us no good if the Zwi becomes aware of us."

"I hope Sadie is able to survive until then," Nachum said.

Alex tilted his head and asked, "Survive? Are you saying her life's in danger?"

"No, I don't think so. But certainly, after so many men having her, you know," he paused and scrunched his face, "she might not be the same woman you fell in love with."

"So what am I supposed to do? Give up on her?" Alex said, pinching his brow.

"Please, I meant no disrespect, Alex. But let me ask you how you plan on befriending any of these men? You'll need to dress like a gentleman and make the impression that you're wealthy, or you'll never be offered an invitation."

"Purchasing a nice business suit is easy, and as far as our supposed wealth," Alex said with a shrug, "Jan and I are in the beef importing business. We're here from Poland looking to make deals with new suppliers. We plan on visiting Buenos Aires regularly and would love to have some fun while away from our wives. But what's most important is that we strike up a friendship, establish trust."

"How is that done?"

"There are several ways," Jan chimed in. "As you can imagine, with my appearance, people are more cautious to open up to me because of my physical flaw. But I use this to my advantage because once I engage the target in a conversation, I reveal my anxieties, fears, and desires, which establishes empathy," Jan said and shrugged. "Most are quick to trust strangers they see as imperfect."

211

"Another key," Alex said, resting his elbows on the table, "is to be a good listener. People are enamored with those who are fascinated with their lives."

"You make it all sound so easy. But how will you prove you're in the beef importing business?"

"We'll get business cards printed," Alex said, holding out two fingers like he was displaying a phantom card. "The Warsaw Beef Company, or something like that. We'll use your phone number as our business line while we're in the city."

"Clever gentlemen. I hope it works."

"I don't see why not," Alex said with a shrug. "It's all in how we present ourselves. After all, Jan and I were able to convince a cunning general we were loyal Russian soldiers; we can certainly pull off this deception."

CHAPTER FIFTY-THREE—TANGO NIGHT

Sadie came downstairs early, curious to find out the source of the music. Halfway down the carpeted staircase, she saw several musicians tuning their instruments, and seated on a stool by the bar, was Shayna sipping her coffee.

Sadie reached for a delicate china cup and saucer and poured from a ceramic coffee pot and said, "Good morning, Shayna, are we having music tonight?"

Shayna slipped a lock of her brunette hair behind her ear and said, "It's Thursday night, tango night. I trust you know how to dance the tango, Sadie."

"I took lessons, though I was told my technique was questionable," Sadie said, dipping a tiny spoon into the sugar bowl and sprinkling it into her coffee.

Shayna scoffed. "You think these men care? As long as they can get their clammy hands on you, it doesn't matter how you dance."

Sadie lifted herself onto the stool next to Shayna and said, "Where are you from?"

Shayna put her cup down on the wooden counter and looked at Sadie with her brown eyes and said, "I'm so tired of telling every new girl my sad story. I'm sure it's not much different from yours, so what's the point?"

"Oh, all right," Sadie said, taken aback by Shayna's rudeness.

They sat for a while in silence before Sadie asked, "Perhaps you don't mind answering a question."

Shayna flipped her hand in invitation and said, "What's that?"

"Do we always call the members by their first names?"

"First of all, it's not their real name, it's their *member* name, so they can remain anonymous. Only the madam knows their true names."

"That makes sense," Sadie said, taking a sip of her coffee.

"I noticed you had the pleasure of that pig, Theodore, last night."

Sadie nodded and leaned in closer to whisper, "Thank god he finished while I was still dancing for him."

"He always does that," she said, shaking her head. "He can't keep it hard unless he plays with it himself. That's why the madam gave him to you on your first night."

"Oh, I didn't know," Sadie muttered.

Shayna patted Sadie's hand and said, "Let me give you some advice, sweetie. I've been at *The Tango* a year now. It's best not to think too much. Just do what the madam wants and you'll be golden. Life here's not so bad compared to the other brothels. We only attend to one man each night, which doesn't last too long, and we get the entire day to ourselves, with no one to bother us."

"But the madam says we can never leave. We're trapped here like prisoners."

214

Shayna furrowed her brow and puckered her lips. She got close to Sadie's face and whispered, "Watch what you say. Apparently, you have no idea who you're dealing with. Just uttering those words can get you dragged out of here, like the trash. Trust me, Sadie, I've seen it."

Sadie's eyes filled with tears, though she tried holding them back. She wiped them away with the back of her hand, pushed her stool back, and stood up. She offered Shayna a last glance, wondering if in time she would turn as callous, before she headed up the stairs, back to her room.

Sadie sat on the edge of her bed and allowed her tears to flow. *What if Alex saw me now?* she thought. *Would he want me after being violated by strange men over and over? Would he want a ruined woman?*

She rose from her bed, stepped over to the small window, and pulled back the curtain. Her view of the neighboring building's brick wall greeted her, and caused her to sigh, thinking of it as a symbol of her life— a dead end.

But a thought buried deep within her, refusing to die, rose to the surface of her consciousness. *Alex would never give up on finding me, I'm certain of it. I've never met anyone with more integrity. I know he's out there searching for me.*

A burst of hope filled Sadie's heart. She stood up and walked over to her vanity table and looked at herself in the mirror. She would need to pull herself together. After what Shayna told her about getting a pass with Theodore, Sadie figured that the madam would likely set her up with a more virile man tonight.

"Sadie, wake up and get yourself ready," she heard through the grogginess of her late afternoon nap.

Sadie forced her eyes open, and standing at the foot of her bed, with her hands on her hips was the madam.

"What time is it?" Sadie said, pushing herself up onto her elbows.

"It's eight o'clock, and our members will start to arrive in an hour. Get yourself ready. Tonight you will have a very special guest. In fact, I believe you already met him at *El Choclo*."

Sadie put her hand to her mouth and said softly, "Do you mean Mr. Rivlin?"

The madam held up a finger and said, "His *Tango* name is Ignacio, and you will be his date tonight."

"You want me to entertain Mr. Rivlin, I mean Ignacio?" she said, rubbing the back of her neck. "Are you sure that's a good idea?"

"You've been requested by Ignacio himself, that's quite an honor, Sadie. Now go and make yourself gorgeous. He wants you to wear that outfit you wore at *El Choclo*," she said, pointing to it hanging off a hook on the wall.

Sadie looked over and saw the dress that Mrs. Stillman made for her.

"But what if he's displeased with me?" Sadie asked, feeling her stomach rumbling from the sudden onset of nerves.

The madam shook her head and said before exiting the small room, "Now that would be very disappointing, wouldn't it, Sadie?"

CHAPTER FIFTY-FOUR—SOMETHING BREWING

Ezra put down his newspaper and pinched the bridge of his nose, trying not to lose his temper. His two sons, Michael and Aaron, were causing a ruckus, typical of rambunctious five-and six-year-old boys. "Can you please stop screaming?" he finally shouted.

His wife Chaya stepped in from the kitchen. "Michael, Aaron, go to your rooms and let your father be," she said, pointing with a wooden spoon.

"I can't stand this anymore!" Ezra said, stood up, and grabbed his suit jacket.

"Where're you going? Dinner will be ready soon," Chaya asked, her arms spread out wide.

"I have something to do," he said, ignoring her indignation and closing the apartment door behind him. He headed down the six flights of stairs and out onto the street. Once he stood on the sidewalk, Ezra exhaled. His life, in only a few short weeks, had gone from fabulous to shit. The two weeks aboard the MV *Alcantara* with Sadie, were the happiest he had ever been. With her on his arm, he was finally the man he thought he ought to be. Someone admired, respected, and important. But with Mr. Rivlin's command ordering Sadie to *The Tango* and sending him back to Warsaw to recruit more *Polacas*, took all of that away from him.

He walked down the avenue and entered the park. At this late afternoon hour, the pathways were mostly empty, which allowed Ezra to exhale, releasing all his internal tension before he returned to his family. He found a bench and sat down, pulled a cigar from his jacket pocket, and lit it.

He took a puff and recalled the conversation he had with Mr. Rubenstein of the Ashkenazum in the dining hall of the MV *Alcantara*. Ezra exhaled a long stream of smoke and nodded to himself. Mr. Rubenstein told him that with his experience as an agent he could work as an instructor with Ashkenazum, the rival organization to the Zwi Migdal. *What if Mr. Rubenstein was serious and offered me a position?* Ezra thought.

The idea of getting back at Mr. Rivlin for destroying his happiness by taking Sadie away, caused Ezra to smile. Of course he could never cross someone like Mr. Rivlin on his own, but under the protection of Mr. Rubenstein, perhaps it was possible.

Then an idea occurred that brought Ezra to his feet. Perhaps there was also a way, through Mr. Rubenstein's help, that he could get Sadie released from *The Tango* and returned to him. After all, the man had powerful connections enough to rival Mr. Rivlin.

"Wait a second," he said aloud. He reached into the breast pocket of his jacket and removed his wallet, and tucked within, he found Mr. Rubenstein's business card.

Give me a call when you're ready to talk, he'd told Ezra.
He walked briskly through the park, full of new purpose.

CHAPTER FIFTY-FIVE—SHOWTIME

Displayed in sparkling silver trays upon a long table, covered with a crisp white cloth, was an array of curious foods.

"What's all this?" Sadie asked Shayna.

"The madam always offers such delicacies on tango night," Shayna said, pointing. "We have lobster, caviar, fried oysters, deviled crabs, duck, geese pate, and this, I believe, is pheasant."

"I've had goose before, but never like that."

"The food's not for us. We can partake only if our member wants us to."

"Yes, I'm well aware. Madam already informed me of the rules for food and alcohol," Sadie said and touched her stomach, still rumbling from nerves. *There will be no eating tonight*, she decided, even if Mr. Rivlin allowed.

*

Sadie had one last look at herself in the six-foot-tall, gilded framed mirror in the Grand Social Hall. She pressed down upon the two curls swirling on each of her cheekbones, making sure they were still in place.

A few minutes before the clock struck nine, the orchestra began with a lively tune, inspiring two of the French girls to take to the dance floor. They moved about like fluttering butterflies, darting to and fro, until the doorbells rang, and they quickly ceased.

"Here we go, ladies," the madam announced.

As if a performance was about to begin, everyone took their places. Shayna, Becca, and Nava lounged upon a sofa, while the French girls, Dominique, Eloise, and Amelie posed seductively by the bar.

For a moment Sadie stood still, unsure where to go, until Shayna crooked a finger at her, reminding her where she belonged. Sadie forced a smile, walked over, and stood alongside the sofa, gripping onto its wooden frame.

Unlike last night, where most of the outfits were tight-fitting bodices with long cotton skirts in a variety of styles and colors, tonight's dress was formal. Sadie was wearing the outfit that Mr. Rivlin requested, which drew glares of jealousy from the other girls. Dominique said a dress like Sadie's was called *haute couture* in Paris, which meant it was expensive, modern clothing created by a leading fashion house, like *Stillman's*.

As midnight approached, a few of the girls were downstairs entertaining their members, while others were either amusing their men in one of the themed rooms or already done for the evening and had retired to the privacy of their bedrooms.

As the hours marched on, Sadie hoped at some point the madam would resign herself to the fact that Mr. Rivlin was not coming, and dismiss her for the evening. But at thirty minutes past midnight, the doorbells jingled and the madam's eyes widened. "That's him," she declared.

Frederick hustled to the door, while Sadie tried to compose herself, sitting upright on the edge of a fancy French-style chair that madam called a *Bergere*. She clutched her sweaty palms together on her lap and tried to force a sincere smile.

The madam seemed anxious as well and snapped at the orchestra leader, commanding him to summon his musicians back from their break, ready to perform upon Mr. Rivlin's arrival.

Sadie heard conversations coming from the vestibule, and from the upbeat sound of Frederick's voice, she surmised that it was indeed Mr. Rivlin, or *Ignacio*.

"Where is she?" the words bellowed over the music playing behind me.

"Ah, Ignacio, it's nice to see you," the madam said, greeting the man as he stepped into the Grand Social Hall.

"Ah, Madam Marguerite, you're looking as lovely as ever."

"You honor us with your visit," she said and turned to face Sadie. "I'm sure you remember Sadie."

"I certainly do," he said, slurring his words.

A shudder of shakes swept through Sadie's body as if there was a chill in the air, and she said meekly, "Hello, Ignacio."

"No need to be shy," he said, grabbing Sadie by the hand and pulling her close.

She tried to speak, but with the sharp smell of whiskey on his breath, all she could do was utter was a grunt.

222

"I've been thinking about this one," he said, wrapping his arms around Sadie's waist.

Pressed against him, she was inches from the sweat stains creeping down his white shirt collar.

"Come on, let's go upstairs," he said and turned to the madam. "Is the *Roman Room* free? I feel like Julius Caesar with my Cleopatra."

"Hail Caesar," the madam said. "Please, allow me to escort you and your queen."

CHAPTER FIFTY-SIX—CLUB DEL PROGRESO

From the shadows, Alex followed a round-faced man departing *The Tango*. He walked a few blocks to the *Club del Progeso*. Alex waited twenty minutes before entering the restaurant and approaching the maître d'. After a pause to size him up, Alex was escorted to a table, a few feet from where his target was seated.

While Alex waited for a glass of wine, he overheard the waiter addressing the man as Mr. Mosconi while serving him the house specialty—the *cochinillo*, a brick-oven baked, suckling pig.

In between bites, Mr. Mosconi wrote in a notepad, and paid him no mind nor the two other couples sitting nearby. The only time he looked up was when he raised and wiggled his wine glass in order to get the attention of the waiter, who would quickly hustle over to refill it.

After gulping down the wine, Mr. Mosconi put down his pencil, and removed his eyeglasses to rub his tired eyes. It was at that moment, Alex decided to strike up a conversation.

"I hear the *cochinillo* is their specialty," he said, catching his attention.

Mr. Mosconi pointed at the half-eaten suckling pig with his knife and said, "It's the best in the city."

"It's not something we eat in Warsaw," he said with a charming smile.

"Oh, you should try it."

"I just placed an order," Alex said, gesturing to the waiter on his way to the kitchen.

"What brings you to Buenos Aires?" Mr. Mosconi asked and took a gulp of his red wine.

"I'm here on business."

"What do you do?"

Alex rose from his chair, reached into his pocket, and handed Mr. Mosconi his recently printed business card.

Mr. Mosconi looked and it and read aloud, "The Warsaw International Trading Corporation—Importers of Argentine Beef. Impressive, Mr. . . . ." he paused to read the card again, "Bartek Borkowski."

"It's a pleasure to meet you, sir," Alex said, reaching out to shake his hand.

"My name is Enrique Mosconi, I'm with an Argentine energy company, engaged in oil and gas production. Please join me. There's no need to eat alone."

Alex held up his palm. "Are you sure, Mr. Mosconi, I don't want to intrude. It looks like you're busy," he said, looking over to the notepad.

"It's nothing important. Please sit," he said, gesturing to the empty chair, "and call me Enrique."

Alex nodded and took a seat, "Thank you, Enrique."

"So tell me, Bartek, how long are you in our city for?"

"About a month. I'll be meeting with the major beef exporters while I'm here."

"Well, everyone knows our cattle is the best in the world, and so are our pigs," he said, shoving a piece into his mouth.

Alex lifted his wine glass to toast, "Here's to the pigs!"

Enrique burst into laughter. "I like you, Bartek."

Allowing some time for more wine and conversation, Alex said, lowering his voice, and glancing from side to side, "Tell me, Enrique. Where can a man have fun while away from the wife and kids? If you know what I mean?"

Enrique wagged a finger. "I do indeed," he said with a sly smile.

Alex held out his palms and said, "I'm listening."

"I'll tell you what, I shouldn't do this because we just met. But you seem trustworthy. Tomorrow night meet me in front of this address at nine o'clock," he said, writing in his notepad and ripping a page out.

Alex took it and read, "*The Tango*? Are you taking me dancing, Enrique?"

Enrique smiled. "Not quite. *The Tango* is a members-only brothel, with the most beautiful ladies in all of Buenos Aires."

"A brothel," Alex said with a devilish grin.

Enrique put down his fork and squinted his eyes. "Don't tell me you've never been to one before."

Alex shrugged, and said with a smirk, "I may have stepped into one or two in Warsaw."

Enrique laughed and wagged a finger. "I doubt your whorehouses can compare to *The Tango*. Why don't you come and see for yourself? Perhaps after your visit, you may have an interest in applying, I could be your sponsor. Then whenever you're in our wonderful city, you'll have a place to enjoy yourself."

Alex tried not to exhibit too much enthusiasm. "That sounds perfect," he said with a warm smile.

"Excellent, Bartek, then let's toast to new friends."

"To new friends," Alex said and held up his glass just as a glistening suckling pig arrived at the table.

CHAPTER FIFTY-SEVEN—TURF WAR

"Ezra, please come in," Mr. Rubenstein said, stepping around his large wooden desk to shake his hand.

"Thank you for seeing me, sir," Ezra said, grasping the oversized man's beefy paw.

"Of course, please sit. How are things with the Zwi?"

He sat down, rubbed his fingertips along his forehead, and said, "Not so good. That's why I've asked to see you."

Mr. Rubenstein flipped his hand, gesturing for Ezra to continue.

"When we spoke on the ship, you mentioned an opportunity of joining your organization as a trainer, and I was wondering if you were serious."

Mr. Rubenstein sat back down behind his desk, folded his hands across his large belly, and said, "I remember you said were getting tired of sea travel and being away from home. Is that what's troubling you?"

Ezra nodded.

He looked at him in silence for a moment before he said, "If you're going to bullshit me, Ezra, you should leave now."

Ezra jerked his head back at the insinuation. "Why would you say that, sir?"

Mr. Rubenstein rose from his chair and walked over to the large window. He stood and gazed out onto the *Rio de La Plata* and said, "The number one quality I look for in a man that I bring into my organization is honesty."

"But what I'm saying is true, sir."

He turned to face Ezra and said, "It may be true, but that's not what brought you here today, is it? Does this have something to do with how our friend Mr. Rivlin appropriated your prized *Polaca*?"

Ezra tilted his head and said, "How did you know?"

Mr. Rubenstein squeezed himself into the wooden armchair next to him and smiled. "You're angry with the ruffian for taking Sadie from you, and trust me, I'd be too. I've seen her, she's a worthy trophy."

Ezra rubbed his mouth and shrugged. "I didn't think that sharing my personal life with you was worthy of your time, sir," he said, while privately relishing that he didn't need to broach the matter himself.

Mr. Rubenstein closed his eyes and shook his head. "How do you think I grew my organization which now rivals the great Zwi Migdal for control of the brothels in Buenos Aires?"

Ezra shrugged.

"It's by paying attention to my people—caring for them. That's how you build loyalty. Rivlin's a drunken fool who wields power over his people through violence and intimidation."

Ezra nodded, and thought it ironic for him to say that, since he knew the Ashkenazim operated similarly.

"That type of behavior I reserve for my enemies; not for those who have taken an oath of loyalty to my organization. Do you understand me, Ezra?"

"I think so," Ezra muttered.

"Good," he said, patted Ezra's knee, stood up, and walked around his desk to his chair. "I want you to forget this training-my-agents nonsense. You're better than that."

"All right, thank you, sir. But what do you have in mind?"

"If you're agreeable, I'd like you to join my inner circle. I need a sharp mind for big changes that are about to happen," he said, lighting his cigar.

"Your inner circle?" Ezra said, not believing his ears.

Mr. Rubenstein took a puff of his cigar, tilted his head back, and exhaled. "Of course I can't share my plans until you've taken the pledge, but what I can say is that the power paradigm in this city is about to shift."

Ezra rubbed the stubble on his chin and thought how sweet it would be to see Mr. Rivlin get what he deserved, so he nodded quickly and said, "Yes, I'm interested."

He pointed at Ezra with his cigar and said, "Are you willing to swear a binding oath of loyalty to the Ashkenazim, meaning once you're in, you're in. It's a lifetime commitment. Can you take such a pledge?"

Ezra thought for a moment and realized that turning down such an invitation was a death sentence. He smiled and said, "I am, Mr. Rubenstein."

"Excellent," he said, rubbing his hands together. "If what I'm planning succeeds, I promise you—you'll get your *Polaca* back."

Ezra took a breath and said softly, "Sadie."

CHAPTER FIFTY-EIGHT—IGNACIO

Sadie gazed into her vanity mirror and gently touched the purple bruise under her right eye and winced. She wasn't sure if the tears rolling down her swollen face were from sadness or caused by the punch leveled upon her from Mr. Rivlin.

The clock on her nightstand said ten o'clock, which meant she should be making her way downstairs to face the madam. But just as she rose and reached for her robe, there was a knock at her door.

"Yes?" she said meekly.

The door opened and in walked Madam Marguerite.

Sadie held her breath, unable to speak.

"Sit down, Sadie," she said, pointing to the bed, "and let me look at you."

Sadie offered a pained smile and sat at the edge of her bed. The madam joined her and put two fingertips under Sadie's chin and observed her face. "Does it hurt?" she said, pressing upon her contusion with her other hand.

Sadie flinched. "I'll be alright," she said, at the less-than-gentle touch.

"Don't be so sure," the madam said, causing Sadie to wonder what she meant. "I need to know every detail, starting with the moment you and Mr. Rivlin entered the *Roman Room*."

Sadie rose from the bed and stepped over to the small vanity chair and sat down. Facing the madam, she took a deep breath and began, "Mr. Rivlin was very drunk."

The madam nodded.

"The moment we entered the *Roman Room*, he poured himself a whiskey. He took a sip, spun around, causing his drink to spill, and garbled at me to take off my clothes."

"And did you?" the madam asked.

Sadie nodded and looked down to her feet. "He gawked at me and wiped the drool dripping down his chin with the back of his hand. Then he grabbed my shoulders, pulled me in close, and kissed me," she said and closed her eyes. "He shoved his tongue nearly down my throat, forcing me to gag from its sickening taste. I jerked my head back and as I did, I tripped over the small table behind me and fell to the marble floor."

"Was that how you got your black eye?"

Sadie shook her head. "No, he stood over me and pointed to the bed. I got to my feet and stepped alongside him, while he struggled to try to remove his trousers. A few moments later, he closed his eyes and wobbled back and forth. I thought he was going to pass out. He regained his focus and looked down at me and told me to spread my legs. I held up my hand, asking him to pause for a moment while I reached over to the box on the nightstand and took out a sheath. *What the fuck is that?* he barked at me. *It's a sheath, Ignacio, you need to wear it—the madam's rules.*"

"You said that?" the madam asked, pinching the bridge of her nose. "I should have told you the rules don't apply to the *Balebos*."

"Oh, I didn't know, I'm sorry."

The madam made a rolling motion with her hand for Sadie to continue.

"I scooted to the edge of the bed and tried to put it on him, but he wasn't hard and I struggled. He smacked my hand away, knocking the sheath to the floor. He grabbed the back of my head and pulled me in close and told me to suck him. *Make it hard,* he shouted. I tried, but the smell disgusted me and I pulled away.

"His cheeks turned beet red, and he yelled, *What the fuck is wrong with you*, and shoved me to the bed. He climbed on top and straddled me with his knees. He spat into his hand and did it to himself until he was finally hard. I squirmed, trying to reach for another sheath, but he pushed down on my shoulders," Sadie said, choking up between heaving tears.

"Come on, Sadie, tell me what happened next."

Sadie shrugged. "I wouldn't let him enter me without one on, just like you told me. I think because he was so drunk, I was able to push him off of me and get to my feet. 'Let me try again,' I said."

"He lunged at me and shouted, *You fucking bitch*! But I was able to avoid his grasp and he fell off the bed onto the floor."

"Oh my, Sadie," the madam said, shaking her head.

"He got himself up and clutched a handful of my hair with his left hand and punched me with his right," she said, pointing to her face.

The madam shook her head and pinched her lips. "Is that when he left?"

"I'm not sure. I lost consciousness and when I came to, he was gone."

The madam exhaled, stood up, and walked to the door.

"What's going to happen now?" Sadie said.

"You're going to get yourself ready for tonight. Go and see Dominique, she'll help you cover up that bruise."

"But what about Mr. Rivlin?"

The madam shrugged. "I don't know, Sadie, but I can promise you, it won't be pretty," she said and closed the door behind her.

CHAPTER FIFTY-NINE—MAXIMO AND PABLO

Enrique shook Alex's hand. "It's good to see you, Bartek."

"So this is the infamous *Tango*?" Alex said, with his hands on his hips, looking up at the imposing brick building.

"Behind this door, my friend, exists paradise," said Enrique, with a naughty grin.

Alex held out his palms. "It's all I've been thinking about since we've met."

"Great, but before we go in, I need to go over a few things."

Alex nodded and said, "All right."

"Once inside we never use our real names; as you probably can imagine why. We've been assigned, what *The Tango* calls—a *member name*. I phoned earlier and let them know I was bringing a guest. Your name will be *Maximo*."

"Maximo? I like it. What's your name?"

Enrique pulled back his shoulders, and said, "I am *Pablo*."

Alex stuck out his hand and said, "It's a pleasure to meet you, Pablo."

"Shall we, Maximo?" Enrique said, pointing to the black entrance door.

Alex held out his arm and said, "After you, Señor Pablo."

Enrique knocked on the door, while Alex stole a look into the shadows across the street and spotted Jan. At the sound of the door swinging open, Alex turned and followed Enrique inside *The Tango*.

A tall, thin man welcomed them and introduced himself as Frederick. "It's nice to see you again, Pablo, and this must be your guest Maximo," he said, shaking each man's hand.

"Thank you, Frederick. Is the madam inside?"

"She is indeed. Please allow me to escort you, gentlemen."

Alex took a breath, to steady his nerves. If Sadie was here, he was worried that she might react in a way that would expose him as a fraud. His plan, as discussed earlier with Jan, was to confirm Sadie's presence at *The Tango*, and quickly make an excuse to depart; because lingering too long would put them both in danger.

Alex had second-hand knowledge of brothels in Warsaw; unlike many of his army buddies. From the stories shared, Alex pictured them as dirty, rundown establishments, with tired, sad women offering themselves to desperate and pitiful men.

Even with *The Tango's* reputation as an elegant establishment, featuring beautiful women, experts in lovemaking, it was little solace imagining Sadie being reduced to a sex slave for the carnal pleasure of rich and callous men.

"Ah, Pablo, it's nice to see you," said an elegant, middle-aged woman standing before them, accepting a kiss on each cheek.

"It's good to see you, Madam Marguerite. Please allow me to introduce my good friend, Maximo."

"It's a pleasure, Maximo," she said, offering Alex her hand.

Alex smiled. "Thank you for your hospitality," he said and kissed the madam's soft hand.

"So tell me, Maximo," the madam said, leading them into the Grand Social Hall, "what's your pleasure?"

Alex looked over to Enrique and rolled his eyes. "My pleasure? What do you mean?"

The madam laughed. "What attributes of a woman stimulate you?"

"Oh, well," Alex stammered, "I'm not sure."

The madam squinted and asked, "Is this your first time in a brothel, Maximo?"

"Yes, I'm afraid it is," he said, looking over to Enrique's furrowed brow.

"Well, there's no reason to worry," she said, taking Alex by the hand. "I have just the lady for you."

"Ah, Amelie," Enrique said, stepping away and approaching a slender woman with long, shiny black hair, casually reclining upon the armrest of a sofa.

"Pablo," Amelie said with a heavy French accent, "it's been too long, *mon amore*. I've been *aching* for you."

Enrique looked over to Alex and said, "Enjoy yourself, my friend. You're in good hands, I'll see you later," and took Amelie by her hand.

Alex watched Enrique and Amelie climb a wide, sweeping staircase.

"Please, Maximo, would you mind stepping into my office?"

"Into your office?" Alex said, puckering his brow.

"Yes, I need to fill out some paperwork. It's how we verify your identity and finances. After all, we must protect the integrity of *The Tango*," she said, opening an unmarked door toward the back of the Grand Social Hall.

Alex took one last look behind him, observing several young ladies mingling among themselves, but alas, none were Sadie. He took a breath and followed the madam into a back room. He had barely crossed the threshold when he was grabbed by a large, muscular man.

"What's this?" he said as he struggled and looked to the madam.

"Shut the fuck up," said a voice from an adjacent, darkened room.

Alex's gaze followed the voice and watched a well-dressed man stepping into the light.

"Tie him up," he said, pointing a gun at Alex.

Alex was pushed into a wooden chair, while his arms and legs were bound with heavy rope, and he asked, "Who are you?"

The man now directly in front of Alex, leaned on the edge of the desk, deftly lifted a cigarette out of a golden case, and lit it with an engraved lighter. He took a puff and exhaled the smoke into Alex's face. "The question is, who the fuck are you?"

Alex looked over to the madam and shrugged. "My name is Maximo?"

"Let's try this another way. Manny," he said, cocking his head.

Suddenly a devastating punch from Manny slammed into the side of Alex's face; the force of which knocked him, along with the chair he was tied to, hard to the floor.

Alex felt the warmth and metallic taste of blood pooling inside his mouth.

"Pick him up."

Once back upright, Alex spat a glob of blood onto the carpet.

"Was that necessary?" the madam moaned, looking at the mess of blood and saliva.

"All right, my name is Bartek Borkowski. I'm a businessman from Warsaw. I was just looking for a good time."

"It's best to tell the truth, unless you want to be softened up some more."

Alex stayed silent, while his eyes darted back and forth trying to size up his predicament, which was dire no matter how he played it. But if he confessed now, he might be able to learn if Sadie was inside *The Tango*, which was the intended purpose of the mission.

"My name is Alexander Kaminsky, I'm a college professor of history in Warsaw. I'm looking for my fiancée, Sadie Wollman. Is she here?"

The man shrugged, looked over to the madam, and back to Alex. "I don't know this name."

Alex ran his tongue along the open wound inside his mouth. At this point, he realized his cover was exposed and there was nothing to lose by speaking the truth. "Sadie and I were to be married until one of your agents, a Mr. Porkevitch, tricked Sadie's parents into a fake marriage, some kind of farce you call a *stille chuppah*. I'm here for Sadie, and demand you release her."

The man laughed.

"May I ask your name?" Alex said.

The man smiled and nodded. "My name is Antonio Catalano, *The Tango's Rufiano*, and I tell you what. Before I kill you, Alex, I'll allow you to get one last look at your Sadie," he said and nodded to the madam.

The madam left the room and a few moments later she walked back in, followed by Sadie.

Alex instinctively jerked his bound body, trying to stand up. "Sadie," he said breathlessly.

"Alex!" Sadie blurted out.

It was the first time he had seen her since her bedroom in Warsaw. He stared at Sadie, taking her in. She looked different. She had cut her hair, but there was more to it than that. Like a gray silk veil covering a lamp, something had dimmed her light. Alex's heart tugged, desperately wanting to break free from his restraints and embrace his tortured love.

Antonio pulled down on his silk suit jacket, brushed off a piece of lint, and said, "Come, let's give these two lovebirds a chance to say their farewells."

The moment the door closed, Sadie leaned over and kissed Alex, wrapping her arms around him and the ropes binding him to the chair.

When they finally released, Sadie asked, "How did you find me?"

"It doesn't matter. We only have a few—" he suddenly stopped and stared at her cheek. "Is that a bruise? Did someone hit you?"

Sadie gently touched under her eye and nodded. "Mr. Rivlin did last night," she said, and lowered her eyes in shame.

"Mr. Rivlin? Who's that?"

"He's the boss of the Zwi Migdal. He tried to . . ." she paused, "you know. But he was too drunk. He got frustrated and punched me."

"Oh my god, Sadie. I must get you out of here."

"But how?" she said with tears cascading down both cheeks. "There's no way, don't you see? I'm a prisoner."

"I know you are. But you must remain strong."

"Oh, I want to," she said, placing her palms upon Alex's cheeks and kissing him again.

Suddenly the door swung open and in walked the madam, Mr. Catalano, and his strongman.

"Visiting hours are over."

"You piece of shit," Alex growled. "Before this is over, I'm going to kill you."

Mr. Catalano chuckled and shook his head.

As Alex watched Sadie being led from the room, all he could think was, *Was that the last time I'll ever see her?*

CHAPTER SIXTY—QUEEN BEE

"He's ready to see you now," said a man with a flattened boxer's nose.

Ezra snuffed out his third cigarette, stood up, and looked at the familiar-looking man, and said, "Don't I know you?"

The man ignored Ezra and beckoned him with a curling of his hand.

As he stepped into the office, he saw Mr. Rubenstein sitting at his desk.

"Please, Ezra, join us. I'm sorry to keep you waiting."

"That's all right, sir," he said, taking an empty chair in between two men.

"Let me introduce you. This is Enrico Bastian," he said gesturing to Ezra's right, "he's my Lieutenant. If anything was to happen to me, Enrico would become *Balebos*."

Ezra reached out and shook the man's hand.

"And this gentleman is Juan Nunez, my *Consejero*. He provides me with legal and business advice."

Ezra and Juan shook hands with Ezra.

"And this gentleman," he said, pointing to the large man who greeted Ezra, "is Luis Firpo, also known as the *Wild Bull of the Pampas*. He was the heavyweight boxing champion of Argentina and now has the responsibility of keeping me safe."

"Of course," Ezra said wagging his finger, "I thought I recognized you."

Luis, standing off the side of Mr. Rubenstein's desk, just nodded.

"Well, Ezra, we've been discussing the logistics of bringing you into our organization," Mr. Rubenstein said, "and we've come up with a bold idea."

Ezra shrugged, looked to Juan and Enrico, and back to Mr. Rubenstein, and said, "What would you have me do?"

Mr. Rubenstein gestured to Enrico, who leaned forward, tilted his head to look at Ezra, and said, "I understand that you've been told how we're seeking absolute control of the brothels in Buenos Aires."

Ezra glanced over to Mr. Rubenstein and nodded.

"In order to do this, we must crush the Zwi Migdal, which, as you can imagine, won't be easy. I'm sure you're well aware, they have a powerfully entrenched organization with tentacles seeping deep into the community of government and law enforcement."

"I'm aware," Ezra said and shrugged. "I've been with the Zwi for over nine years."

Enrico pointed a finger in the air. "We've made progress, but in order to strike the final blow, we must eliminate the Queen Bee."

Ezra squinted at Enrico and then over to Mr. Rubenstein. "You mean Mr. Rivlin?"

Enrico patted Ezra on his back and said, "Exactly."

"How is that possible? He's so well protected."

"That's where you come in," Enrico said.

Ezra sat straight up, his eyes bulging. "Me?" he said, pressing a finger into his chest. "You want me to kill Mr. Rivlin?"

Mr. Rubenstein shrugged, held out his palms, and said, "You told me he's sending you back to Warsaw next week. Make up some excuse about an idea for recruiting you want to discuss with him. Then once you're face to face, you'll pull out a gun and shoot him. He'll never suspect you."

Ezra gripped the wooden armrests of his chair and clenched his jaw. "You want me to sneak a gun into Mr. Rivlin's office and assassinate him?"

"You came to me, Ezra, wanting to join my organization," Mr. Rubenstein said and shrugged. "This is what needs to be done."

Ezra snorted and realized he wouldn't get far by turning them down, especially after making his lifetime pledge of loyalty to the Ashkenazim. With no choice but to accept, Ezra took a breath and said, "Even if I'm able to get a shot off, I'll never get out of there alive."

"You'll have help," Mr. Rubenstein said. "His bodyguard, Benjamin, has been on our payroll for months."

Ezra closed his eyes for a moment, took a breath, and said, "Can you explain to me how this is going to work?"

"Benjamin will pat you down for a weapon before you enter Rivlin's office. Once you're in, you'll approach the desk, pull your gun, and shoot

Rivlin, preferably in the head. Then you and Benjamin will calmly walk out."

"You make it sound so easy," Ezra said, feeling beads of sweat running down his chest.

Mr. Rubenstein shrugged and said, "It's not easy, I know. But if you remain calm, it can be done, and once it is, Ezra, I'll send you, Enrico, and Juan over to *The Tango*, where you'll take your reward."

Ezra stared at Mr. Rubenstein for a moment, then said, "You mean Sadie?"

Mr. Rubenstein smiled and nodded. "Yes, Ezra, I mean Sadie."

CHAPTER SIXTY-ONE—SHOOT OUT

With his hands bound in front of him, Alex was escorted by Manny, Antonio's bodyguard, through *The Tango's* rear door and into a darkened alleyway where a black motorcar was waiting. Manny opened the back door and gestured for Alex to get in.

Alex ducked his head, slid into the back seat, and Manny followed. Meanwhile, Antonio sat up front next to the driver and said, "Let's go, Josef."

As the motorcar pulled out of the alleyway and onto the street, Alex asked, "Where are you taking me?"

Antonio snickered. "I'm taking you to the tragic conclusion of your life."

*

As the motorcar drove through the streets of Buenos Aires, Alex stared out the window, dwelling on his heart-wrenching, momentary encounter with Sadie. Her bloodshot, tired eyes, and bruised face, spoke to the trauma she was under.

He knew he had to do something soon before things got even worse. He tugged at the ropes binding his wrists, but there would be no escape.

About twenty minutes later, they were beyond the city limits and into the countryside. After making its way along a dirt road, the motorcar drove out onto an open field and stopped.

Alex recalled the last time something like this happened. He had barely survived that night after being shot and almost dumped into the Vistula River. He doubted that this time, he would be able to overwhelm his captors.

"This is it," Antonio said.

Alex was urged with a less than gentle shove to exit. He stood alongside the motorcar, while Antonio barked out, "Open the trunk and get the shovel."

"Okay, boss," Manny said and walked over to the back of the motorcar.

Alex felt his heart racing. They were apparently planning to kill him and bury his body where he would never be found. He tried to focus on his breath as he quickly surveyed the surrounding area to determine if making a run for it was feasible. But in an open field with nothing to duck behind, by the time he was a few feet away, he would have been shot.

The moment Manny opened the trunk, Alex heard a gunshot and watched Manny collapse to the ground. Then the blur of a figure leapt from the opened trunk. It was Jan.

Another shot rang out, but this time it came from Antonio who fired at Jan, hitting him in the arm and causing him to drop to one knee. Jan fired back, but it was too late as Antonio leapt back into the car.

Alex watched the tires spin for a second or two, before catching traction and speeding away, leaving them in the desolate, darkened field with Manny coughing up blood and exhaling his last breath.

"Are you alright?" Alex asked, dropping to the ground next to Jan.

"Help me with my shirt."

"You need to untie me first," Alex said, holding out his wrists.

Jan grimaced and unbound Alex.

With his hands free, he removed Jan's blood-soaked shirt and examined the wound. "You'll be okay. The bullet just skimmed your arm," Alex said, ripping Jan's shirt into long strips.

Once tended to, they got to their feet. Alex looked at Manny sprawled upon blood-stained weeds and said, "How did you get yourself into the trunk?"

"When you were inside *The Tango*, I looked for another way into the club. That's when I found the motorcar idling in the alleyway by a back door. When his driver got out to take a piss, I picked the lock of the trunk and slipped inside. I figured that they would take me to their headquarters. About ten minutes later, I heard voices and we were moving. I bounced around until we stopped, and waited for that unsuspecting dolt," he said pointing to Manny, "to open the trunk; then I shot him, and to my surprise there you were."

Suddenly remembering, Alex blurted, "I saw Sadie; she's there inside *The Tango*."

Jan put his hand on Alex's shoulder and squeezed. "Is she all right?"

"She was beaten by that fuck Rivlin," he said, pointing in the direction the car sped away.

"So what do we do now?" Jan said, holding pieces of his blood-soaked shirt over his wound.

Alex looked toward the flickering lights of Buenos Aires and said, "We need to find our way back and rescue her."

CHAPTER SIXTY-TWO—EZRA'S REVENGE

"Ezra, please, you're pacing like a lion in a cage. Come, sit down and tell us what happened," Mr. Rubenstein said, seated behind his desk while Enrico stood off to one side, with his arms folded across his chest, and Juan casually leaning upon the window sill.

Ezra took a deep breath, lowered himself in the chair next to Benjamin, and began. "It was like you said, sir, Benjamin did a quick frisk, and I entered Mr. Rivlin's office with my gun tucked away in my jacket pocket. When I walked in, I was surprised to see not only Mr. Rivlin, but also Antonio Catalano, *The Tango's Rufiano*. Mr. Rivlin said he was pleased to see me and that it was perfect timing."

Mr. Rubenstein held out his hands, and asked, "Why was that?"

"Apparently someone showed up at *The Tango* last night, acting as a prospective new member, and was looking for Sadie."

"Did they tell you who?"

Ezra nodded. "It was Alex Kaminsky, her lover from home. I caught a glimpse of him from the car when we pulled out of the Warsaw train station. Apparently, he followed us to Buenos Aires."

"Is that so?" Rubenstein said.

"Yes. He approached a *Tango* member under the guise of a businessman looking for a good time and got himself an invitation. Little did Alex know that this member assumed he was a fraud and decided to

251

play along. He phoned ahead and warned Madam Marguerite of the coming deception. So when Alex showed up, Antonio was waiting."

"But how did they know it was her Polish lover?" Rubenstein said, biting down hard on his cigar.

"Apparently, he confessed when he was being questioned by Antonio."

Ezra shared the story, complete with details of the shootout in the field, and how Antonio drove off, leaving Alex and Jan stranded somewhere in the countryside.

"Did he say anything else?"

Ezra nodded. "He wanted to know why I didn't warn him about Alex."

Rubenstein held out his arms. "Warn him about what?"

"That he was a hero in the Polish war against Russia. 'Trained assassin,' as Antonio said. But honestly, I had no idea. I just thought he was another jilted lover, like all the others. How in the world did they know this about them?"

"The Zwi have eyes and ears everywhere," Rubenstein said and took a puff on his cigar.

Ezra nodded and said, "That's when Antonio turned to me and growled, 'You're going to pay the price for putting my life in danger.' It was at that moment I acted. I took a breath to steady my nerves and glanced over at Benjamin. I rose to my feet, and slipped my hand into my pocket, and pulled out the gun. I aimed at the space between Rivlin's eyebrows and fired. Benjamin did the same, shooting Catalano."

Rubenstein stared at Ezra for a long moment and said, "Bendik Rivlin and Antonio Catalano are both dead?"

"Two for the price of one," Ezra said, holding up two fingers, and sighed, feeling his body releasing his built-up tension.

Rubenstein slapped his hands together. "You've done well, Ezra. You too, Benjamin," he said, looking over to the large man sitting next to Ezra.

"Thank you, boss," Benjamin said.

Rubenstein looked over to Enrico. "You and Juan, get over to *The Tango* and lock down the place."

Enrico nodded and stepped toward the door.

"Oh, and one more thing, Enrico."

"What's that boss?"

"I want Sadie Wollman removed from *The Tango* right away," he said, tapping his finger on his desk, and shared a warm smile with Ezra.

CHAPTER SIXTY-THREE—POWER SHIFT

"How's the arm?" Nachum asked, walking into the kitchen.

Alex looked up from dressing the wound, and said, "He'll live."

"You sound disappointed," Jan said with a smirk.

"I've heard some interesting news," Nachum said, joining the men at the kitchen table.

Alex put down the ointment and leaned in. Jan shifted in his seat, anxious to hear what Nachum had to say.

"Have you heard of the Ashkenazim?"

Alex shrugged. "No, who are they?"

"They're the Zwi Migdal's *enemigo*, their rivals."

"The Zwi have competition?" Jan asked.

Nachum nodded. "It's run by a man named Leo Rubenstein. They have grown in the past three years to nearly as large as the Zwi, and after today, who knows."

Alex held out his palms. "What are you talking about, Nachum?"

Nachum took a moment to look at Jan and Alex, and rubbed his chin. "A very reliable source has told me that earlier today the Ashkenazim took out Bendik Rivlin, the *Balebos* of the Zwi Migdal and Antonio Catalano, the *Rufiano* of *The Tango*."

"Catalano," Alex said, wagging his finger, "that's the man who tried to kill me."

"Except I'm the one who got shot," Jan said, gently tapping his wound.

Alex squeezed Nachum's shoulder. "Are you saying that the boss of the Zwi Migdal is dead?"

Nachum nodded vigorously. "And Catalano, *The Tango's Rufiano*."

"Would that mean *The Tango* is unprotected?" Jan asked and looked over to Alex.

Alex jumped to his feet, knocking his chair over. "Let's go, Jan, if we get there before the Ashkenazim, we can get Sadie out."

*

Alex and Jan ran the half-mile to *The Tango*. Once they turned the corner, they saw standing out front, the man who betrayed Alex—Enrique Mosconi, or Pablo, his member name.

"That's Mosconi," Alex said.

"Who's he speaking to?" Jan asked, trying to catch his breath.

"Frederick. I met him too. He works at *The Tango*."

They watched from across the street as Mosconi shook hands and departed, leaving Frederick standing alone.

"Let's go, now's our chance," Alex said, patting Jan on his elbow.

Alex walked briskly, crossing the street, while Jan circled down a few dozen feet down, sealing off the sidewalk if Frederick decided to make a run for it.

"Good day, do you remember me? It's Maximo," Alex said, his face inches from Frederick's.

255

"Indeed I do. You're the Polish spy," he said, expressing no fear in his eyes or demeanor. "I thought Antonio killed you last night."

"He tried," Alex said, as Jan approached.

"Well, look at you," Frederick said, admiring Jan's pale complexion.

"We've come for Sadie. If you don't want to end up like your Rufiano, you'll open the door and not get in our way."

Frederick frowned and said, "I'm sorry, but you're too late. Sadie was taken away about thirty minutes ago."

"What do you mean? Where is she?"

Frederick shook his head. "I have no idea."

"I don't believe him," Jan said. "Let's take a look for ourselves."

"Go ahead and try," Frederick snickered. "*The Tango's* under Ashkenazim's control now. They have armed men in there. I've been thrown out."

"Do you know who took Sadie?"

"It was two men. But one of them did say something that was interesting."

Alex held out his hands. "What was that?"

"The taller man said to Sadie that they were taking her to Ezra. I believe he's the agent that brought her here from Warsaw."

"Ezra Porkevitch?" Alex said.

"Yes, that's him."

Jan held out his hands. "Why are you helping us?"

Frederick shrugged. "Sadie was a lovely, innocent girl. She deserves better than this."

Alex looked at Jan. "Come on, let's go. Thank you, Frederick," he said, and they took off down the street.

CHAPTER SIXTY-FOUR—SADIE'S FREEDOM

"Which one of you is Sadie Wollman?"

Before Sadie could respond, all six ladies gave it away by turning their heads toward her.

"I am, sir," she said, with a timid shrug, while feeling her palms turning clammy.

The man in the black suit beckoned her. "You're coming with me."

"What's going on?" the madam said, charging into the Grand Social Hall.

"Are you Madam Marguerite?"

"Yes, and who the fuck are you?"

"My name is Enrico Bastian, and this is Juan Lopez, we're with the Ashkenazim. We've taken control of *The Tango*. Mr. Rubenstein, our *Balebos*, has asked for Sadie Wollman to be brought to him," he said, reaching out and grabbing Sadie by her wrist and tugging.

"Hold up," the madam said, stepping in between them. "What's happened to Mr. Catalano?"

Enrico sighed. "Antonio Catalano and Bendik Rivlin are both dead."

Shrieks of surprise came from the ladies, who moments before, had hurried downstairs upon hearing the ruckus of the men forcing their way in.

"Who killed them?" the madam asked.

258

"Ezra Porkevitch," Enrico said.

"Ezra?" Sadie gasped, rubbing her sweaty palms together. *How on earth did Ezra pull off such a heroic act?*

"That's right and you're his reward, let's go," he said, pulling Sadie toward the front door.

"But what about us," the madam said, with her arms spread, "what's going to happen to *The Tango*?"

"As far as I know, it's business as usual. Don't worry, someone will be in touch. Now we need to go," he said, escorting Sadie.

*

After a ten-minute ride, the motorcar stopped. Sadie looked out the window and recognized Ezra's apartment building. She opened the door, stepped onto the sidewalk, and saw Ezra standing a few feet away, with his hands proudly perched on his hips.

Sadie stared at Ezra, trying to absorb all that had occurred over the past day and night. Questions flooded her mind. *Did Ezra really have something to do with the killing of Mr. Rivlin? And where was Alex? Is he still alive?*

"Welcome home, Sadie," he said with a smug smile.

"Ezra, what's happened? This man says you killed Mr. Rivlin," she said, pointing to Enrico.

"Come with me," he said, taking her hand. "I'll explain everything upstairs."

"You look terrible," Ezra said, closing the door behind him.

Sadie spun around, flailing her arms. "What do you expect? Rivlin punched me in my face," she said, tapping the bruise under her left eye.

"That fuck!" Ezra said, staring at Sadie's bruise. "Well, you won't have to worry about him any longer."

Sadie dropped her arms and felt the stress that brought tears to her every night begin to drain away. "I need to sit down," she said, lowering herself to the sofa.

Ezra sat next to her, and put his arm around her, and tilted his head to look at her. "It's going to be all right, Sadie. I'll protect you."

Sadie looked at him, her hands shaking, and said, "Is it true, Ezra? Did you kill those men?

"I shot Rivlin," Ezra said and shrugged, "but Benjamin, Rubenstein's man, he shot Catalano."

"But why, Ezra? Why would you do that?"

Ezra pulled his head back and squinted. "You don't know?"

Sadie shook her head.

Ezra sighed, took Sadie's hand and caressed it between his, and said, "I did it for you, Sadie. To protect you from those men."

Sadie's mouth hung open. Her heart, frozen in fear since that day in Warsaw when her parents signed her over to the Zwi Migdal, began to soften. She leaned her head upon his shoulder, closed her eyes, and whispered, "Thank you, Ezra."

Ezra squeezed her. "I'm going to take care of you from now on."

"But what about Alex?" she blurted out, suddenly remembering his appearance at *The Tango*.

"Oh, yes, Alex," Ezra said, standing up from the sofa, and stepping up to the window overlooking the harbor. He turned to face her and said, "Alex was killed by Antonio Catalano in an empty field on the outskirts of the city. I'm sorry, Sadie."

Sadie put her hand to her mouth, as tears rolled down her cheeks, and her body jerked in uncontrollable heaves. She wiped the tears away and suddenly pulled back from Ezra. "Alex came for me," she sighed.

"It was a bold effort, but I'm afraid it's over. It's just the two of us from now on," Ezra said.

CHAPTER SIXTY-FIVE—JEALOUSY

"Where can I find Rubenstein?" Alex asked.

Nachum shook his head. "You can't just walk into Ashkenazim headquarters, demanding they turn Sadie over to you."

Alex sighed. "Don't concern yourself with our methods. We'll figure it out."

"Oh," Nachum suppressed a laugh, "like the way *Pablo*, or whatever your name was, almost got the two of you killed."

"That was unfortunate," Jan admitted. "But that's the nature of espionage; sometimes you get shot."

Nachum sighed. "All right, gentlemen. Leo Rubenstein's office is not far," he said, writing an address on a notepad and handing it to Alex. "He owns a building in the *Recoleta* neighborhood along *Plaza Rodriguez Peña*."

Alex tore off the page and patted him on his shoulder. "Thank you, Nachum," he said and turned to Jan. "Why don't we go scope it out?"

*

"This is it—1766 Paraguay," Alex said, standing on the southern end of the park, looking across the street at the tall stone building.

"Rubenstein chose a nice neighborhood to manage his brothel business from," Jan said, looking around at well-dressed pedestrians strolling by. "Do you think Sadie is in there?"

"Hard to say without knowing why they took her from *The Tango*," Alex said, pursing his lips. "Why would Ezra kill Rivlin and take Sadie?"

"Alex, don't you get it?" Jan said, shaking his head.

Alex pouted and shrugged.

Jan put both hands on Alex's shoulders and said, "I think the question you need to ask yourself is why would Ezra Porkevitch risk his life for Sadie."

Alex stared at Jan, shaking his head. "It can't be," he mumbled under his breath, considering the unimaginable—losing Sadie to Ezra.

"I'm afraid so."

"She must hate him for what he did to her. Ezra Porkevitch destroyed her life. How could she be in love with him?"

"I don't think she is," Jan said, shaking his head. "It's Ezra who's in love with Sadie."

Alex nodded. "Yes, that must be it," he said. But brewing deep within his heart, a pang of suspicion sprung into life. It was small, but like a virus, Alex knew that this jealousy would spread until it consumed him.

He gazed outwards, unfocused. He felt his body soften, his shoulders slouch over, and said, with tears welling up, "We must find her quickly, Jan, before it's too late."

CHAPTER SIXTY-SIX—SADIE'S TORMENT

The brilliant sunshine rising over the sea found its way through the slightly parted opening of the heavy drapes, and shone a beam upon Sadie's face, stirring her awake. She held out her palm to block it and sat up. "Ezra?" she called out. But there was no response.

Sadie found her clothes folded neatly on a bench at the foot of the bed. She dressed and made her way into the living room, and called out again, but there was silence. She walked into the kitchen and saw a note on the table, with her name written on it. She unfolded it and read:

Good morning, Sadie,

I've left to attend to business matters, but I'll return soon to take you to lunch. Your belongings will be brought over from The Tango later today. In the meantime, make yourself comfortable, and please do not leave the apartment. It is not safe to wander the streets unaccompanied.

All my love, Ezra.

She put the note down. "All my love?" she scoffed and put the letter down. *He can rot in hell,* she thought, puckering her face.

She walked back into the living room, opened the door, and stepped out onto the patio, featuring a grand, sweeping view of the Rio de la Plata. As far as she could see in either direction, hundreds of boats and yachts filled the vast array of slips in the harbor.

Sadie leaned her hands upon the railing, closed her eyes, and felt the sun's warmth upon her face. But it did nothing to soothe her rage. She gritted her teeth and pounded the railing with her fists.

Ezra has destroyed my life, and now Alex is dead. Sadie looked at the activity of the city harbor and screamed. But her cries of pain from the twelfth floor got twisted in the wind and went unheard. For a brief moment, she thought how quickly it could all end by climbing over the railing and jumping to the cobblestone street below.

Frustrated, she fled back into the apartment, and threw herself onto the sofa, and wept into a pillow. She lay there a while, drowning in waves of overwhelming sorrow. *What will happen to me now? Does Ezra really think that I would fall in love with him, now that Alex is gone?*

She thought of the last time she saw Alex, tied to that chair. He had come for her, risking his life, and now he was dead. Memories of their last kiss opened a new flood of sobs that shook her body.

Sadie pushed herself up, gripped the sofa's arm, and squeezed. Anger rose from a place within her she never knew existed. "This will not be my life," she shouted.

She stood up, walked back into the bedroom, and looked at herself in the mirror. She fussed with her hair, and remembered what Mr. Stillman once said to her onboard the ship, "You pay attention to my wife, she'll make you the star of Buenos Aires."

Sadie wiped the tears from her face, took a deep breath and stood up tall and gazed at her reflection, and thought, *I will become the star of*

265

Buenos Aires, and use my fame and power to exact revenge upon Ezra for what he's done to me.

CHAPTER SIXTY-SEVEN—GOLDEN TROPHY

"You look dazzling, my dear," Eleanor Stillman called out to Sadie.

Sadie smiled. "I'll make sure to tell everyone at *El Choclo*, it's a *Stillman*."

"You're a lucky man, Ezra," Eleanor declared.

Ezra smiled. "Indeed, I am," he said, taking a moment to drink in every delicious curve of Sadie's figure, clothed in the snug-fitting, glittering, golden gown.

Eleanor touched Sadie's arm, leaned in, and said, "Come see me at the store this week, I have something new I'd like to show you."

"I'd love to."

"Excuse us, Eleanor," Ezra said, "Mr. Rubenstein's expecting us."

Ezra escorted Sadie, his trophy, through the rush of couples anxious to capture a glimpse of the fabulous former *Tango Polaca*.

"There he is," he said, pointing to Mr. Rubenstein seated at the same table where he saw Mr. Rivlin a week earlier.

"Don't you look fabulous, Sadie," boasted Mr. Rubenstein, seated alone in the semi-circle, banquette. "Please, join me."

Ezra held Sadie's hand, assisting her as she slid in next to the large man.

"It's nice to see you, sir," Sadie said. "I would like to thank you for removing me from *The Tango*."

"You want to thank me?" he said, with a hand to his chest and his eyes bulging out. "I had nothing to do with it. This was all Ezra's doing."

"I couldn't have done it without your support, sir. By the way, where are Enrico and Juan?" Ezra said, looking out onto the crowded restaurant.

"They're attending to some unfinished business. But let's not talk about them," he said, waving his hand imperiously. "Sadie, would you like champagne?"

Sadie's eyes gleamed, and she said, "Yes, I would love some."

Mr. Rubenstein held up his chubby arm to summon the waiter.

*

Just as they finished their first bottle of Moët, Eleanor stopped by the table and asked if Sadie could be excused. "I would like to introduce her to Mr. Coppola, the fashion photographer."

Once alone, Ezra quietly asked Mr. Rubenstein if there was any word about the whereabouts of Alex.

"Not yet, but we're out looking for him," Mr. Rubenstein said with a sigh. "This may take time. If he's an actual spy, I'm concerned that Enrico and Juan won't have the skills to track him down."

Ezra rubbed the back of his neck, and said, "I can't have Alex, all of a sudden, make an appearance. Sadie thinks he's dead."

Mr. Rubenstein tilted his head and frowned. "Is that what you told her?"

Ezra nodded. "She needs to make a clean break from him."

"Sadie's psychological well-being is the least of my concerns. What's more important is that we find him before he becomes a liability to our brothel business. Our clientele is already on edge after removing Rivlin."

"Maybe I should give Enrico and Juan a hand?"

Mr. Rubenstein shook his head. "Absolutely not. You're going to take over for Catalano as *The Tango's* new *Rufiano*."

"Me?" Ezra said, putting his hand over his chest.

"I need a good man in there. It's our most important property."

"What do I know about running a brothel? Especially *The Tango*?"

Mr. Rubenstein pulled a cigar out from a silver case and offered it to Ezra, who declined. He reached into his pocket for a guillotine cutter, snipped off its end, and lit it with an elegant silver lighter, engraved with his initials, and took a puff. Ezra watched him exhale a stream of white smoke.

He pointed with his cigar, and said, "As you are aware, Ezra, the city's most important people frequent *The Tango*. For god's sake, even the mayor's a member. I need you there. You'll be my eyes and ears."

Ezra nodded and took a moment to look out onto the crowded dance floor, where people were mingling and socializing before the music began. He spotted Sadie speaking with a man he assumed was that famous photographer and knew it wouldn't be long before she became the sensation of Buenos Aires society.

269

"I understand, sir," Ezra said, but he couldn't help wondering, *What if Enrico and Juan fail in their mission to find Alex?*

CHAPTER SIXTY-EIGHT—UNDER THE MOONLIGHT

Jan jiggled the twisted wire in the lock and heard the tumblers fall. "We're in," he whispered.

He turned the knob and slowly pushed open the back door to *The Tango*. Alex followed him inside the dark office, where a few days ago, he was tied to a chair kissing Sadie, possibly for the last time.

Jan placed his ear against the office door, nodded, and opened it. Alex and Jan were inside the Grand Social Hall. A small table lamp was lit, providing enough illumination to navigate toward the staircase. Alex indicated to Jan with a finger-walk to make their way to the upper floors.

During their conversation earlier, Alex expressed to Jan his idea of seeking out Madam Marguerite. "She may know where Sadie was taken."

"What about security? When we were there last, Frederick said the Ashkenazim had men inside."

Alex shrugged. "If there are, we'll need to immobilize them."

"Immobilize?" Jan asked, wide-eyed.

Alex ran his finger across his throat, imitating cutting it open.

Jan nodded.

They stepped gingerly up the staircase, and within moments were on the second floor.

Alex whispered, "Let's see if we can find one of the girls to show us to the madam's room."

Jan nodded and they headed down the hallway and stopped at the first door. Jan twisted the knob and pushed the door open. The room was mostly dark, except for the moonlight flooding the wooden floorboards under the window. They approached the bed and saw it empty.

"This was Sadie's room," Alex whispered.

Jan squinted and asked, "How do you know that?"

He waved two fingers by his nose and said, "I can smell her."

"All right, Alex. Let's try the next room."

As they stepped back into the hallway, they heard shouts of women's voices coming from the floor above them. Alex pointed a finger toward the ceiling, and said, "Let's go."

They charged up the stairs and down the hallway to the opened door.

Alex entered the room first and saw all six women huddled around a body lying in the bed. Alex stepped around them to see what had frightened them, and under the light of the full moon, streaming through the unshuttered window, lay Madam Marguerite in a pool of crimson blood.

Alex put his hand to his mouth to suppress his shock. He stepped closer and saw the slain woman on her back, with her arms spread wide. The madam's nightgown was soaked in blood, clinging to her lanky frame.

"What happened?" Jan asked, joining Alex.

Alex pointed and said, "Her throat's been cut."

"Who are you?" asked a woman with a French accent.

"I'm Alex, Sadie's fiancé, and this is Jan. We came to see if Madam Marguerite had information of Sadie's whereabouts."

"You should've asked the killer."

"Who is that?" Alex asked.

"Ezra Porkevitch did this. I'm surprised you didn't see him on your way up the stairs. He just left here a few minutes ago."

"Ezra killed Madam Marguerite?" Alex asked.

"But why?" Jan said.

"They got into an argument downstairs regarding the Ashkenazim taking over *The Tango*. She ran upstairs to her room, and Ezra followed. There was a scuffle. We all heard it from the second floor, and by the time we got here, Ezra was headed back down the stairs, covered in blood, and the madam was dead."

Alex looked over to Jan. "Come on, let's go. Maybe we can catch him," he said, and they ran from the room, charged down the stairs and out into the empty street.

CHAPTER SIXTY-NINE—MURDER

It was well after midnight when Ezra woke Sadie.

"Ezra, is that you?" she said, hearing sounds coming from the bathroom. With no response, she pushed the door open, and saw to her horror, Ezra washing blood from his hands. "Are you hurt?"

"Something very bad has happened, Sadie. We need to leave the city as soon as possible. Pack your bag."

Sadie held out her arms. "What are you talking about?"

Ezra squeezed out the washcloth, looked at his reflection, and wiped the streaks of dried blood from his face. "Madam Marguerite is dead."

"Is that her blood?"

Ezra held out his hands and nodded.

"I don't understand," she said, gripping and shaking his arm.

"It just happened. Mr. Rubenstein appointed me *The Tango's* new *Rufiano*, so I thought I'd pay the madam a visit, and tell her the news that I was in charge," he said, throwing the bloody washcloth into the sink, and gesturing for them to go to the bedroom.

Ezra sat alongside Sadie on the edge of the bed and continued, "When I arrived, the madam made it very clear she wasn't going to cooperate with me, or the Ashkenazim. She asked me if it was true that I killed Antonio, which I didn't—it was Benjamin, not me. I shot Mr. Rivlin. But she wasn't listening to anything I was saying. She just continued ranting about how I ruined her life. I told her she was free to leave if she wasn't happy. That angered her more. She cursed at me and ran upstairs and locked herself in her bedroom. I followed after her and banged on the door, saying that it doesn't have to be this way, and she should give me a chance."

"Where were the girls when this was happening?"

"They came out of their rooms and gathered in the hallway, watching me. That was until the madam opened her door and demanded they go back downstairs. Then she looked at me, and crooked a finger at me to enter," Ezra said, and stood up and walked over to the window. He pushed the draperies back and looked out onto the moonlit harbor, and turned to Sadie. "She said that she was going to ruin me for taking Antonio away from her."

"Was the madam in love with Antonio?" Sadie asked.

Ezra shrugged. "I didn't know what to say. I wanted to apologize, but before I could utter a word, she charged at me holding a knife, trying to stab me. I leapt out of the way, causing her to stumble and fall to her knees, dropping the knife. When I bent over to pick it up, the madam jumped onto my back and clawed at me with her fingernails," he said, pulling his shirt to show the bloody scratch marks on his chest.

Sadie grimaced at the sight of them.

"After several attempts, I was able to flip her off me and onto the bed. Then, I don't know what possessed me, I grabbed her hair and pulled her head back, and with the knife, still in my hand, I slit her throat."

"Oh my God, Ezra!" Sadie said, putting her hand over her mouth. "How could you do such a thing?"

Ezra shook his head. "I don't know. Maybe it had something to do with her being the madam of *The Tango* where I almost lost you."

"What did you do next?"

"I left her there, bleeding out. I ran from the bedroom, down the staircase, and out onto the street."

"But what about the girls? Weren't there witnesses?"

"Yes, and I'm sure they've called the police by now. That's why we need to leave," he said, throwing items of clothing into a suitcase.

Sadie held out her hands. "But where will we go?"

"We'll head down to the harbor. I know a fisherman who will take us to Montevideo. That's in Uruguay. Now hurry, pack your things, before it's too late."

CHAPTER SEVENTY—THE HARBOR

"That must be him!" shouted Alex, pointing to a man climbing into the backseat of a black motorcar. "Come on," he said, taking off in a full run.

Just as the car engaged its gears and slowly pulled away, Alex reached the rear-passenger seat window and looked inside. There was a man he assumed was Ezra, and when he saw his face smeared in blood, he knew it was him. Alex punched his fists hard upon the glass, and screamed, "Where's Sadie, you fuck?"

Ezra leaned forward and said something inaudible to the driver, and the motorcar increased its speed, leaving Alex and Jan standing in the middle of Junin Street, watching it disappear around the corner.

"Dammit," Alex said, panting, trying to catch his breath.

Jan patted Alex on his back, and said, "Come on, let's go back to Nachum's."

That was the first time Alex had seen the face of the man who took Sadie from him. These thoughts reignited the cauldron of hatred that had been brewing for weeks. He imagined his hands around Ezra's neck, squeezing out his last breath.

They walked a few blocks from *The Tango* when Alex stopped to look at Jan and said, "Do you remember what the Polish Ambassador, Mr. Duda, said to us?"

Jan shook his head. "About what?"

"That if we were able to find Sadie, we should take her to Montevideo, in Uruguay. That's because people flee there to escape the Zwi Migdal, as well as skirt the law."

"I remember. So what?"

"Ezra just killed the Madam of *The Tango*. I'm sure, even in Argentina, murder is a capital offense, which means he'll be on the run. Perhaps he's headed for Montevideo, and taking Sadie with him."

Jan nodded and wagged a finger. "You're right. We should go to the harbor," he said, and both men took off in a full run along Avenue Cordoba.

*

Ten minutes later, drenched in sweat, Alex and Jan stood on the wooden dock. The full moon, now directly overhead, casting a sparkling light upon the choppy waters of the Rio de la Plata.

Alex looked out and spotted an old fishing boat, bobbing up and down, puttering away from the docks. "There it is," he said, and shouted, "Sadie!"

Then, as if commanded by the almighty, the clouds parted and a beam of moonlight shone upon the fishing vessel, offering Alex a vision of Sadie and Ezra standing side by side in the moon's reflection.

Even though the boat was now hundreds of feet away, he heard her scream, "Alex!" just as a cloud passed by, closing the curtain on their reunion.

Alex turned to Jan, his eyes bugging out. "We need a boat," he said, looking around at the dozen or so wobbling around in their slips.

CHAPTER SEVENTY-ONE—MONTEVIDEO

"Is that Alex?" Sadie hollered, her arm outstretched, pointing off into the distance at a man standing on the dock, waving his arms.

"Where?" Ezra said, standing alongside Sadie in the stern of the fishing boat.

"On the dock, right there," she said, jerking her arm.

"That can't be him, Sadie, he's dead. Now come on, let's go sit below," he said, urging her down the steps to the ship's galley.

"That's Alex—it's him. He's alive!" she said. "Turn the boat around," she pleaded to the boat captain.

Ezra shook his head. "We can't go back, and besides that wasn't Alex, he's dead. I promise you."

"I just saw him," she said, pointing. "You lied to me."

As a cloud drifted by, obscuring the moonlight, Sadie stood staring into the darkness. Her mind became a battlefield between hope and despair. She grasped the handrail wrapping around the boat's stern, and continued her musings: *If that was Alex, how would he find me now?*

*

Sadie stayed topside for the entire six-hour voyage waiting for the sun to rise and provide a vision of a boat transporting Alex, but all she saw was passing clouds and birds crisscrossing the sky.

By the time they reached Montevideo, it was late morning. Sadie refused Ezra's helping hand as she climbed from the fishing boat onto an abandoned dock.

"What is this place?" she asked, reaching for her bag.

Ezra thanked the boat captain and joined Sadie. "Watch your step," Ezra warned, "the dock's old and falling apart."

The awkwardly crooked, wooden dock had missing planks, leaving open gaps to the blackish-water several feet below. She stepped gingerly, and when they finally reached the shore, Sadie exhaled, and said, "Why are we being dropped off here?"

"Uruguay is a sovereign country; we can't just enter without going through customs. When I was with the Zwi, we used this dock to send our people back and forth, without interference from the government."

Before taking another step, Sadie stopped and turned to gaze out onto the streams of sunlight, brightening the sea, and thought, *That was Alex, I know it was him.*

"Come, Sadie, we shouldn't linger."

*

"Whose apartment is this?"

"The Zwi own it," Ezra said, pulling back the drapes, and peeking out to the street below. "Well, that was until the Ashkenazim took control."

Sadie glanced around the furnished apartment. "Are we safe here?"

281

Ezra shrugged. "For now. If anyone does come by, they probably won't know anything about Rivlin. Word of his demise may have not reached Montevideo yet."

"Eventually, it will, and you'll be a fugitive."

"You worry too much, Sadie," he said, moving closer, putting his hands around her waist and pulling her in tight.

Sadie pushed him away. "Don't touch me," she snarled.

"Hey, come on now," Ezra said, holding out his arms. "Do you really think that was Alex?"

Sadie nodded. "It was him, and you're a liar and a murderer," she said and cringed as the words passed her lips, wishing she could take them back.

Ezra squinted, his cheeks turned purple and he said, "I thought by now, you would have learned that I'm no one to be trifled with."

"I'm sorry, I didn't mean it," she said, swallowing hard. Unless she settled him down, he was certainly capable of making her another one of his victims, like Madam Marguerite or Mr. Rivlin. But to her dismay, she knew there was only one way to soothe his brutish behavior.

Not since learning that she would soon be sent off to *The Tango* did she need to deal with Ezra's sexual urges. While he started off gentle on the steamship from Hamburg, he slowly morphed into a rough and demanding defiler.

Even though while frightened, and knowing he may hurt her in order to induce pleasure, it seemed like a wise choice to give herself to him, rather than allowing his anger to boil over.

She took a step closer, and said, "Ezra, I'm sorry," and reached out for his hand, and placed it on her hip. "Everything is so stressful; I don't know what I was thinking."

Sadie watched Ezra's eyes soften. She smiled and led him to the bed.

CHAPTER SEVENTY-TWO—THE GABRIELLA

The smell of cigar smoke caught Alex's attention. "I think there's someone on this boat."

Jan knocked hard on the fishing boat's hull.

"What do you want?" answered a gravelly voice.

"Can we charter your boat?" shouted Alex.

"Come back in the morning."

Alex climbed on board, and looked down the steps toward the galley, and said, "We don't want to fish. We need to get to Montevideo. We can pay you?"

"All right," said the man, emerging from down below. "Why on earth would you want to go to Montevideo in the middle of the night?

"I'll explain on our way," Alex said to the bearded man, with a cigar cinched between his yellowed teeth.

"It'll cost you seventy pesos," said the man, sticking his grizzly face inches from Alex, "and you need to pay me now."

Alex held out his hands, trying to establish a reasonable personal space between them. "You got a deal," he said, reaching into this pocket.

"That's great!" the fisherman said. "My name's Mateo, and my boat, she's called the *Gabriella*. Welcome aboard, gentlemen."

*

Eleven hours later, the *Gabriella* approached the coastline of Montevideo. Alex stood alongside Mateo and asked, "Where do you think they disembarked?"

"From what you told me, most likely at the old docks to the west of the harbor."

"Will you look at that!" Alex said, his attention drawn to a large steamship docked in the harbor. "What's that?"

"That's the SS *Pennsylvania*. She's over six-hundred feet long."

"Pennsylvania? Does she sail to America?"

Mateo nodded. "Her port of call is New York City."

"New York," Alex murmured and thought back to when he and Sadie boarded the SS *Amerika* in Hamburg, only to be pulled off by the authorities at the last moment. He turned to Jan, who joined him topside, and said, "We need to get ourselves passage on that ship to America."

"To America?" he said, wide-eyed.

Alex patted Jan on his back, and said, "To New York, my friend."

"That's all well and good, but right now, we need to find Sadie, and Montevideo looks like an imposing city. Where do we begin?"

Holding on to the wheel and pushing on the throttle to slow the boat down, Mateo said, "You say your Jewish girl was taken by the Zwi Migdal. Is that right?"

Alex nodded.

"I've been known to ferry those *Rufianos* with their *Polacas*, from time to time. From what I've overheard, they keep an apartment a few

285

blocks from here," he said, saddling up alongside the dilapidated wooden dock.

Alex shared a look with Jan. "That's good to know. Thank you, Mateo."

"Oh, and I nearly forgot," he said, scratching his beard. "The apartment is on the top floor of a brothel. Don't ask me which one. That's all I know."

"Thank you," Alex said, as he and Jan offered Mateo their farewells, and disembarked the *Gabriella*.

CHAPTER SEVENTY-THREE—THE BROTHEL

Still groggy, Sadie opened her eyes and saw Ezra sleeping beside her. She sat up and looked around, unsure of her whereabouts.

She swung her feet off the bed, rubbed the sleep from her eyes, stood up, and groaned from the sharp pain in her right hip. Clutching the source of the discomfort, she bent her knees and reached for her clothes on the floor.

Once dressed, Sadie walked over to the window and looked out onto the street below. It was dusk, and the gas lamps were being lit.

While Ezra slept, Sadie felt lucky that he was able to be more gentle with her, though she knew he had it in him to be rough. She shook her head in disgust, thinking about the pleasure he received by forcing himself into her. How different he was from the cruise, when he confessed how he wanted to please her, more than himself. *What had brought about this change in him?*

Sadie imagined finding a knife and stabbing him repeatably while he slept. *Wouldn't that be liberating*, she mused, though she lacked the courage to do so.

Boisterous voices startled Sadie out of her murderous musings. She assumed it was coming from another apartment. The disturbances intensified with sounds of women laughing and heavy footfalls stomping upon the staircase outside the doorway to the apartment. She smelled hints of cigar smoke.

"What are you doing?" Ezra said, lifting himself up onto his elbows.

"What is this place?" Sadie asked with a furrowed brow.

Ezra inhaled and sat up. He listened to the sounds and smiled. "Oh, it's the brothel downstairs."

Sadie stared dumbstruck for a moment, then uttered, "We're in a brothel?"

Ezra nodded. "Don't worry, you're staying with me. Unless you start acting up again," he said with a smirk.

Sadie pursed her lips and turned to look out the window. "How long will we stay here?"

"That's a good question," he said, rising to his feet, stepping close to her, and wrapping his arms around her.

She pushed him away and looked with disgust at his naked body. "Get dressed unless you want the world to see you."

"Who's going to care seeing a naked body through the window of a brothel?" he said, taking Sadie in his arms.

She cringed and squirmed away. "Please get dressed," she pleaded.

He laughed, and said, "All right, Sadie."

Sadie kept her focus on the street below, ruminating about her sighting of Alex until Ezra interrupted her thoughts. "We can't stay here long. Eventually, the Buenos Aires police will figure out I left the city.

Once the local police know that I'm running from the law, it will only be a matter of time until they find me."

"So what are you going to do?"

"You mean what are *we* going to do."

Sadie shrugged.

"Did you notice that steamship in the harbor?"

"I did."

"That's the SS *Pennsylvania*. It sails to New York City tomorrow night."

Sadie watched him slipping on his socks and waited for him to continue.

He looked up at her, smiled, and said, "We're going to America, Sadie."

"You taking me to America?" she said, with her jaw hanging open.

Ezra nodded. "We're going to start a new life together, just the two of us."

"But I don't want to go to America with you. I want my life back with Alex."

"You must stop dwelling upon that dead man. It's time to move on."

"Never," Sadie said, and returned her gaze back onto the street below.

"This is what we're going to do," Ezra said, ignoring her melancholy. "We'll go downstairs, have a few drinks with the madam, and then try to get some sleep. In the morning, I'll buy us first-class passage. It will be like old times, Sadie, when we sailed from Hamburg. Except, you're not the same innocent girl you were back then," he said, with a smirk.

Sadie turned from the window and held out her arms. "I don't understand how you're so cavalier with people's lives. You've murdered two people, and who knows what's happened to Rebecca and the other Warsaw girls you deceived with your schemes. Now you want to run off to America with me, and leave your wife without a husband and your children without a father. You're a despicable man."

Ezra smiled, held out his hand, and said, "Come, Sadie, let's go meet the madam. I'm sure she'll be fascinated with you."

CHAPTER SEVENTY-FOUR—THE DREAM

"I'm exhausted," Alex said, sipping a coffee at an outdoor café. "What time is it?"

Jan looked at his pocket watch. "It's ten."

"We should keep looking."

"I agree, Alex, but I'm getting exhausted going from brothel to brothel, asking if anyone has seen a good-looking redhead with a bearded man," he said, looking at the activity surrounding the SS *Pennsylvania*.

"You're right, but what choice do we have?"

"All right, but in the meantime, let's find a bench under a tree; I need a few hours of sleep," Jan said.

Alex looked at the massive steamship dwarfing the buildings standing before it, and nodded. "That's a good idea," he said and dropped a few coins on the cafe table.

While Jan found an out-of-the-way place to shut his eyes, Alex took a walk along the harbor, doing his best to avoid the busy dockworkers loading supplies on board the steamship. He sighed, watching the queue of people waiting to buy passage to America, and fantasized he was on the line with Sadie.

He wandered over to the winding assembly of people seeking travel, and asked a young man, "What time's she sailing?"

The man's eyes widened, and a broad smile filled his face, expressing his anticipation of sailing to America, and said, "Six tonight, but you shouldn't wait too long. I hear only steerage is left."

*

Alex and Jan agreed to take turns sleeping.

"It's best for one of us to keep an eye out. You never know, we might spot Sadie and Ezra walking the streets," Alex suggested.

Three hours later, with no luck, Alex gave Jan a gentle nudge to wake him.

"What time is it?" he asked, swinging his legs around.

"It's one-thirty. How are you feeling?" Alex asked, sitting down next to Jan.

Jan exhaled and stretched his arms. "I'm okay. Why don't you get some rest, and I'll scout the vicinity."

"Pay attention to the docks. The SS *Pennsylvania* pulls out at six tonight."

Jan patted Alex on his leg. "I'll come back for you in a few hours."

The cool breeze coming off the *Rio de la Plata* soothed Alex into a deep slumber, and moments later into a vivid dream.

The three of them stood in the park.

"We're going to America," Sadie said, leaning her head upon Ezra's shoulder, his arm wrapped around her back.

"You're not serious. You can't go with him," he said, pointing at Ezra.

"We're in love. Ezra has proven himself. He was the one who rescued me from The Tango, not you, Alex."

"But I came all this way. I thought you loved me."

"I did love you, but that was a foolish mistake. My father was right, I must marry a Jewish man and raise Jewish children. Ezra is a Jew, you are not."

"But I thought that didn't matter, Sadie."

Sadie took a step toward him, pointed a finger inches away from his face, and said, "It matters, Alex. Hashem commands it."

*

"Alex, wake up," Jan said.

Alex opened his eyes and sat up quickly. "I just had a nightmare. Sadie was running off with Ezra to America."

"That was no dream," Jan said. "Quickly, we need to get on that ship."

"What are you talking about?"

Jan pointed with an outstretched arm. "I just saw Sadie and Ezra boarding the SS *Pennsylvania*."

Alex jumped to his feet. "Let's hurry, Jan," he said, and they took off, running at full speed for the ticket office.

CHAPTER SEVENTY-FIVE—THE JEWISH JEZEBEL

"It's not the Presidential Suite, but we'll make do," Ezra said, as the bellhop accepted the coin, and excused himself.

Sadie sat down on the bed, rubbed her eyes, and said, "I'd like to get some rest if that's all right with you."

"That's fine," he said with a shrug. "I'll take a walk and get myself acquainted with the ship's amenities."

Sadie nodded, flipped off her shoes, and lay down upon the bed.

Unlike the voyage on board the MV *Alcantara*, Ezra knew no one. While he was able to purchase first-class passage, he wouldn't enjoy his special VIP treatment, such as dining at the captain's table. But he would be assured one thing of great importance, his anonymity. After all, he was running from the law.

The topside deck offered a sweeping view of the *Rio de la Plata*. Ezra leaned his elbows on the wooden railing and enjoyed the sun setting in the western sky. This was the first time he had, since the mad scramble of escaping from Buenos Aires, a moment to reflect on what had occurred.

Why did I allow myself to react so impulsively? I wish I'd known Antonio Catalano was the madam's lover. I might have been less provocative in my approach.

294

For a few glorious days, Ezra had become one of the most powerful men in the Ashkenazim, an organization now in control of the Buenos Aires brothels and sex-trade business. But that prestige was short-lived. Instead, he was on a thirty-day cruise to America, in order to avoid capture by the Buenos Aires police, on the charge of murder. Such a predicament, not even the powerful Mr. Rubenstein, could help him escape from.

Two children, followed by their parents, strolled by along the deck, causing Ezra to think about his own family he left behind. In a day, or two at most, a police detective would visit his apartment, and explain to his wife, Chaya, that her husband was a suspect in the murder of a well-known brothel-madam. She, of course, would be shocked and dismayed and worried about her future without him. But with the substantial bank account he provided for her and the boys, he knew his family would be taken care of, at least financially.

Chaya and the boys had become accustomed to his absence, since his work took him away from home for months at a time. At first, Chaya would complain, but over the past few years, she said little, realizing that it did no good, and more importantly, she enjoyed the lifestyle Ezra's lucrative career provided.

Ezra thought back to when they first met. It was before getting himself involved as an agent with the Zwi Migdal. Several years before the Great War began, Chaya's family had immigrated to Argentina from a *shtetl* in what would now be considered southern Poland.

He first saw her at synagogue on the high holy day of Yom Kippur. After services, while the congregation mingled outdoors, Ezra gathered his nerves and approached. Apparently, both Ezra's and Chaya's parents noticed the mutual attraction, and several months later, in the same synagogue, they were married.

After the birth of their two boys, Ezra got a job working for the finest furrier in Buenos Aires. This was his first job in sales, and to his surprise, he became Goldblum's number one salesman.

Barely one year into working for the prestigious firm, he met Mr. Luis Zwi Migdal, founder of the notorious organization, who came into Goldblum's looking for a fur for his wife. Impressed by Ezra's charm and good looks, he recruited him into his organization.

Ezra rose quickly into one of the Zwi's top agents and would soon spend at least half the year away from home, distancing himself from his wife, while enjoying the fruits of his labor with hefty commissions and beautiful women.

During one of Ezra's recruiting trips overseas, Mr. Migdal and his minions were taken out by a power-seeking group led by Mr. Rivlin in a coordinated attack. When Ezra returned home, he was greeted with a choice of offering his loyalty to the new *Balebos* or finding himself shot and dumped into the *Rio de la Plata* with his former cohorts.

He pushed himself off the railing and shook his head, thinking about how he was unable to take advantage of the recent leadership change due to his foolishness. He figured that a public scandal would ensue, and the quick demise of Ezra Porkevitch and Sadie Wollman would be the talk of dinner parties for a few weeks, that is, until something new and exciting took its place, extinguishing them from people's consciousness.

The police would turn the city upside down searching for his whereabouts. By the time they figured out that he must have gone to Montevideo, he would be out to sea, and out of reach of the authorities.

After exploring the ship, Ezra decided to head back to the cabin to check on Sadie. Just as he turned the corner, he saw coming in the other direction, a well-dressed, middle-aged woman, with the same bellhop who had helped him with his valises, leading the way.

They both arrived at the entrance to her cabin at the same time.

"Here you are, Miss Adler," the bellhop said, inserting the key into the door.

Ezra stopped walking, his passageway obstructed with the rolling-cart full of the lady's belongings.

"My apologies, Mr. Porkevitch," the bellhop said, "I'll be out of your way in a moment."

Ezra held out his palm, offering his patience, and tilted his head to look between the woman's impressive amount of luggage, and said, "Good evening, Miss Adler. Are you heading back home to New York?"

"I am, sir," she said. "I've spent four weeks in Buenos Aires and the last two weeks here in Montevideo. Such a lovely place."

"Yes indeed," he agreed. "My name is Ezra Porkevitch. My fiancée is resting in our cabin," he said, pointing to the doorway behind her.

"Oh, we're neighbors. I would love to meet your fiancée, Mr. Porkevitch. But right now," she said, placing her palm on her forehead, "I'm exhausted and need rest."

"Of course, Miss Adler. Perhaps I will see you later this evening."

Once Ezra was able to pass, he stood in front of his cabin door for a moment, while a thought fluttered about in his mind about Miss Adler. *I know this name.* As he reached for his key, he remembered a story that Henry Stillman shared with him about a madam in New York City, who was once connected with the Zwi Migdal, and had been lured by Mr. Rubenstein into the Ashkenazim. Her name was Polly Adler, and she operated several high-end brothels throughout the city. *They call her the Jewish Jezebel*, Henry had told him.

Ezra looked at her cabin door where she'd just disappeared behind, and thought that his fortunes were about to change, yet again. If Miss Adler was in Montevideo for the past two weeks, she would have no idea about the demise of Rivlin and Catalano. At least for the voyage his identity was safe. He smiled and thought, *I have a month to develop a relationship with this Jewish Jezebel.*

CHAPTER SEVENTY-SIX—WILD BULL OF THE PAMPAS

Alex sat down on his bunk. "We'll need to make do," he said, with an exasperated sigh.

"I don't mind sleeping down here in steerage," Jan said with a shrug, "but how are we going to get up to the first-class deck?"

"And then what? Accuse Ezra of kidnapping Sadie and demand he hand her over to us?"

"He could slip and fall overboard," Jan said, shifting his eyebrows.

Alex chuckled and whispered, "Or accidentally drink rat poison."

"Too risky," Jan said, shaking his head. "We need to get ourselves booked into first-class."

"I told you, I tried," Alex said. "Every cabin was sold out."

"We could try to lure Sadie away and hide her down here in steerage," Jan said, looking around at the fellow passengers sharing the bare-bones accommodations, deep into the ship's hull.

Alex shook his head. "Once she's gone missing, the ship's security would turn the place upside down searching for her," he said and paused for a moment, allowing himself to ponder the options. "I think we should just wait until we arrive in New York, then make our move. In the meantime, we need to make sure Sadie knows we're here."

"How would we do that?"

Alex cocked his head over to the young man mopping the steerage cabin's metal floor. "On our way down here, we passed the storage closet where they keep uniforms. We can pretend we're part of the maintenance crew, and casually mop the decks, polish the railings, or something until we find Sadie."

"That could work," Jan said.

"Perhaps I could steal a few minutes with her, and share our plan, it would—"

"Anyone in this bunk?" interrupted a tall muscular man, with a crooked nose, and a bag slung over his shoulder.

Alex looked up and shook his head. "It's all yours."

He flung the bag onto the bunk and offered his hand to Alex. "My name is Luis Firpo," he said.

"It's good to meet you, Luis," he said, shaking hands. "My name is Alex Kaminsky and this is Jan Mazur."

"You have an accent. Where you boys from?"

"We're from Poland," Alex said.

"Poland! I've been there. Great country," he said, sitting down on his bunk.

Jan shared a look of surprise with Alex, and said, "What brought you to Poland?"

Luis shrugged. "I used to be a professional prize-fighter. I was there for a match with your champion, Henryk Chmielewski," he said and smiled. "I beat him in the first round."

"You're a boxer?" Jan asked.

"I was known as the *Wild Bull of the Pampas,* the undisputed heavyweight boxing champion of Argentina for six years."

"That's very impressive, Luis," Alex said with a smile.

"Thank you."

"Why are you going to New York?"

"I'm fighting an exhibition bout with the heavyweight, Jack Dempsey."

"Jack Dempsey?" Jan said, holding a finger to his cheek. "I read about him. Isn't he the heavyweight champion?"

"He certainly is, and a great one at that. But this is just a fundraiser for charity. We'll throw a couple punches for a few rounds, nothing serious, and they'll pay me $10,000. Easy money."

"That's exciting," said Jan. "But why are you in steerage? A champion like you should be in first class."

"I've been retired for three years, so I'm tight on cash. But I may splurge on the voyage home," he said with a laugh.

"It's good to meet you, Luis," Alex said, standing up. "We're going to stretch our legs topside. Would you like to join us?"

Luis slapped his knees, stood up, and held out his powerful arm, and said, "Please, amigos, lead the way."

"Alex is hoping to catch a glimpse of his fiancée," Jan said. "She's traveling in first class."

Luis turned with a puckered forehead and asked, "Why in the world would she be up there, while you're down here?"

"Come on," Alex said, patting Luis on his back, "I'll tell you the story on the way."

CHAPTER SEVENTY-SEVEN—SADIE MEETS POLLY

"Oh, that's Miss Adler. I met her earlier," Ezra said, raising his hand and waving.

Sadie turned her head, and saw a woman, probably in her mid-forties, with short, brown, curly hair, waving back.

"Ah, Miss Adler, it's good to see you again. Please allow me to introduce my fiancée, Miss Sadie Wollman," Ezra said.

He's introducing me as his fiancée? Sadie thought. *Does his deception have no limits?*

"My dear, it's a pleasure meeting you," Polly said, sitting down, and turning to Ezra. "You found a rare beauty."

"Thank you, Miss Adler," Ezra said.

"Please call me Polly."

"It's nice to meet you, Polly," Sadie said, with a polite smile.

"Are you alone?" Ezra said, looking behind her.

"Yes, I'm heading over to my table," she said, gesturing.

"Please join us. We would love to dine with you," Ezra said, pulling out a chair next to Sadie.

"That's very nice," she said, sitting down and looking over to Sadie. "Tell me, dear, how did the two of you meet?" she asked, taking Sadie's hand and cradling it between hers.

Sadie didn't know what to say. Certainly the truth wasn't an option.

Filling the awkward pause, Ezra said, "We met in Warsaw on my last business trip, and fell in love."

Polly nodded and squinted her eyes, as if she doubted the story, and said, "It must have been hard for you leaving your family and friends."

"Would you mind pouring me some wine, Ezra?" Sadie said, hoping to change the conversation to something less revealing.

"Of course," he said, reaching across the large round table for the carafe.

"What brought you to Montevideo, Polly?" Sadie asked, placing the cloth napkin upon her lap.

"I'm a businesswoman," she said, with a swagger. "I had meetings with my investors."

"A businesswoman?" Sadie asked curiously. "May I ask what is it that you do?"

Polly leaned in close, while keeping a watchful eye on Ezra, and said softly, "I own gentlemen's clubs in Manhattan."

Sadie tilted her head and squinted. "Gentlemen's clubs?"

Polly looked over to Ezra and shrugged.

Ezra leaned in and whispered into Sadie's ear. "They're brothels."

Those words released a rush of blood to Sadie's face. Her eyes darted back and forth between Ezra and Polly and said, "Brothels? Isn't that interesting?"

Picking up on the underlying tension, Polly said, "If you don't mind me asking, what do you do for a living, Ezra?"

Ezra took a sip of his wine, swallowed, and smiled. "I was an agent with the Zwi Migdal. But I'll be looking for a new line of work when we get to New York."

Polly wagged a finger back and forth and asked, "So is that how the two of you met?"

Sadie looked at Ezra with wide eyes, worried about how he was going to answer.

"Yes, Sadie and I met on my last visit to Warsaw."

Polly smiled. "I'm familiar with how the Zwi works. So tell me, Ezra," she said, jerking her head over to Sadie, "was she one of your *Polacas*?"

Ezra shrugged and nodded. "That was the intention until we got to know each other. It's strange how love works."

"Strange indeed," Polly said, nodding.

"Excuse me, miss," a waiter said, lifting the carafe. "Would you like some more wine?"

"Yes, that would be nice," Sadie said, and looked up, and nearly dropped her wine glass. It was Jan. They locked eyes for a moment until he shifted his gaze slightly toward the dining hall entry doors. Sadie glanced over and saw Alex just beyond the maître d' station. She sat for a moment, waiting for Jan to leave, and smiled, hoping Polly or Ezra couldn't hear her heart pounding against her ribcage.

Finally, she mustered up the nerve, stood up, and said, "If you would excuse me."

Polly clasped onto her wrist and said, "I hope I didn't upset you, my dear."

"No, not at all. I just need to use the ladies'," Sadie said, trying to offer an authentic smile.

She stepped briskly through the dining hall, ignoring the dozens of eyes gawking at her. Once she passed the maître d' station and went through the double doors, she saw Alex. He was wearing a blue workman's jumpsuit with the ship's logo sewn onto the breast pocket.

Sadie put her hand over her mouth.

"Follow me," he whispered and opened a door to a linen closet.

They both slipped inside. Sadie put her hands around his neck, and drew him in tight, and said, "Is it really you?"

"It's me, Sadie," Alex said, and they kissed.

She allowed herself to be lost in the moment, her body weightless, for just a minute. But the sensation was snatched away as soon as Alex released her. "We can't linger for too long. I just wanted you to know that I'm here," he whispered.

"What am I supposed to do?" Sadie said, maintaining her hold upon him.

"We must wait until we disembark in New York."

Her eyes stung, with teardrops paused upon each eyelid. "You expect me to last a month with that man? He's a murderer."

"I know about the madam, I was at *The Tango* looking for you, the night it happened."

"I can't go back to him now," she said, with streams of tears rolling down her cheeks.

Alex squeezed her, and said, "You have to. It's almost over and we'll be together."

Sadie lifted her chin, and they kissed one last time.

Alex pushed her back and patted away the tears from her face. "You need to compose yourself. Don't let him suspect anything."

Sadie took a breath. "All right," she said, opening the closet door, and swiftly shutting it behind her, leaving Alex behind.

Just across the hall, she noticed the ladies' room. She quickly entered to freshen up before returning to the dining hall.

CHAPTER SEVENTY-EIGHT—THE CAPTAIN'S TABLE

Occasionally first-class passengers would wander over to a section of the main deck that was visible from where Alex had stood for the past two hours, hoping for a glimpse of Sadie.

"It's getting late," Jan said, looking out onto the sea. "I'm heading down."

Alex sighed. "All right, I'm coming too," he said, walking toward the stairwell leading to the steerage quarters.

"I know you're anxious," Jan said, following Alex down the narrow corridor, "but you need to be patient. We have three more weeks until we reach port."

"I know," Alex said and sighed. "I just told Sadie she needs to be patient."

Once down below, they stepped inside the stench-ridden steerage cabin and were greeted by a cacophony of snores, coughs, and farts from the two-dozen men sleeping in their bunks.

"You're finally back," Luis said, sitting up. "I've been waiting for you."

Alex sat down and removed his shoes. "Hi, Luis, how was dinner with the captain?"

"Oh, it was fine. Captain Velazquez is a big boxing fan. He saw me fight in Buenos Aires."

"That's great, Luis. I'm sure you ate better than we did," Jan said.

"Listen," Luis said in a whisper, and leaned forward, resting his elbows on his knees. "While I was at the captain's table, I saw your girl Sadie seated a few tables away."

Alex grabbed Luis' arm. "How did you know it was her?"

"From your description. She's as beautiful as you said, even more so than I imagined."

"All right, Luis, then what?" Alex asked, his heart beating like a war drum.

Luis held up a finger. "What you didn't tell me was the man she was with was Ezra Porkevitch."

"You know him?" Alex asked.

"My security job was with Mr. Rubenstein, *Balebos* of the Ashkenazim. I was in his office when Ezra was offered a position in the organization, in exchange for killing Rivlin."

Alex looked over to Jan, then back to Luis. "You worked for Rubenstein?"

Luis nodded. "As added incentive, Mr. Rubenstein offered Sadie as his reward. When Ezra shot Rivlin in the head, Sadie was taken from *The Tango*, and brought to Ezra's apartment."

"Did Ezra see you at the captain's table?" Jan asked.

"No, but I walked over and greeted him. Ezra remembered me, and was thrilled that I approached, probably because I'm a recognized celebrity, and he introduced me to his fiancée."

"His fiancée?" Alex said loudly, which triggered demands to *keep quiet* from a few men trying to sleep.

"I'm afraid so. But if it makes you feel any better, Sadie seemed rather subdued."

Alex took a deep breath, trying to temper his anger.

Luis lifted a finger in the air. "There was someone else seated next to Sadie, who I also met before. Her name was Polly Adler, she's a madam of several brothels in New York City."

"Where did you meet her?" Alex asked.

"At Mr. Rubenstein's office. He's a business partner with her. She was there asking for money to deal with a gangster trying to take control of her brothels."

Jan held out his hands and shook his head. "I don't understand—why are you sharing this with us?"

Luis shrugged, looked around, and whispered, "Because I'm using the excuse of this fight with Dempsey to immigrate to America. I'm not going back. The prize money will set me up nicely to start a new life. The Ashkenazum and the Zwi, they're all the same scum."

Alex placed his head in his hands. "I don't think I can stand another minute of this."

Luis leaned over, patted Alex on his arm, and said, "You may not have to. I have an idea."

CHAPTER SEVENTY-NINE—POLLY'S PROPOSAL

Ezra tapped a piece of clinging ash off from his cigar and watched it float above and beyond the railing, and out to sea. He took a sip of his red wine, and asked Polly, "What's the weather like in New York this time of year?"

"It's wonderful. I love autumn. The city gets terribly hot and humid in the summer."

"I think I'm going back to the cabin," Sadie said, rising from her chair. "I'm ready for bed."

"Wait," Ezra said, pushing his chair back. "I'll come with you."

Polly held up her hand. "Oh, Ezra, please stay a little longer with me. There's something I would like to discuss with you."

Ezra looked over to Sadie. "Go on without me, I'll only be a little while."

Sadie nodded. "Good night, Polly."

"Good night, dear."

Polly waited for Sadie to be out of earshot before she spoke. "I need to talk to you about her."

Ezra narrowed his eyes and asked, "About Sadie?"

Polly nodded.

Ezra held up his hands. "I know what you're thinking, and the answer is no."

"Listen to me," Polly said, wagging a finger, "that young lady could light up Manhattan, and make you a rich man."

"I don't know. Sadie was not happy at *The Tango*, plus to be honest, I've become rather attached to her."

Polly waved her hand, dismissing the comment, and said, "What's your plan when you get to New York? How are you going to make money?

"I don't know," he said and shrugged. "Maybe ask you for a job."

Polly snorted. "A job? That's funny. You think you and that pretty girl of yours will be happy being shoved into one of those run-down tenements on Houston Street, living off your meager wages from a *job*," she said with a snarl.

Ezra squinted, realizing he was already missing his luxurious lifestyle in Buenos Aires. "All right, Polly, what do you have in mind?"

"I own a brothel on Seventy-fifth Street, called the *Majestic*. It's the *Tango* of Manhattan. Very upscale with a clientele of famous actors, powerful politicians, and wealthy businessmen. I would love to add Sadie to my lineup," Polly said, lighting up a cigarette.

Ezra mulled over Sadie's likely reaction to returning to the life of a *Polaca*. "She's not going to like it."

"Most don't at first," she said with a shrug. "But my ladies are treated like royalty; like princesses. Eventually, they succumb and enjoy the privileged lifestyle I provide."

Ezra tilted his head back, and exhaled a plume of cigar smoke into the star-filled sky over the SS *Pennsylvania* pushing its way up along the Brazilian coast, and said, "But what about me?"

Polly smiled, obviously pleased Ezra agreed with her plan concerning Sadie. "I would like you to run the day-to-day operations of the *Majestic* as its director," she said, leaning in, and resting her elbows on the small cocktail table. "There's a beautiful apartment in the back of the building with its own private garden. You can live there with Sadie. You'll see her during the workday, and at nighttime, she'll be in your bed—the best of both worlds."

Ezra imagined what it would be like being in charge of New York's premier brothel and the recognition it would afford him. This was an opportunity he couldn't pass up. Yes, it would take a Herculean effort to convince Sadie, but what were her options? She knew no one, and he doubted she spoke English. However, there was the consideration of sharing Sadie with other men, but he figured that would be a worthy trade-off for being the director of the *Majestic*.

He would accept Polly's offer, but wait until they arrived in New York before sharing the news with Sadie. There was no need to upset her and ruin their remaining time at sea.

"All right, Polly, I'll be your director," Ezra said, reaching across the table to shake Polly's hand.

Polly grinned and shook her head, and said, "Oh no, Ezra, a handshake will not seal this deal."

Ezra held out his hands and looked confused. "What then?" he asked.

Polly stood up, took Ezra's hand, and said seductively, "Come with me to my cabin."

Ezra squinted, absorbing the nature of her request, and said, "Okay, let's go."

CHAPTER EIGHTY—CARD GAME

"What time did you tell him?" Alex asked, looking at his pocket watch.

Luis sighed. "I told you—midnight."

"Maybe he couldn't find his way down here and gave up?" Jan said.

Alex stood up from the makeshift card table, and wandered around the cavernous storage space, filled with large wooden containers and crates bound for New York Harbor.

"Hello," a voice called out from the other end, echoing off the steel hull.

"Over here, Ezra," shouted Luis, and whispered to Alex and Jan, "Here he comes."

Ezra marched along the wood planks laid out as a walkway in between the soaring towers of shipping containers, and as he approached, he stretched his arm out, preparing to shake hands. "Luis, sorry I'm late. I was *busy* with my fiancée," he said, shifting his eyebrows up and down, "if you know what I mean."

The plan was to confront Ezra calmly, but once those defiling words passed his lips, Alex attacked. "You fucker," he shouted, tackling Ezra onto his back, and getting off a solid punch to the side of his face before he was pulled off by Jan and Luis.

"What the hell?" Ezra said, getting to his feet, and spitting out a glob of blood from his mouth.

"I should kill you right now," Alex said, struggling to break free from Jan and Luis.

Ezra pushed his tongue against the inside of his mouth, feeling the wound. "I recognize you—you're Alex," he said, jerking his chin toward them.

"Sit down," ordered Jan.

"Just make sure he doesn't touch me again," he said, cautiously pulling over a small, empty crate, and lowering himself.

"All right, Alex, I'm going to let you go," said Luis. "Try to remain calm, and we'll deal with this like we agreed upon."

There was no denying the fear in Ezra's eyes, which Alex responded to with a nod and an imperceptible smile. Once released, he rolled back his shoulders, to relieve the tension from being restrained, and said, "All right," with a long exhalation.

"That was clever of you, Luis, to lure me down here for a card game with these thugs."

Alex jabbed a finger and shouted, "You're calling *us* thugs?"

"Sadie was right. That *was* you on the dock in Buenos Aires."

Alex nodded.

Jan said, "Alex has agreed to make you a deal."

"A deal for what?" Ezra scoffed.

"A deal for your life," Alex said with a scowl.

Ezra's eyes darted back and forth. He rubbed his palms on his pants leg, and said with a less aggressive tone, "What is it you want from me?"

Alex furrowed his brow and spoke deliberately. "When we arrive in New York, we'll all disembark the ship together. The moment we touch American soil, you'll leave Sadie with me. If not, that will be your first and last day in America."

Ezra shrugged. "What choice do I have, but to accept?"

Alex looked at him and shook his head. *Why is he so quick to concede?* he wondered.

"But what about the next two weeks?" he asked. "Do I just pretend that all is normal?"

Alex leaned in, squinted his eyes into slits, and said, "If I find out that you so much as touched her, I'll kill you, and I'll do it slowly. Do you understand me?"

Ezra nodded. "I understand. Is it all right for me to leave?" he said, rising to his feet.

Alex flicked his wrist, dismissing him. As he walked away, Alex called after him, "Don't think just because we're down here in steerage, we can't get to you in first class."

Ezra turned his head to look at Alex and nodded.

Once he was out of earshot, Alex said, "This is a mistake, letting him go. We should at least tie him up and keep him hidden until we reach New York."

Luis shook his head. "What do you think will happen when he's reported missing? The ship's security will search and find him, and you'll be held in custody. Once we dock, they'll hand you over to immigration, who will arrange to send you back to Poland. Trust me, it's best to be patient, and deal with this in New York."

"You want me to be patient, Luis, for the next two weeks, while I'm pacing the floor in steerage?"

"It's the only way."

CHAPTER EIGHTY-ONE—NEW YORK HARBOR

Ezra and Sadie carried their valises down the canvas-covered gangplank onto the landing at Chelsea Piers. They waited in line, along with other first and second-class passengers who would need to pass through customs before being allowed to exit onto the streets of Manhattan.

Ezra put an arm around Sadie, pulled her in tight, and said, "We've made it, my love, we're in America."

Sadie offered a barely perceptible smile, keeping her solemn gaze straight ahead.

"Come now, don't be so glum. We're going to have a wonderful life. I've arranged an apartment for us in an upscale neighborhood. As soon as we pass through customs, we'll catch a taxi and get settled."

Sadie remained silent.

Ezra, unperturbed by Sadie's melancholy, wondered what Alex and Jan were thinking about now, as they were probably being ushered onto a ferryboat and transported over to Ellis Island for processing, along with the hundreds of fellow passengers from steerage. He smiled at his cleverness, and their stupidity, over the deal he was coerced into making two weeks earlier. Apparently, they weren't aware of the procedures entering America requiring the separation of the classes into two groups.

He chuckled, thinking about their frustration, watching from the ferry, as it pulled away from Manhattan's west-side, and making its way across the harbor to the immigration facility on Ellis Island. Ezra was confident that in a city of six million people, that neither Alex nor Jan would be able to locate them.

Once they had passed through customs, Ezra pushed his way through the crowded street. "We need to go uptown. Let's grab a taxi on the other side."

Sadie shrugged and followed.

In the taxi, she asked, "Where're we going?"

"Don't worry," he said, patting her knee. "I've got everything worked out."

*

"This is it," Ezra said, tilting his head back and gawking at the imposing fifteen-story, golden-colored brick building on the corner of Seventy-fifth Street and Broadway. "Come, Sadie, let's go inside."

Just as they were about to step into the building's vestibule, Ezra's name was called out. He turned and saw Polly getting out of a taxi.

"What is she doing here?" Sadie said, sounding frightened.

"Hi, Polly, good timing."

Polly spoke with the driver regarding her luggage and then approached. "Come, I'll get the two of you settled," she said, opening the front door.

"What is this place?" Sadie asked, looking about the marbled entry foyer.

Polly looked over to Ezra. "You haven't told her yet?"

"I was about to," Ezra said, with a furrowed brow.

"Tell me what?" she asked sharply and stood her ground.

"Let's talk privately," he said, reaching for her hand, which she jerked away.

Sadie folded her arms across her chest and said, "Tell me now."

Ezra sighed.

"Tell her, Ezra," Polly said impatiently, with her hands on her hips.

"This is the *Majestic*, one of Polly's brothels. She's given us an apartment to live in. It has an outdoor garden," he said, hoping to soften the blow still to come.

Sadie's nostrils flared. "What else, Ezra?"

He rubbed his chin and pursed his lips. "I've accepted the position as the director of the *Majestic*," he said and paused. But Sadie remained expressionless.

"Tell her the rest, Ezra. I'm tired, and would like to get some rest," Polly insisted.

"You'll also have a position, Sadie. Similar to the one you had at *The Tango*," he said, and watched Sadie's face turn beet-red. "But you'll stay with me each evening, like a couple."

Sadie took a step toward Ezra, and before he could react, she slapped him across his face and sprinted for the front door.

"Go get her, Ezra," Polly ordered.

Ezra sighed, put down his valise, and ran after her. While she struggled to try to open the front door, he grabbed her.

"Let go of me," she screamed, trying to break free from Ezra's grip as he pulled her back.

"Follow me," Polly said and walked down the hallway.

"I'm sorry, Sadie," Ezra said, tugging her along. "This is for the best, or we'd be living in squalor, and I'm sure you wouldn't like that."

CHAPTER EIGHTY-TWO—ELLIS ISLAND

"Where are you taking us?" Alex asked a uniformed man, as they were shepherded onto a ferryboat.

"Steerage passengers go to Ellis Island for processing and a health exam."

"But what about the first-class passengers?"

The man pointed to the dockside. "They go through customs here."

Alex turned to Luis. "Did you know about this?"

"No, how would I?" Luis said with a shrug.

Alex pushed his way, followed by Jan and Luis trying to keep up, to the ferryboat's stern.

As they pulled away from the shore, Alex strained for a look at the passengers milling about on the street, some waiting for taxis. "Dammit! We should have taken him out when we had the chance. Why'd we wait?"

"I'm sorry," Jan said.

"I shouldn't have listened to you!" Alex said, putting his hands to his head. "How will we ever find them now in a city as large as New York? We don't even know where to start looking."

"Actually, I think we do," said Luis.

Alex dropped his hands and asked, "What are you saying?"

"Remember when I met Ezra and Sadie?"

"Yes, in the dining hall."

Luis nodded. "Seated with them was Polly Adler, the madam who runs a string of brothels in Manhattan. If we find her, I bet she can lead us to them."

Jan wagged a finger. "That's helpful. At least it's a place to start."

Alex answered the immigration officer's questions, while, at the same time, his mind swirled in a sea of doubt. *What if this is my last chance to rescue Sadie?*

"Sir, I've asked you a question," the officer said.

"I'm sorry, I thinking about someone who got separated from me."

"You shouldn't worry. People wait outside for their families who get separated while on the line."

Alex shook his head. "No, she was in first class, and disembarked at the piers in Manhattan."

"Oh, that could be a problem," the officer said. He then tapped the file on his desk and said, "Now please, Mr. Kaminsky, I have one more question. Do you have a way to make a living in America?"

Alex took a breath and then said, "Yes, I have a friend at Columbia University who says there's a position available. I was a professor at the university in Warsaw."

*

Alex rubbed his eyes, still sore from the doctor gripping each eyelid with a metal tool, and yanking it back to examine for some type of disease. By the time he was done and walked out onto the docks, it was nearly sunset.

He looked around at the dozens of people waiting for the remaining members of their family to make it through, and then hop onboard one of the ferries heading over to Manhattan or to New Jersey. Since there was no sign of Jan or Luis, Alex wandered over to the water's edge and looked across the harbor at the New York City skyline, sparkling due to the sun setting behind him.

Alex sighed. Somewhere upon that imposing island, dwarfed among its vast forest of towering skyscrapers, was Sadie. *But how will I ever find her?*

Using Luis' suggestion, they would search Polly's brothels, and hopefully discover something to lead him to Sadie. But sadly, time was not on his side.

As he sulked, a terrible thought crossed his mind: *Ezra calls Sadie his fiancée; what would happen if they actually married before I got to her?*

CHAPTER EIGHTY-THREE—SADIE'S LAMENT

The garden, enclosed by brick walls on three sides, featured a tulip tree boasting autumn colors of orange, gold, and yellow leaves, and offered shade upon a small table and chairs where Sadie sat and tried to make sense of the last two weeks on board the steamship.

Ezra, usually jovial in public, seemed anxious, and on edge. During conversations, his eyes would nervously dart about, observing the comings and goings of fellow passengers, as if he were expecting one to suddenly approach him.

Meanwhile, Polly sought out her company at every opportunity, seeking to strike up a conversation, as if she wanted to be her girlfriend. But at the back of her mind, Sadie doubted her sincerity, and apparently, her suspicions were right.

During the voyage, Sadie also had to deal with Ezra's unbridled libido. She hoped that her lack of enthusiasm would have tempered his lust, but instead, he climbed on top of her nearly every night.

Several times he repeated his favorite complaint, "You lie there like a dead fish."

Now as she sat in the garden of the *Majestic—dead*, was exactly how she felt inside. But there was still an ember of life glowing within her core—Alex. *But what happened to him? Why didn't he try to see me again? Where is he now?*

During a brief moment, while Ezra was speaking with a customs official, she discreetly asked one of the uniformed men standing nearby, "Where do the steerage passengers disembark?"

He pointed across the river and said, "They continue on by ferry to Ellis Island, before they're allowed into the country."

"Do you mean to say that we're separated from them?" she asked.

"That's correct, miss."

Sadie sighed. *How will he find me now?* she lamented, then noticed a small wooden door encased within the brick wall. She jiggled the handle, but it was locked. She pounded her fist upon it. But even if she could escape, where would she go? She couldn't speak the language, nor did she have any money.

Sadie paced the small patio like a caged lion. She wanted to cry, but there were no more tears left. A squirrel caught her attention, as he ran by her feet and scampered up the tree, hopped onto the top of the brick wall, and disappeared over the other side.

Returning her gaze to the garden, she noticed something tucked behind a small pile of left-over bricks glittering in the morning sun. She bent over and grabbed a pair of garden shears. She gently touched the blades, testing their sharpness. *They have an edge*, she thought.

A cloud passed by and blotted out the sun, pushing Sadie deeper into her sadness. The dark moment caused her to remember the story of a girl she once knew from the neighborhood. Though no one knew for sure, except the girl's parents, if she really took her own life.

Sadie was not friendly with the girl but had seen her at social gatherings from time to time. She noticed that she was shy, withdrawn, and appeared to be troubled.

"She slit her wrists and bled to death in her bathtub," Sara had told her.

That image haunted Sadie for years, and she couldn't imagine how someone could have the ability to take their own life. But there she stood, with the garden shears in her hand, contemplating her life as a sex slave, and suddenly the sin of suicide seemed to be her only escape. *What if Alex can't find me? How long do I have to live like this?*

She stepped off the patio and onto the flower bed, slipped the scissors back where she found them, and walked back inside to the apartment. The question now, that would occupy her mind for days to come: *Would I have the courage to take my own life?*

CHAPTER EIGHTY-FOUR—THE ALGONQUIN

"There's plenty of room for both of you," Luis said, throwing out his arms.

Jan sat on the tufted sofa and put his feet up on the ottoman. "I've never seen a hotel guest room so large."

"Are you sure it's all right for us to stay here?" Alex asked.

Luis flipped his wrist, dismissing Alex. "You're my entourage. All boxers have 'em. That's because of the jerks out there who want to test their skills against the champ. You boys step in and prevent me from knocking them on their asses."

"Sounds dangerous," Jan said with a chuckle.

Alex joined Jan on the sofa and said, "I doubt we'll be here much, except to sleep. I want to spend every minute searching for Sadie."

"Maybe Mr. Jacobs could help. He's the promoter, the guy who sets up the fight. I'm meeting him in the lobby at six for dinner. Why don't you join us?" Luis said.

Alex nodded. "Sure, if you don't mind."

*

"Well, look who it is," shouted a voice from across the hotel lobby. "The *Wild Bull of the Pampas* right here in New York City," said a jovial man, wearing a well-tailored black business suit, and walking toward them, hand outstretched.

329

"It's good to see you, Mr. Jacobs," Luis said, gripping the man's hand.

"And who are these gentlemen?" he asked, taking an extra moment to look at Jan.

"These are my traveling companions. Alex Kaminsky," he said, patting him on his shoulder, "and Jan Mazur."

"Will you be joining us for dinner? There's a great steakhouse a few blocks away," he said, removing his hat and rubbing his hand over his bald head.

"If that's all right with you, Mr. Jacobs," Alex asked.

"Absolutely, I'm sure the maître d' will make arrangements for a larger table, and please—call me Mike."

*

"Are you ready to show the world that the *Wild Bull of the Pampas* can still deliver that devastating right hook?" Mike asked, as the waiter, standing alongside, opened a bottle of wine.

Luis squinted and said, "I thought this was an exhibition fight. You know, nothing serious."

Mike pushed his chair back onto its two rear legs and roared. He then leaned forward, nearly catapulting him into the table, and slapped his palms together, and said, "Of course, I was just joking," as Luis forced a smile.

"I'm sure you'll put on a good show for the fans. You know we've sold out. The Hippodrome may not be Madison Square Garden, but it seats over five-thousand people."

Luis nodded. "I'll do my best, sir."

"I'm sure you will," he said and turned to Alex. "Where're you boys from?"

"Jan and I are from Poland."

"Poland? How did you meet Luis?"

Alex took a quick look around the restaurant, and said, "Maybe this is not the best place to have that discussion."

Mike pursed his lips and nodded. "Of course. After dinner, we can head back to the *Algonquin*. There's a nice spot in the men's smoking room where we could talk."

*

Mike puffed on his cigar, listening to Alex tell his tale.

"That's quite a story," Mike said, dropping chunky ash into the pewter tray on the table next to his leather chair.

"Do you know Polly Adler?" Jan asked.

"*Pfft*," he blurted out. "Every man with a nagging wife knows Polly. But finding your girl won't be so easy. She runs a tight ship."

"Can you tell me where her brothels are?" asked Alex.

"Sure I could. But if Sadie is as special as you say, Polly would place her in the *Majestic* on West Seventy-fifth Street. That's her premier spot and also where she lives. You'll never get her out of there without help."

Alex rubbed his chin and looked over to Jan. "I think we can manage."

"You have no idea who you're dealing with. Polly is connected with the police. Not even that good-for-nothing gangster Dutch Schultz is able to get his greedy paws on it. At least that's what I'm hearing."

Alex shook his head.

"Do you have any suggestions?" asked Luis.

Mike nodded slowly, and said, "Why don't you boys come to the fight tomorrow night, and afterwards, I'll introduce you to someone who might be able to help."

"Thank you, Mike," Alex said, "we'll be there."

"I just need to warn you, he's the meanest son of a bitch you'll ever meet."

Alex shrugged. "You never met Russian General Tukhachevsky."

CHAPTER EIGHTY-FIVE—THE GIRLS

"There's something we need to discuss," Polly said, closing her office door.

"What's that?" Ezra asked.

"You may have gathered by now that the Ashkenazim are my investors. They pay for this extravagance," she said, flicking her hand in the air.

Ezra nodded, and rubbed the back of his neck, while he considered sharing the news of how Mr. Rubenstein offered him a position with the Ashkenazim in exchange for assassinating Rivlin, and then his impulsive blunder of murdering Madam Marguerite, which had caused him to be on the run. *Perhaps now is not the best time*, he thought.

"What I didn't tell you," she continued, "was the reason for my trip."

Ezra held out his hands, expressing for Polly to continue.

"I met with Mr. Rubenstein and explained my need for additional financing to deal with the ongoing threats from Dutch Schultz."

"Dutch Schultz?" he asked, with a shrug.

"Dutch is someone you never want to meet, but I'm afraid you'll have no choice. He, and his low-life associates, are frequent clients of the *Majestic*," Polly said, lighting a cigarette.

"What's the problem?"

Polly took a drag, paused for a moment, and exhaled. "He wants it," she said, gesturing around her.

"What do you mean, he wants it?" Ezra frowned.

"He wants the *Majestic*," she said, with an exasperated sigh.

Ezra listened, not knowing how to reply.

Polly tilted her head. "He's a gangster, like those former friends of yours at the Zwi Migdal. He has no qualms of employing his brand of thuggery to take what he wants, unless of course, he's deterred by a force greater than his gang of goons."

"And who would that be?" Ezra asked, anxious for the answer.

"The police precinct captain, the commissioner, and the mayor. We pay them all. Most of whom are our clients anyway," she said, with a shrug.

"Makes sense. It was the same in Buenos Aires. But what do you want me to do?"

"The funds should have been wired into my Wells Fargo account by now. Once it's confirmed, I'll withdraw certain amounts in cash, and you'll distribute it to this list," she said, handing him a sheet of paper.

Ezra reached for it, and pretended to browse the names, while wondering what Rubenstein would think if he knew it was him responsible for doling out his cash. Either he would be relieved, or more likely, upset that he disappeared without speaking with him first.

"All right, Polly," he said, swallowing hard.

Satisfied, she slapped her palms on her desk and stood up. "Let's introduce Sadie to the girls. I've arranged for breakfast in the dining room."

*

"Come now, Sadie, they're waiting for us," Ezra said, while Sadie fussed with her hair.

She pursed her lips and turned to face Ezra. "All right, let's go," she said with a sharpness to her tone.

Ezra opened the door of their room and gestured with an outstretched arm. Sadie rose to her feet and walked down the hallway.

Unlike the lineup of Jews and Parisians at *The Tango*, the ladies awaiting them were a mix of Irish, German, and Italian descent. Ezra thought of them as attractive enough, but none approached Sadie's exquisite beauty.

Ezra watched Polly's enthusiasm as she presented the *new lady of the Majestic.* The girls wore their casual day clothes, and sat around a large, wooden dining room table, sipping their coffees, splurging on muffins, and barely taking notice of Sadie. *Probably jealous*, Ezra thought.

"And this good-looking gentleman is Mr. Ezra Porkevitch, our new director," Polly said, placing her hand on his shoulder.

"What's a director?" asked a tiny girl, who looked no more than sixteen years old.

"Good question, Irene," Polly said, causing the girl to broadcast a charming smile. "A director is your boss. He's in charge now."

"But what about you, Polly?" she said, with sad eyes. "Are you leaving us?"

"Of course not. This will allow me more time to spend on making sure you girls get what you need, while Mr. Porkevitch will see to the day-to-day operations."

"Oh," Irene said, with a blank stare, obviously not understanding.

"Now, girls," she said, waving her finger, "I want you to welcome Sadie. She doesn't speak any English, so you need to help her out. Be kind to her. You all remember what it was like when you first started."

The girls nodded, though clearly making an effort to show their disinterest by putting extra butter on their already buttered toast or more sugar in their tea.

Polly smiled and was about to step away, when she said, "Oh, I almost forgot. We're expecting Dutch and his *charming* associates tonight. So be on your toes, ladies. Mr. Porkevitch will be here in case you need him."

A collective groan swept over the room, causing Ezra to wonder if he was up to the challenge.

CHAPTER EIGHTY-SIX—THE FIGHT

Alex froze halfway across Sixth Avenue and stared. He had never seen a more extravagant building. Not only was the Hippodrome large; it took up an entire city block, stretching from Forty-third Street to Forty-fourth Street. But it was the design that stirred Alex's imagination. It reminded him of his studies of the ancient Greeks, who gathered to cheer on the charioteers as they raced around the similarly named hippodrome.

"Watch out, Alex," Jan shouted from the sidewalk, "you're going to get run over."

"It's magnificent," he said, running to catch up.

"It is, did you see the marquee?" Jan said, pointing above its grand entrance.

Alex looked up and read:

HEAVYWEIGHT EXHIBITION BOUT
TWO WORLD CHAMPIONS
JACK DEMPSEY
THE MANASSA MAULER
VS
LUIS FIRPO
THE WILD BULL OF THE PAMPAS

"We're guests of Luis Firpo," Alex said to the man in the ticket booth.

After giving their names, Alex and Jan each held a ticket for admission. They pushed their way through the packed lobby, where another uniformed man ripped their tickets in half, allowing them entry into the auditorium.

They found their seats after climbing two flights of stairs up to what was called—the Second Balcony.

"I've never seen anything so grand," said Alex, gawking at the fifty-three hundred seats, now being filled up with spectators.

Jan pointed to the architectural details, the private boxes overlooking the boxing ring on the large stage, and said, "It more like an opera house than a boxing venue."

Alex nodded. "It's elaborate for a sporting event."

They excused themselves as they squeezed past people seated in their row until they found their seats.

"I suppose we should go backstage after the fight," Alex said.

Jan nodded and rubbed his chin. "I hope whoever Mike is introducing us to, can help."

"Me too, unless Dempsey knocks Luis out and no one is in the mood to give us a hand," Alex chuckled.

"It's just an exhibition fight. No one's supposed to get hurt."

Alex shrugged and waved his finger about. "These men are professional fighters. Once they get in the ring, and five-thousand people start cheering them on, who knows what will happen."

*

Twenty minutes later, the house lights dimmed, and the fighters were introduced to the roar of the sold-out house. Luis wore a shiny red robe, with a black silhouette of a bull sewn on its back, while his opponent, Jack Dempsey, wore a nameless, terrycloth white robe.

After the introductions, the fighters huddled in the center of the ring. The referee gave his instructions, Luis held out his gloves, and Jack gently tapped them. Moments later, the bell rang, and the first round commenced.

Even though their seats were several hundred feet from the stage, Alex could hear the furious pounding of punches both fighters inflicted upon each other.

Jan tapped Alex's arm and said, "Either they're terrific actors, or they're taking this seriously."

"I told you," Alex said, keeping his eyes on the action.

According to what Luis told him, the fight should go no more than five rounds. But it was now into the eighth. With each round, the fighter's punches connected with more force and ferocity.

A few seconds into the ninth, a sharp right jab connected with Luis' chin, knocking his head back. The crowd watched in awe as his mouthpiece flew across the ring, followed by an arching spray of his blood.

"Did you see that?" Alex said, rising to his feet and pointing.

The sight of blood ignited the spectators, now shouting for more.

339

Dempsey pounded his fists together and shuffled his feet, expressing his renewed spirit. The referee stepped in front of Luis, as he wiped the blood from his mouth with his boxing glove, and seemed to be asking him if he was all right. Luis nodded, and shoved the ref out of the way, giving the blood-thirsty crowd what they were shouting for.

Like two gladiators, Dempsey and Firpo provided a show worth the price of admission. By the time the final bell rang at the end of the tenth round, both fighters could barely stand. While Luis never hit the canvas for a ten-count, it was clear who was the better fighter.

As the photographers and newspaper men mobbed the ring, Alex and Jan made their way down from their perch. By the time they arrived, the die-hard fans were crammed against the ring, as the two men, their gloves removed, were signing autographs and posing for photos.

"He looks like he's ready to collapse," Jan said, pointing to Luis.

Alex put his hand on Jan's shoulder. "Let's try to talk to him."

Just as they began to push their way closer to the ring, a commotion diverted everyone's attention. A man was climbing into the ring shouting, "You're no wild bull, Firpo, the only bull you are is bullshit!"

Luis, still glistening in sweat, walked over to the man, dressed in a fine-looking business suit, and said, "Who the fuck are you?"

"I'm Mad Dog Coll, and I just lost five-hundred bucks on you piece of shit," he said.

Mike Jacobs, the fight promoter, stepped in between. "Come on, Mad Dog, this was an exhibition fight, no wages were taken."

Alex's eyes were glued upon the short man with blood-thirsty eyes, wondering if he was going to pull a gun. Then all of a sudden, like a storm cloud pushed aside from a gust of wind, allowing the sun to shine its warmth upon the earth, Mad Dog laughed, and said, "I was joking. It was a great fight. Thank you, Luis."

Alex exhaled.

Luis shook hands with Mad Dog. They exchanged a few words, and Luis looked out beyond the ring and spotted Alex and Jan. He gestured toward the backstage entrance, an indication that they should follow him into the dressing room.

Once inside, Mike Jacobs said, "Mad Dog, I would like to introduce to you, Alex Kaminsky and Jan Mazur. These are the men I told you who need a favor getting a girl out of the *Majestic*."

"Is she your girl?" Mad Dog asked, cocking his chin at Alex.

Alex nodded.

He looked back at Mike and said, "You know Dutch has his grubby hands on the place, and word is, Polly has sought financial help from the Jews in Argentina. It won't be easy."

"If it was easy, Mad Dog, these gentlemen wouldn't be here asking for help."

He held up his hands. "It's not a problem. I can get your girl, but what can you do for me in return?"

Alex had already contemplated this question and had no qualms selling his soul for Sadie's wellbeing, and from what he was told, Mad

Dog would be the closest thing to the devil he would ever meet. He took a breath, and said, "Whatever you need done."

Mad Dog smiled. "Excellent!" he said and shook Alex's hand.

Alex glanced over to Jan, whose eyes expressed his concern about the potentially dangerous deal that he had made, and Alex hoped he wouldn't regret it.

CHAPTER EIGHTY-SEVEN—DUTCH SCHULTZ

Sadie quickly learned that the *Majestic* was nothing like *The Tango*. There were no such things as *member names*, such as Mr. Rivlin's *Ignacio*, nor did the one-member-per-night rule exist. According to what Sadie was told by a German-speaking redhead, "We work all night, and into the wee hours of the morning, and what's worse, sometimes we might do three guys in a night."

Moments before the *Majestic* opened for the evening, all twelve ladies, including Sadie, stood side-by-side in what Polly called—*the lineup*.

"A man will walk the line," Polly said to Sadie in Yiddish, imitating a client, "and examines each girl, until he lands on the one who turns him on, and if it's you," she stopped, pointing at Sadie, "he'll take you upstairs."

Sadie swallowed hard.

"Make sure you smile and don't get flustered if he suddenly grabs your ass or demands a kiss."

Kissing also wasn't allowed at *The Tango*, and she wondered if the men were required to wear sheaths, though she was beginning to doubt it.

The ladies chatted among themselves, waiting for the first customers to walk in. The German redhead, probably feeling sorry for Sadie, asked her, "Where're you from?"

Sadie tried to smile. "I'm from Poland."

"Is that where you got your dress? It's beautiful."

"Oh, thank you. But no, I got this in Buenos Aires."

The redhead offered a clumsy smile, hinting that she did not understand. As Sadie was about to explain, a ruckus by the front entrance halted their conversation.

"That's probably Dutch and his boys," muttered the redhead.

Sure enough, a man dressed in a finely-tailored suit that looked like the silk ones on display at *Stillman's* sauntered in. He sported several oversized gold rings, and an equally impressive gold watch. Following in his footsteps were three men, also wearing expensive clothing and jewelry, along with fancy suede hats.

"Good evening, ladies," Dutch said, eyeing the ladies.

"Good evening, Dutch," replied several of them, along with a smile that offered a glimpse into their mortal fear of the man.

"Dutch, allow me to introduce to you our new girl," Polly said, hustling over. "This lovely lady is Sadie. She's from Poland and doesn't speak English, so if you—"

"It doesn't matter," he said, interrupting Polly. "Love is a universal language."

Sadie took a step back at the aggressive tone of his words. She didn't need to understand them to get their meaning; plus, he smelled like he had bathed in a tub of whiskey.

Dutch reached out and grabbed Sadie's wrist and yanked her hard. The force forward caused her to trip on an edge of the Persian carpet and fall to her knees.

"Get up," Dutch shouted, his eyes bugging out.

"There's no need for that," Polly scolded and bent over to help Sadie.

"I'll decide what's needed," Dutch said and elbowed Polly out of the way, causing her to tumble into a table, knocking over a ceramic oriental vase that crashed onto the marble floor.

"Just one moment," came Ezra's voice, as he suddenly appeared. "What's going on here?"

"Who the hell are you?" Dutch said with a growl.

"Ezra Porkevitch," he said, offering his hand. "I'm the new director of the *Majestic*. What seems to be the problem?"

"There's no problem, Director. Now get the fuck out of my way. I'm taking this one," he said, squeezing Sadie by her neck, and pushing her toward the stairs, causing her to stumble, before she grasped the handrail.

"Hold on now. There will be no roughhousing here," Ezra insisted.

Dutch released Sadie and confronted Ezra. "Who the fuck are you to tell me what to do?"

Ezra shrugged. "I already told you, sir, I'm the director of the *Majestic*."

"Is that so?"

Ezra smiled and nodded.

Just as Sadie was about to tell Ezra not to interfere, Dutch gave him a swift punch to his gut, causing Ezra to double over.

"Please, Dutch, don't," shouted Polly, running over and standing in between the two men.

"Fuck off, Polly," he said, pushing her out of the way, and delivering a solid punch to the side of Ezra's jaw.

Ezra held up his hands, unable to defend himself. "Stop," he pleaded.

But Dutch didn't stop. He continued his assault, while his men cheered him on. Soon Ezra was on the floor, curled up in a ball, trying to protect himself from Dutch's sharp kicks.

Sadie screamed in Yiddish for him to stop.

Dutch put his hands on hips and stared at Ezra lying on the floor, with blood trickling out the side of his mouth. Covered in sweat and breathing hard, he grabbed Sadie. "Let's go now," he said and dragged her upstairs.

"Sadie!" Ezra cried out, pushing himself off the floor.

She turned to him. He no longer looked like the same man who had taken control of her life. The beating had drained his power. Hopefully, its cost would only be a few hideous minutes with Dutch, which would be well worth the price of seeing Ezra get his due.

As she looked away, Ezra said, "Sadie, I'm sorry, please forgive me."

CHAPTER EIGHTY-EIGHT—POLICE PROTECTION

With his arms folded across his chest, Alex leaned against Mad Dog's black Ford Model A Touring Sedan and looked across the street.

"I hate to say it," Mad Dog said, "but there's no way I can get your girl out of there now."

"I don't understand," Alex said, looking at two men standing in front of the entrance to the *Majestic*. "Are you telling me that you're afraid of those two men?"

Mad Dog pushed his face inches from Alex's and snarled, "I ain't afraid of nothin'. But I'm no dummy either. Those suits are NYPD. Polly got herself police protection after that visit from Dutch and his boys two days ago. Apparently, they tore the place up. I hear some of the whores were badly beaten."

"Beaten?" Alex said, worried that Sadie could have been hurt. "But why would the police protect her? She runs an illegal business."

"What does that matter when you pay off the right people?"

Alex furrowed his brow. "She would need deep pockets for this kind of protection."

"Maybe that's why she traveled to Buenos Aires," Jan suggested.

Alex pursed his lips and nodded.

"I'm sorry I couldn't help out," Mad Dog said, patting Alex on his shoulder.

"That's all right," Alex said. "By the way, what was the favor you were going to ask me if you did get Sadie out of there?"

"Oh, right," Mad Dog said with a chuckle. "I wanted you to take out that swine, Dutch Schultz. But, as I thought about it, why should I give you the pleasure?"

Alex snickered. "I wouldn't want to deprive you."

"Why do you hate him so much?" asked Jan.

"I used to be part of Dutch's gang. But that fucker had the balls to pay his men a flat salary, like we had a *job* or something. I told him that's not how things work. We're supposed to get a cut in the action, you know—a percentage."

Alex and Jan both nodded.

"I was bringing in over half the revenue. I did everything for that man. One time, there was this guy, an owner of a speakeasy who refused to sell our bootleg, so I killed him. The charges were dropped, which Dutch said I should have thanked him for. He was annoyed with me for causing *an unnecessary distraction*. After that, our relationship began to sour.

"A year later, me and a few of the boys robbed a dairy in the Bronx, and Dutch wouldn't give me my cut. That's when I demanded to be an equal partner, but he refused, so I left and formed my own gang. A few weeks later a shooting war started between our gangs and last May, my brother Pete was gunned down while up in Harlem," he said and paused a moment. "I went into a rage and over the next few weeks, I hunted down and killed four of Dutch's men. Then they retaliated; you know how it goes. By the time it settled down, over twenty men on both sides were gunned down."

"Why are you telling us this?" Alex said, thinking it was strange to hear this man's confession.

"I don't know." He shrugged. "Maybe it's because I like you. I never spoke of it before to anyone outside the gang."

Alex nodded, not knowing how to respond.

"After that, I got into kidnapping my rivals and demanding ransom. No one would report me to the police, because you know, we're all trying to go unnoticed. It was a good racket for a while, until we tried to grab one of Dutch's guys who was lounging outside a social club up in the Bronx. There was a shootout on the street and a five-year-old boy was killed."

"That's terrible," Alex said.

Mad Dog nodded. "By the way, my real name is Vincent Coll. But after that night, the press gave me a new name—*Mad Dog*, and it stuck."

Jan reached out and squeezed Mad Dog's forearm, and said, "I'm sorry about your brother."

"Thank you, Jan," he said and looked across the street. "I wish there was a way I could help you boys."

"That's okay. It's better we take care of it," Alex said. "But we need to get inside tonight. Sadie could be hurt."

"We can pretend we're customers," Jan said. "That would at least get us in the front door."

Alex gnawed at his knuckles and nodded slowly. "We can cause a diversion. Maybe an explosion," he said, lifting his brow. "I'll need to find Sadie first, this way we can escape while everyone is attending to the chaos."

"And where are we supposed to find explosives?" Jan asked.

"Explosives?" Mad Dog said with a smile. "Maybe I can help after all."

CHAPTER EIGHTY-NINE—THE COWARD

Once Dutch and his gang of hoodlums finally left, Ezra hobbled over to the door and locked it. He exhaled with a groan and clutched his side. He feared that besides the bruise on his leg, the kicks he endured from Dutch also cracked a rib or two.

He didn't need to look at his pocket watch to know that it was several hours past midnight. Ezra limped over to the stairs and clutched onto the railing.

"Sadie's already back in her room," said Polly, walking down the corridor toward him.

"Are you all right?"

Polly nodded. "I'm fine, but those animals hurt two of the girls. Nothing broken, thank goodness, they're battered and bruised. They'll heal in a few weeks," she said dryly.

"What about Sadie? Is she okay?"

Polly nodded. "Yes, she's fine, just sore. Dutch, as you now know, is not a gentle man."

"That's for sure," he said. "I better go and check on her."

"One second, Ezra," Polly said, now standing alongside him. "You seem to have disappeared after Dutch knocked you around."

Ezra pursed his lips. "What do you mean? I was here. Maybe I went to my room for a while, you know, to attend to my ribs. It hurts when I breathe."

"Is that so?" Polly said, crossing her arms. "Then why did I just see you come out from the basement door? Were you hiding down there?"

Ezra held out his arms. "What did you expect me to do? There were four of them."

Polly shook her head. "I didn't expect you to cower in fear. Your actions speak poorly of your character. You can pack your bags and leave as soon as it's light."

Ezra took a breath, grimaced, and said, "If that's what you want, Polly. I'll go and tell Sadie."

"Oh no, Ezra, just you. Sadie stays. She's who I wanted in the first place. I thought I might be able to find a place for you here, but after your performance here tonight, I don't think it's going to work."

"You can't just throw me out. Where am I supposed to go?" Ezra pleaded.

Polly shrugged. "If I were you, I go back to Buenos Aires, and get your old job back with the Zwi," she said, stepping around Ezra and bounding up the stairs.

He watched Polly disappear and sighed. One thing he knew for sure, he wasn't leaving without Sadie.

When he got to his room, Sadie was lying in the bathtub, her head laid back, and her eyes closed.

"Are you asleep?" Ezra asked softly.

She opened one eye and said, "Leave me alone."

Ezra thought she looked pale. Her cheeks were sunken, her hair wet and matted. While her physical beauty was still evident, whatever vibrancy she possessed on the inside had vanished.

"I want to tell you that when you're done with your bath, you need to pack your things. We're leaving. Polly is throwing us out."

Sadie opened both eyes this time. "Is that so?" she said.

Ezra nodded. "Please hurry. I want to get out of here as soon as possible."

Sadie closed her eyes and said, "I'm not going anywhere with you."

"What do you mean?" he said, full-throated. "You have to, Polly said."

Sadie smiled. "No, Ezra, she didn't. While you were hiding in the basement like a little boy, Polly said that you would be leaving without me."

Ezra stood, speechless.

"Now, if you don't mind. I would like my privacy."

"Are you sure, Sadie? You'll be all alone."

Sadie laughed. "I've been alone since that first day you ripped me from my home and life in Warsaw," she said, taking the washcloth, folding it, and placing it over her eyes.

CHAPTER NINETY—SOOTHING THE BEAST

Sadie waited until she heard the door close, before lifting herself from the bathtub. *Is he finally gone?*

After many months, and thousands of miles, Ezra Porkevitch was out of her life. She patted herself dry with a large white towel and slipped on the bathrobe. *Maybe it won't be so bad,* Sadie considered, with a sigh.

She certainly had the comforts of her own private bedroom, luxurious bathroom with a bathtub, and a private outdoor patio garden, while the other girls were crammed into small rooms, and shared a communal bathroom.

Sadie sat by the vanity table, looking at her reflection. Her *Eton Crop* hairdo had lost its style. *I need a haircut, or maybe I should let it grow out? Perhaps Polly will have an opinion.*

She sighed, wondering if the *Majestic* would end up becoming her home. *What would Father and Mother think of their shaina-maidel now?* But to be fair, she couldn't believe it herself that she was now living the scandalous life of a *Polaca*.

She shook her head, and thought, *Could it be that my God-given beauty has been more a curse than a blessing?* Nevertheless, she would need to make the best of her circumstances. At least Polly seemed to be supportive of her, especially after last night's fiasco. "If you could take care of Dutch, you could handle anyone," Polly told her.

While Sadie fussed with her hair, she recalled what happened.

Once Dutch finished pummeling Ezra, he dragged Sadie up the stairs to the guest rooms. Sadie knew that unless she took control, she would not only get a beating, but be viciously raped as well.

Dutch tossed her into the room like a ragdoll and slammed the door. Sadie fell hard to the floor and looked up at him. His cheeks were blood-red, his huge nostrils flared out, reminding Sadie of a bull ready to charge.

Without the ability to speak a language he understood, Sadie rose to her feet and took a breath to compose herself. Dutch stared at her, his eyes pulsing like a beating heart. Sadie smiled as she cautiously approached. She reached out and took his hand and gently tugged, bringing him over to the bed.

She undid the buttons on his sweat-soaked shirt, and removed it, nearly gagging at the sudden waft of his sour body odor, but kept her poise and continued. She undid his belt and gestured for him to stand, while she removed his pants.

While his temper had soothed, his loins had not. While sitting on the edge of the bed, she reached out and trying not to cringe, touched his erection. He closed his eyes and moaned. Sadie realized, unlike her previous encounters at *The Tango*, she might not escape from this one unscathed.

While continuing to fondle him, she looked in vain to the bedside table, hoping to see a small box or container, like the one Madam

Marguerite kept for the sheaths. *Would he let me put it on him?* she worried. Then she remembered what the French girl Dominique had told her when she first arrived at *The Tango*.

"You must learn how to *tailler une pipe,* which means how to give a blow job. I will teach you."

While Sadie never had that lesson from Dominique, she thought about it while looking at Dutch's uncircumcised, engorged penis, rising from a rough thicket of black pubic hairs. She leaned in close and was greeted by a wretched smell.

Sadie realized afterwards that it probably wasn't more than a minute or two that it took for Dutch to climax, though it felt much longer. She was surprised that he didn't collapse on the bed and pass out. Luckily, instead, he was able to pull up his pants, stumble from the room, and make it downstairs and out onto the street with his gang.

When she got back to her room, she gargled with mouthwash that was sitting on a shelf in the bathroom, over and over, hoping to remove that bitter taste. But it lingered.

After her bath, and Ezra's departure, she stepped out into the garden. The sun was rising, and a soft glow washed across the tops of the brick wall, where a few pigeons perched, soaking in its warmth.

The sight of the birds stirred Sadie's memory of her first date with Alex in Saxon Gardens. She chuckled, thinking back on how they desperately tried to clean the pigeon poop off from Alex's jacket. But quickly sighed, as her fond reminder soured to guilt, worried that Alex may still be out there, searching for her.

How could I give up on him? she thought, as her tears swelled. She sat down on the metal garden chair and listened to the pigeons cooing. Sadie could no longer hold back her tears. *But even if Alex did find me, why would he want me now? I'm no longer that innocent, chaste girl, admiring him from the front row of his history class at the university.*

CHAPTER NINETY-ONE—THE REUNION

"How do I look?" Jan asked, running his palm down along the jacket, smoothing out the creases.

"You both look good, now that you bathed and shaved," Mad Dog said with a chuckle.

Alex straightened his tie and patted Mad Dog on his back. "Thank you. We would have never had a chance of getting into the *Majestic* without these suits."

"Here, Jan, hide this in the inside pocket," Mad Dog said, handing him a stick of dynamite.

"We're going to owe you big time for this," Alex says.

Mad Dog smiled, his eyes twinkling in the late afternoon sunlight streaming through his apartment window. "Not to worry, my friend. If things work out as I'm expecting, I'll soon have a share of the *Majestic*."

Alex jerked his head back. "What do you mean?"

Mad Dog shrugged. "I'm going in with you, and have a little *come-to-Jesus-moment* talk with Polly. She can't afford police protection forever, and after your little commotion, I'm sure to convince her that I can offer a more reasonable solution."

"All right," Alex said with a nod. "Just make sure Jan and I make our escape with Sadie."

Mad Dog squinted, and said, "You do your part, and I'll do mine, and I'll see you on the other side."

*

"Good day," Mad Dog said to the two undercover policemen standing guard in front of the *Majestic*.

Both men instantly closed ranks, blocking the entrance. "How can we help you gentlemen?" one of the square-jawed men said.

Mad Dog held out his palm, and plainly visible was a folded up ten-dollar bill. The man looked down, noticed it, and shook Mad Dog's hand.

"We're here for the ladies, gentlemen," Mad Dog said, making the exchange of the bribe.

The man nodded and said, "One moment please."

Two minutes later, Alex, Jan, and Mad Dog were inside the vestibule being greeted by the madam.

"Welcome to the *Majestic*, gentlemen, my name is Madam Polly, would you please follow me."

Alex glanced over to Jan and rolled his eyes. They stepped into a large salon, featuring exquisite architectural elements and wood-carved furniture. Alex also noticed that none of the ladies were present, *probably waiting to be summoned after we pay*, he presumed, as they followed the madam into her office.

The madam sat behind her desk and took a moment to observe the three men. "Aren't you Mad Dog?" she said, pointing.

"I am," he said, obviously pleased to be recognized, "and these are my good friends, Alex and Jan. They've just immigrated from Poland, and I want to show them some of the finer things New York City has to offer."

"Poland?" Polly said and paused. "I have a Polish girl here, very pretty," she said with playful eyes.

"What do you think?" Mad Dog said, putting his arm around Alex. "A little taste of home?"

Alex offered Polly a polite smile, and said, "That sounds good."

"And what about your albino friend? What's your fancy?"

"Oh, I'm married. I'll just sit and wait."

Polly scoffed. "That's never stopped anyone before. But suit yourself."

"I'll pick someone out there," Mad Dog said, flipping his hand as though brushing her comment aside.

"Whatever makes you happy. All you need to know is that we have the most beautiful ladies in all the city."

"That's what I heard," Mad Dog said, handing Polly a wad of cash.

Madam Polly counted the bills, dropped it through the slot of a safe box bolted to the floor, and reached behind her to press a button on the wall. "Gentlemen, let's go meet the ladies of the *Majestic*."

Here we go, thought Alex, following the madam into the salon. She swept her arm to the comfortable-looking furniture adorning the well-appointed room. "Please, make yourself comfortable, the ladies will be here momentarily."

Mad Dog and Jan sat on the green velour sofa, while Alex stood and paced the floor.

"Settle down, Alex," Jan whispered.

Alex held up his palm, nodded, and took a deep breath. But his stillness was short-lived upon hearing the sound of women's shoes clicking upon the wooden floor above. Jan and Mad Dog rose and stood beside Alex, as the parade of ladies descended the staircase in single file.

Alex stared intensely at each of the ten women, who, as they reached the salon, stood in a line-up for their perusal. But alas, Sadie was not among them. He looked over to Jan, who gave a subtle shrug.

Just as he thought, *where's Sadie?* He heard footsteps coming down the stairs. Alex turned and saw her. It took Sadie until she got halfway down to realize that it was Alex at the bottom of the staircase waiting for her. She froze, her mouth hung open, before regaining her composure and proceeding.

"This is the Polish girl I told you about," Polly said.

As Sadie continued down the staircase, Alex sensed pain in her movements. He wondered if she too was one of the girls that Dutch and his gang beat up the other night. Regardless, his eyes were locked onto hers and he felt his heart pounding hard against his chest.

"Yes, I want her," he said in Polish.

Sadie stood before him and offered a smile, but said nothing.

"Did you forget your native tongue, my dear?" Polly asked.

"Sorry," Sadie said in Polish. "Welcome to the *Majestic*."

"Does she please you, Alex? Or would you prefer someone else?"

"She pleases me very much."

"Well then, go ahead, Sadie, take your compatriot upstairs."

CHAPTER NINETY-TWO—SHOWDOWN

Sadie pushed Alex into the room, closed the door, wrapped her arms around his neck, and kissed him.

Alex pulled away first and said, "We must hurry."

"What do you mean?"

"There's no time to explain. In a few minutes, we'll hear an explosion—that will be our cue to make a run for the front door. There's a car with a driver waiting on the street," he said pointing, "ready to take us to a safe place."

Sadie held up her hands. "An explosion? Will people get hurt?"

"It's a small stick of dynamite. Just enough to cause a distraction."

"Oh, Alex," she said, leaning her head on his shoulder, "I never thought you would find me."

"I told you, I would never give up," he said, stroking her hair.

She squeezed him tightly. "I love you," she said and pulled back to look at him.

"I love you too," Alex said, wiping the tears from Sadie's cheeks.

Then it came. A muffled blast that shook the room, releasing streaming tails of dust from behind the wood trim in the coffered ceiling, followed by a brief moment of perfect silence.

"Come, let's go," Alex said, taking Sadie's hand.

They ran toward the stairs and stopped.

"Oh my god," Sadie shouted, pointing to where the front entrance used to be.

Ceiling beams had collapsed, bringing down enough plaster and debris to block their escape.

"Is there another way out?" Alex asked.

"Yes, through the garden, follow me," Sadie said, running down the stairs. "This way." She pointed toward her bedroom.

"Wait a second, Sadie," Alex said. "I need to find Jan."

"Jan is here?"

"Yes, he's the one who set off the explosive," Alex said, searching the salon. "Jan," he shouted.

"Jan," Sadie yelled.

After a minute of frantic searching, Sadie said, "There's no one here."

"Maybe he got out," Alex said. "Come, show me the way."

They ran down the hall, into Sadie's room, and out into the garden.

"This door leads to an alleyway and out onto the street, but it's locked," Sadie said, breathing hard.

"I'll kick it open," Alex said, taking a few steps back for a running start.

Sadie suddenly saw Ezra lurking behind the swung-open door leading to the bedroom, holding a brick in his hand.

"Ezra, don't!" she shouted, as he smacked it down hard onto the back of Alex's head, knocking him to the ground.

"Alex!" Sadie screamed and rushed to him, helping him get to his feet.

"Out of my way," Ezra roared, knocking Sadie aside, and tackling Alex to the ground. "I'm going to get rid of you once and for all."

Sadie desperately looked for something to stop Ezra with. He had Alex pinned to the patio, and he reached for the brick, holding it high. Just as was about to strike, Sadie grabbed the garden shears, tucked behind the pile of bricks, and in one swift motion, swung them hard, burying them deep into the side of Ezra's neck. The brick fell harmlessly from his hand, and he stared at Sadie for a moment, with the scissors' handle sticking out of his neck.

Sadie swallowed hard, just as Ezra grabbed the handle and pulled it out, releasing a streaming fountain of blood arcing into the air and splattering onto the patio.

Still sitting on top of Alex, where moments before, he was about to deliver the death blow, he looked at Sadie with wide eyes, his life fading fast, and said, "I love you, Sadie."

Sadie scoffed at the remark, lifted her foot, and kicked him hard in the chest. Limp, he fell off Alex; his last breath extinguished before hitting the ground.

"Are you all right?" Sadie said, dropping to her knees, attending to Alex.

Alex pushed himself up onto his elbows and touched the back of his head. "He hit me pretty good," he said, looking at his blood smeared upon his hand.

"One second," Sadie said, "I'll get a towel from the bathroom."

When she returned, Jan was standing alongside Alex.

"Jan, where did you come from?" Sadie asked.

"Down the alleyway, and through here," Jan said, pointing to the open door. "Come now, we need to get out of here."

Sadie gave Alex the wet towel, he held it to the back of his head, and the three of them ran to the street and to the waiting motorcar.

CHAPTER NINETY-THREE—FAREWELL TO VINCENT

"Quick—get in," Mad Dog said, holding open the car door.

Sadie slid along in first, followed by Alex, then Jan. The door slammed shut, and Mad Dog jumped into the front seat. "Let's go, Patrick," he said to his driver.

"Where to, boss?"

"The place on Orchard," Mad Dog said, turning his head to look at the police cars, and fire trucks pulling up in front of the *Majestic*.

"What the hell happened?" Alex asked. "You said it would be a small explosion. It nearly took the entire building down. Did anyone get hurt?"

Mad Dog laughed. "Polly and the girls are fine, and you got what you wanted, didn't you?" he said, jerking his thumb at Sadie.

Alex clutched Sadie's hand and said, "Yes, I did."

"Good, and so did I. Before Jan set off the explosive, I told Polly what was going to happen and that she only had a few minutes to get her girls to safety into the basement. Once we were all there, she asked why was I helping her. I said that you two were sent by the Zwi Migdal who heard about her side-deal with Rubenstein and were there to send her a message."

Jan shook his head. "Why would you tell her that?"

"To prove that she can't trust the police to protect her. Once the bomb went off, she agreed to my offer of a twenty percent partnership, along with financing to rebuild."

"You are the clever one," Alex said.

"Thank you," Mad Dog said and turned to look at Sadie. "You were right about her, she's a knockout."

Sadie sighed and asked, "Where're we going?"

"I have an apartment down in the Lower East Side where you can stay until things settle down. Plus, it will give you time to find your own place."

"That's good of you, Mad Dog," Alex said, "but I have no money to pay you."

Mad Dog smiled. "That's all right. The cash I'll make off the *Majestic* will cover it. Plus, it makes me feel good to do something nice for a change. I'm not always a *mad dog*."

*

Standing on the sidewalk, looking up at the dilapidated tenement building, Mad Dog said, "This is it—125 Orchard Street." He handed Alex a brass key tied to a round piece of wood with 8C painted upon it. "It's not the most spacious place, especially for the three of you. But I'm sure you'll make do. Stay as long as you need to."

"I won't be here long," Jan said. "I'll be heading back home to Warsaw on the next ship heading to Europe."

"What are you talking about, Jan?" Alex asked, surprised.

"You two deserve a life together," Jan said with a warm smile. "I'll just be a third wheel."

"Nonsense, Jan," Sadie said, reaching for his hand. "You'll always be a part of us. Don't leave."

Mad Dog opened the door to his motorcar and pointed. "I think the three of you can figure things out. Right now, I need to get my construction crew into the *Majestic* so Polly can get back into business as soon as possible," Mad Dog said. "Farewell, my friends."

"You were right. You're not always a mad dog. Goodbye, Vincent," Alex said.

Mad Dog smiled and nodded. "Goodbye, Alex, and good luck to all of you," he said, got into the motorcar, and drove off.

"I don't know about you, but I'm starving," Alex said.

"There's a place across the street," Sadie said, pointing, "*Russ and Daughters*. Let's give it a try."

CHAPTER NINETY-FOUR—MOSHE'S MARKET

"Jan, Sadie and I are taking a walk. Should we bring you back something?"

Jan rolled over and held his hand out to block the morning sun streaming in through the window from his eyes. "No, I'm all right, thanks."

Sadie and Alex walked hand in hand along Delancey Street, looking at the variety of street vendors offering an array of fruits and vegetables, pickles, pretzels, and household items.

"I'm going to take the train up to Columbia today and see if I can find my friend Stanley. If I can get a position as a professor at the university, we'll be set. The only problem is that the semester already started. I would need to wait until January. I'll need to find a job in the meantime."

"I can get a job too," Sadie said, admiring the colorful display of fruits and vegetables laid out in baskets under a large banner that said, MOSHE'S FRUIT & VEGETABLE MARKET.

"No, Sadie, I want you to stay home and take care of our children."

Sadie pointed to an empty bench. "We need to talk, Alex. Can we sit down for a few minutes?"

"Just one second," Alex said and picked two red apples. He handed the man wearing an apron two nickels.

"Are you going to eat those now?" asked the man.

Alex nodded.

The man beckoned for him to give them back. Alex handed over the apples.

"Let me polish them up for you," he said, taking a cloth and expertly rubbing the apples until they shone. "Now that looks good enough to eat."

Alex took them back. "Thank you, sir. Are you Moshe?" he asked, pointing to the sign.

"At your service. Please tell me who you are, and who your lovely lady friend is?"

"My name is Alex, and this is Sadie. We're from Poland."

Moshe tapped his chest. "Me too, I'm also from Poland. Are you by any chance looking for a job? I can't pay much, but you can take home anything that's not sold at the end of the day."

Alex looked over to Sadie. "Maybe for a little while. I'm hoping for a position as a professor at Columbia."

"Ah, an intellectual. That's good," Moshe said, offering a big smile to match his rotund shape. "You think about it, and let me know."

"I will, thank you, Moshe," Alex said, and sat down on the bench next to Sadie, handing her an apple.

Sadie crossed her legs and sighed. "Are you sure you want to marry me?"

Alex blinked and shook his head. "Of course I do. Why are you asking me this?"

She grabbed Alex's hand and caressed it in between hers. "I've been with other men."

Alex stared at her for a moment. "Do you mean Ezra?"

Sadie nodded. "And three others, though none of them were inside me," she said, furrowing her brow.

"Okay, Sadie. I thought it would have been worse."

"Worse?" she said, shocked at his reply. "It was awful and degrading."

"Oh, I didn't mean it like that," Alex said, shaking his head. "I just meant, that um . . ."

"Alex, I need to know that you understand that I was a victim of sexual assault. None of it was consensual. You might think you're okay with it now, but years down the road, you might become resentful and use it against me. I also may have some profound trauma to deal with that might turn ugly. I don't want you to regret making the wrong decision."

"Oh my god, no, Sadie. How can this be wrong? I want to marry you because I love you. What's happened is proof that we would both fight for one another. That no obstacle is too big to prevent us from being husband and wife."

Sadie smiled. "I agree," she said and kissed Alex.

"So," Alex said, jerking his head toward the fruit and vegetable stand, "what do you think of me getting a job at Moshe's Market, at least temporarily? Moshe just asked if I'm interested."

Sadie shrugged. "We have to eat, don't we?"

CHAPTER NINETY-FIVE—BON VOYAGE, JAN

"Are you going to be all right? You don't look so good," Alex said, squeezing Jan's shoulder.

"I'll be fine. There will be plenty of time on the ship to catch up on my sleep," he said, looking at the passengers boarding the SS *Amerika.*

"We did get a little carried away," Alex confessed with a sly smile.

Jan rubbed his forehead. "It's true I had too much to drink last night. But, after all, it was your wedding," he said with a shrug. "How often do we celebrate such an event?"

"I'm happy you were able to be by my side as my best man last night. It meant the world to me."

Jan patted away a tear escaping with the back of a finger and said, "I wish you and Sadie nothing but happiness and lots of children. Both of you deserve it."

Alex pointed to a wooden bench and said, "Come sit with me for a few minutes."

Jan nodded.

"Do you think we'll ever see each other again?" Alex asked solemnly.

Jan leaned forward, resting his elbows upon his knees, and said, "What I've learned is that one never knows what the future holds. But I hope so. I'm going to miss you. We've been through quite a bit in our lives."

Alex felt a rush of tears bubbling up from deep within him, and when he looked at Jan, he couldn't hold them back. He heaved uncontrollably. To steady himself, he wrapped his arms around his friend and said in between his sobs, "I could never have found Sadie without you by my side. I owe everything to you."

"That's not how I look at it," Jan said, holding onto Alex.

"What do you mean?" Alex asked, pulling away.

"Without you, I would never have had the confidence to be the person I am today. It's because of you I've had the courage to face the world."

Alex shook his head. "I don't understand. I thought it was because of the story your grandfather told you when we were kids."

Jan shrugged. "That had something to do with it. But without you by side, especially in the war, I would have never amounted to much. You have been my rock, Alex," he said with tears now rolling down his cheeks.

"Look at us, two war heroes, crying like babies," Alex said with a broad smile.

Jan took a deep breath and stood up. As Alex joined him, he put both hands upon his shoulders and said, "Well, my friend, I guess this is it. I want you to know, my brother, that I love you, and no matter if an ocean separates us, if you are ever in need, you let me know and I'll be there."

Alex nodded. "Of course, brother, and that goes for me as well. Bon voyage, Jan."

CHAPTER NINETY-SIX—ONE YEAR LATER

"Look, Nathan, there's Daddy," Sadie said, waving and pushing the stroller through the crowded plaza backdropped by the Romanesque library building of Columbia University.

Alex, speaking to a few students huddled around him, saw Sadie, and waved back. He excused himself and trotted over. "How's my little boy today?" he said, leaning over to look at his son.

"He's good," Sadie said.

"Are you just out taking a walk, or do you need to see me? I have another class in a few minutes."

Sadie shrugged and shook her head.

Alex squinted. "What's wrong, Sadie," he said with concern.

"Nothing's wrong. I just got this letter from my parents," she said, pulling out an envelope from her pocketbook.

Alex took it and looked at the address. "How did they know where we live?"

Sadie smiled and said, "That's because I wrote them a letter two months ago after Nathan was born."

Alex raised his eyebrows and said, "You did? Why didn't you tell me?"

"I know, I shouldn't have. But I wanted to let them know I was all right, and that we had Nathan. I sent a photo."

"That's okay, Sadie. But what's in the letter?" Alex said, tapping the envelope against his palm.

Sadie took a breath and exhaled. "Well," she paused, "it looks like they're coming to America."

"Is that so?" he said, raising his eyebrows. "When shall we be expecting them?"

Sadie stared at Alex for a moment, then said, "Tomorrow. They're arriving tomorrow."

"Tomorrow?" Alex said, opening his eyes wide.

Sadie bit her lip, nodded, and added, "There's one more thing."

Alex squinted and said, "What's that?"

"They've asked to stay with us."

Alex took a breath. "You know the last time I saw your father he said, that if I was able to find you and brought you home, he would never allow me to marry you, never. Now he wants to stay with us?"

Sadie nodded.

"For how long?"

"Forever," Sadie said with a shrug. "They're immigrating here."

*

Sadie waited among the burgeoning crowd of people, motorcars, and taxis by Pier 60, for the first-class passengers from the SS *Amerika* steamship to disembark. It didn't take long before she heard her father's unmistakable baritone voice barking orders to a porter.

Sadie stood up on her tiptoes, trying to peek over and around the crowd pushing its way to the curb where she waited for her parents.

"Father, Mother," Sadie shouted and waved her arms when she saw them approaching.

Her mother waved back enthusiastically, while her father smiled and nodded.

Sadie exhaled, allowing the pent-up resentment and hatred that had coursed through her veins like a virus for the past eighteen months to release upon seeing her parents.

"Mama," she shouted, running and embracing her.

"My baby girl," Mother cried, kissing Sadie's face over and over. "Oh, my darling, how I've longed for this day."

Tears ran down Sadie's cheeks.

"Here you go," Father said, handing his daughter a hankie.

Sadie patted the tears away and looked at the man who nearly ruined her life. "Hello, Papa," she said and leaned in to kiss his cheek.

He surprised Sadie by wrapping his beefy arms around her and pulling her in tight. "Will you ever forgive me?" he whispered.

Sadie squeezed him, and the many months and hundreds of days of her sorrow finally released. Tears gushed, and she heaved, unable to control the convulsions overwhelming her. She held on tight until the moment passed. When she pushed away and looked into her father's eyes, she saw for the first time, tears in his eyes.

"I'm so sorry, Sadie. I had no idea what I was getting you into."

Sadie nodded. "I know, Papa, I know."

"Where's Alex and the baby?" Mother asked.

"They're at the apartment, waiting for us. Come, let's go, I have a taxi waiting."

CHAPTER NINETY-SEVEN—FOUR ACTS

"I'm so excited, I can't stand it," Mother said.

"I know, Mama, me too. Nathan's such a good baby," Sadie said, knocking on the door to her third-floor apartment.

"Coming!"

Sadie heard the tumblers unlocking, and the door swung open. Alex stood, holding Nathan in his arms. No one moved for a moment until Sadie said, "Go on in, unless you want to meet your grandson in the hallway."

"Let me see him," Mother said, rushing over. She stuck her face close to Nathan's, ignoring Alex's personal space she intruded upon.

"Would you like to hold him?" Alex asked.

Realizing her rudeness she said, "Oh, I'm sorry, Alex. It's nice to see you," giving him a swift kiss on his cheek.

"That's all right," he said, handing Nathan to her. "Nathan, this is your *Zeyde*."

Jennie smiled at Alex and cradled Nathan in her arms. "Oh, how he warms my heart," she said, holding him tight to her soft bosoms, rocking side-to-side, with her eyes closed.

"Father, I'm sure you remember Alex," Sadie said.

"Of course," he said, reaching out to shake his hand.

"It's good to see you, sir," Alex said.

"Same to you, Alex."

"Come, let's sit in the kitchen, I have lunch prepared," Sadie said, pointing the way.

*

With lunch done, and Nathan asleep, the family gathered in the living room.

"What's the plan for your wool business?" Alex asked.

"I'll be looking for a location and hopefully find what we need to open Wollman's and Son."

Alex glanced over to Sadie for a moment, before asking Avraham, "Is Hymie planning to immigrate too?"

Avraham nodded. "Yes, he's coming as soon as I send word."

"That's wonderful," Alex said.

"I want you both to know," Avraham began, "that we're grateful to both of you for allowing us to stay in your home until we find our own place. First thing tomorrow morning, we will start looking. We don't want to be a burden. "

"Come on now, Avraham, don't be silly. You're family, and that's all that matters to Sadie and me."

"I like to say something," Avraham said, rising to his feet, and walking over to the window, and gazing out onto the Columbia campus, before turning, and facing Alex. "I don't know how to say this," he said, taking a breath to compose himself. "But the last time I saw you, I said, if you succeed in bringing Sadie back, I'd be grateful, but I would never let you marry her."

"I remember," Alex said, softly.

"Allow me to explain," he said, pulling over a chair, and sitting down. "I was raised to believe that a Jewish marriage is a merger between a man and a woman into a single soul," he said, interlocking his fingers together. "When I heard that Sadie wanted to marry you, I couldn't reconcile not obeying a sacred law."

Alex nodded and said, "I understand."

"But my reaction to preventing this from occurring, resulted in a disaster far worse than the original sin for my daughter," he said, looking over to Sadie. "But thanks to Hashem, and to you Alex, she's safe and here with us today."

Alex reached over and patted Avraham on his leg, and said, "That's all that matters."

Avraham gazed at the floor, and continued, "During the time when Sadie was gone, I had plenty of time to think about what I did. Guilt overpowered me. I couldn't work. I argued over little things," he said, with a shrug and a glance over to his wife.

"It's true," Jennie said, nodding.

"I spoke to our rabbi about this."

"You spoke with Rabbi Zeides?" Sadie said.

"Don't worry, Sadie, the rabbi promised to keep the matter private."

Sadie scoffed, remembering Rabbi Zeides' wife, the *rebbetzin* and *yenta*, who had probably shared Sadie's plight with the entire *shul*.

"The rabbi agreed that interfaith marriage was a sin. But what I did to stop it was a greater sin," he said, sitting up tall in the chair. "When I asked how I could repent, the rabbi held up four fingers and said, *To do Teshuvah, you must do four acts. First, you must leave the sin*, which in my case, couldn't be accomplished until I saw with my own eyes that you were no longer in danger, because of my actions.

"*Next, you must show remorse and shame for your sin.* This was, I must say, not hard to abide by, as I was genuinely ashamed and embarrassed.

"Holding up two fingers, the rabbi said, *You must never commit this sin again.* This, of course, was a forgone conclusion. But the most significant, the fourth act *is a confession spoken out loud*, which if you, and Sadie, would permit me," he said and stood up.

Avraham took a breath, put his palms upon his face, and said, "I have sinned. I have sold my daughter into slavery. I deeply regret my actions, and I declare before Hashem, who knows my innermost thoughts, that I will never violate my daughter's wishes or desires for my own selfish reasons ever again."

He removed his hands, and Sadie saw tears running down her father's cheeks.

"Oh, Papa, that was beautiful," she said and embraced him.

Alex rose, and stood before Avraham, and said, "You're a *mensch*, Avraham."

Avraham smiled and said, "You know Yiddish?"

"He does, Papa, he speaks it fluently, along with Polish, Spanish, German, and English."

"Impressive."

Alex gave his father-in-law a hug and said, "I appreciate your words, but there's something I would like to say."

Sadie reached for and squeezed Alex's hand. He patted it and nodded.

"I too believe that when a man and a woman marry, they are forming a merger into a single soul, and from this union, we have created our precious boy, Nathan. While it is true I was not born a Jew, it doesn't preclude me from becoming one."

"What are you saying, Alex?" Sadie asked.

"For the sake of our family, for the love of my wife, and for raising our child, I will covert my religion to Judaism."

"Oh my, I can't believe my ears," said Jennie.

"Are you sure, Alex?" said Sadie.

"I'm sure. Come, let's pray," he said, and gestured for everyone to stand in a circle and hold hands. Alex closed his eyes, took a breath, and said, "Hear, O Israel, the Lord is our God, the Lord is One. Blessed be the name of the glory of His kingdom forever and ever. You shall love the Lord your God with all your heart, with all your soul, and with all your might. And these words which I command you today shall be upon your heart. You shall teach them thoroughly to your children, and you shall speak of them when you sit in your house and when you walk on the road, when you lie down and when you rise. You shall bind them as a sign upon your hand, and they shall be for a reminder between your eyes. And you shall write them upon the doorposts of your house and upon your gates."

And with that, everyone said, "Amen."

The End

www.ingramcontent.com/pod-product-compliance
Lightning Source LLC
Chambersburg PA
CBHW030828110726
47900CB00006B/1794